daring DESTINY

KAYLENE WINTER

Trigger Warning

Readers,

The stories I create explore real-life challenges and experiences to provide an authentic and heartfelt narrative. I want to acknowledge some sensitive topics present in this story that may be of concern to some readers.

This story features hyperfocus, a type of neurodivergence, and a family member's alcohol addiction (mostly off-page). A sensitivity reader carefully reviewed the portrayal of neurodivergence to ensure it is both informed and respectful.

Thank you for taking the time to read this story. I hope it brings you connection and insight.

With Love,

Kaylene

BRENNAN

Prologue – Present Day

WHAT THE FUCK AM I doing here?

Never, in a million, billion years, could I have predicted I'd end up at my fifteen-year high-school reunion. I mean, who even has a fifteen-year reunion?

Uh, my disorganized, indifferent class, that's who I guess.

We blew past our ten-year and I didn't even notice. No interest. High school sucked, it wasn't for me.

I never fit in.

Until recently, my all-consuming focus has been the company I founded when I was at Foster Business

School, Cognify AI. We revolutionized the real estate industry by turning market data into actionable insights for realtors, offering predictive analytics, personalized property recommendations, and immersive virtual tours, all through an intuitive, graphical interface. We scaled the technology into the hospitality industry, making my company the highest-grossing technology company in the world after we went public.

Shit.

I'm such a fucking turd.

Even my own thoughts sound like elevator pitches.

Chill out, man.

I'm trying to, for fuck's sake. Which is why I'm standing here in the renovated cafeteria at Garfield High with a whiskey in hand and a polite smile plastered on my face. I'm completely out of my comfort zone. Social outings like this make me cringe. I suck at small talk. It's pointless. Irrelevant. *Boring.*

I wouldn't have bothered, except for one reason.

Astrid.

Just thinking her name sends a little thrill down my spine. And, a lightning bolt of remorse.

She was my low-key obsession back in high school, The ultimate in main-character energy. An ice-blonde goddess who glided through the halls, dressed like a superstar as if she owned the place. Kind and compassionate to everyone. Hot as fuck. Every guy wanted her.

Especially me.

Unfortunately, a socially awkward, slightly overweight kid never stood a chance with an it-girl like Astrid. No, she was hooking up with Jake Thompson, the asshole basketball superstar who treated her like garbage but looked like a Greek god.

He's not here tonight, of course. Mr. Big-Time NBA superstar couldn't be bothered.

Oh, how times have changed. Tonight, I'm wearing the BDE crown on my own, I guess. Last month, *Wired* named me the most influential tech CEO of the past decade. I guess it's true, but it's weird for someone who deliberately stayed out of the spotlight to suddenly be recognized everywhere.

Hence, why I've parked myself in a dark corner. Too many classmates I don't care for suddenly want to be my best friend. *No fucking thank you.* Clout chasers are *not* my jam. As soon as Astrid sees I've made the effort, I'll make my escape.

Whoa. There she is. She looks incredible, as usual. My God, after all these years it's uncanny the way she has an effortless way of looking like a million bucks.

Tonight, she rocks a shimmery black dress. It dips low enough to enhance her impressive cleavage but not enough to be obscene. Her long, blonde hair falls in waves over her shoulder. Other than the dark eyeliner, which makes her green eyes pop, her face is clean and natural. Even her jewelry is classy. Simple gold earrings and a matching bracelet. Sky-high black heels make her slim, toned legs look like they go on forever.

God. It's like she walked straight out of some fashion magazine.

It's hard to believe it was three-ish years ago when she reached out to me through my brother Connor, the bass player in Seattle's biggest band, Less Than Zero. Coincidentally, she was his realtor. Sold him a multimillion-dollar house on Hunt's Point, where the richest people in the Seattle area live. When Connor mentioned she wanted to get in touch, I thought it was a joke.

Why would the high-school "it" girl want to talk to me? A guy she never acknowledged?

I did what any self-respecting guy with a past like mine would do.

Ignored her.

She was persistent, though. Turned out she wanted help with this reunion. Apparently, convincing a bunch of thirty-somethings to relive their glory days wasn't as easy as it sounded, even for the most popular girl in the class. She had a brilliant idea and I was, apparently, the one who could help her.

I'm still not entirely sure why I agreed. Maybe it was the challenge. Maybe it was the allure of Astrid-fucking-Gustafsson paying attention to me for once. Whatever the reason, we hit it off.

And, we created something special.

Gazing over at her chatting with some of her old friends, I'm glad she's having fun. She's been so intent about making this a success, this must be a dream come true. It's packed. Our classmates are completely immersed in the interactive experience which, to me, is a much better way to catch up with someone you haven't talked to in fifteen years.

Who wants to listen some rando drone on and on and on about career, marriage and their snotty kids?

No fucking thank you times two.

"Brennan." Astrid's smooth, whisky-tinged voice hits me in the core, as it always does.

She strides toward me. Her smile is forced and tight, which I totally understand. I'm, deservedly, not her favorite person at the moment.

I try to sound casual, like I haven't been keeping my eye on her all goddamn night. "Hey. Congratulations. Your idea's a huge success."

"*Our* idea," she corrects, gazing out at the crowd. "You're the one who made it all happen."

Side by side, we look around the room and for a moment, things feel normal. We're two people who worked hard and used our respective skills to make an innovative concept a reality.

Astrid spent her time gathering key moments from high school from the official photo archive and images pulled from social media. With a team of developers, I created the technology powering the interactive display.

Now, snippets of everyone's lives over the past fifteen years are being projected on sixty-foot walls. It's a living yearbook come to life. With a companion app so people can continuously update and reconnect based on their interests, job titles, and locations.

A culmination of the best and most heartbreaking years of my life.

Maybe she's in a conciliatory mood. I take a step toward her. "Well, it was a team effort."

Astrid holds up her hand to stop me and squints at me incredulously. "Don't even. Not tonight."

I wish I could say her snark catches me off guard. It doesn't.

Truth be told, I'm honestly not sure why she's even speaking to me.

We stand there awkwardly while the room around us buzzes with energy. The digital displays continue to randomly flash images from our high school days. People are laughing, reconnecting, living in the moment. As cool as everything has turned out, the familiar niggle starts to take root in my brain when things get uncomfortable.

I've gotta get out of here.

"Actually, before you bolt, I do need to talk to you. Come outside with me?" Astrid can read me like a book, she knows I won't last long in this environment.

I do my best to keep my voice steady. "Uh, okay. Sure."

Before I can fully process what's happening, Astrid takes my hand and leads me toward the exit. We slip out the back and the noise of the reunion fades behind us.

Outside, the quiet night air is a stark contrast to the festivities inside.

Sweet. Sweet. Relief.

Astrid looks up at the sky. I watch as her shoulders relax and tension melts away.

"God, I needed some peace." She shakes out her shiny, blonde hair. "It's exhausting, you know?"

I nod, because I *do* know.

As I've gotten to know Astrid *for real*, it's something we have in common. She's actually much different than I thought she was as a teenager. She seemed so comfortable around everyone. A naturally gregarious, outgoing person everyone aspires to be.

It's an act, though. She shoulders too many expectations. Cares too much about what people think. Feels pressure to always be perfect. Believes she has no choice but to keep her shit together at all times. It's funny how we're the same in this regard.

It's *exhausting*.

"You hide it well." I can't help but voice what I'm thinking out loud.

She laughs bitterly. "Years of practice."

We fall into another stretch of silence, standing together in the dark.

"So..." she says quietly. "Can we talk?"

"Yeah." I brace myself for what's coming next.

The end. This is probably the last time I'll ever see Astrid. My heart is breaking into a million pieces and I'm not sure how to stop her from...

Without thinking, I reach out and take her hand, comforted by how natural it feels. She doesn't pull away, just flicks her eyes up to me and blinks rapidly. As if she's trying to stop from crying. My heart thunders in my chest. She moves in closer.

Thu-thump.

Suddenly, her lips are on mine.

In the beginning, it's a soft kiss. Tentative, as if she's testing the waters. Then, it quickly deepens and I find myself pulling her flush against my chest. Instinctively, my arms wrap around her as I lose myself in the moment. She tastes like peaches and heaven.

When our lips finally part, our foreheads remain pressed together as we try to catch our breath.

"I didn't mean to..." She clutches at my waist.

"Neither did I," I mutter, though it's a lie. If I could kiss Astrid forever, I would.

I planned to.

We stand there for a moment, holding each other. Neither of us willing to let go. The air between us is charged. Electric.

She gazes up at me, her eyes soft but guarded. "Thank you."

"For what?" I'm genuinely confused.

"For being here tonight. I truly didn't think you'd come" She takes in a huge breath and lets it out, like she's nervous.

Considering the situation, I'm unsure how to respond. "Why wouldn't I be here? It was important to you. To *us*."

She smiles wistfully and tilts her head. "*Brennan*."

"I... Uh..." I don't know how to respond.

Astrid shoots me a look as if to say, *shut the fuck up.*

So, I don't bother finishing the sentence. It's pointless to bullshit her. I'm not capable of giving her what she needs and we both know it.

I'm utter crap at relationships. I don't know how to nurture them. Prioritize them. Communicate properly. I never have. Probably never will.

Astrid should have been different. She's everything I ever dreamed about. My ultimate fantasy. And I had her. Until I fucked up.

Ruined us.

Astrid sucks in a breath. "So...turns out I'm pregnant."

Wait, *what*?

Reality crashes down, unforgiving. Like a hundred million buckets of ice water.

If I can't manage a romantic relationship with someone as perfect as Astrid...

How in the *fuck* can I be a good father?

One

About Three Years Prior

I NEVER GET SICK of these moments.

That certain buzz when you sense you're gonna close a fifty-million-dollar home sale.

The anticipation of millions in commission is within reach.

It's a feeling that never loses its appeal.

Glancing through the marketing materials of my listing, a spectacular Hunts Point estate, I marvel at what an architectural masterpiece this place is. Clean lines, expansive glass windows, perched on the edge of Lake Washington with a view that sells itself.

But, I know even the most stunning properties need the right touch. A perfect story to bring them to life. To make the house irresistible. Plus, a little diversion on the way.

That's where I come in.

My clients will be here any moment so I take a sec to reapply my lipstick and check my outfit—a vintage ivory wool tweed Chanel suit, tailored to perfection, paired with nude Louboutins. I put a lot of thought into the clothes I wear for showings. Expensive but not flashy. My style is carefully cultivated to make high-net- worth people take me seriously without being intimidating.

The telltale sound of the front door chimes means it's showtime. Through the floor-length glass panel of my office, I see Connor McGloughlin and his wife, Ronni enter the lobby. They're every bit the power couple—Connor, with his long, curly hair and rockstar swagger. Superstar actress, Ronni, with her effortless Hollywood glam.

Even though I cater to wealthy clients, it still gives me a little thrill to work with famous entertainers like them. I'm not intimidated, especially not today. It just so happens Connor and I have a shared connection.

"Connor, Ronni, so nice to see you again." I offer a warm smile as I greet them. "Let's get going, we have five perfect locations to tick all your boxes. Security. Seclusion. Serenity."

"Yeah, we're keeping it simple, we need privacy and peace." Ronni clutches Connor's hand.

I guide them to my pride and joy, the black Bentley Bentayga EWB SUV I treated myself to earlier this year when I hit the five-million-dollar commission mark. When I sell the McGloughlins the house I have in mind, I'll be on track to have my best year yet.

Truthfully, I should patent the process I've developed to show homes. First, I start with what I call my "diversion" showings— stunning properties with a few subtle flaws. A breathtaking view but the layout feels cramped. A sprawling private estate with a dated master suite. Stuff like that.

Many realtors do it this way intentionally, but I meticulously plan the specific order of showings. Deliberately build up client expectations just enough. Then, when I finally show them the house I truly have in mind, it's like a revelation.

"It's perfect," or *"Astrid, how did you know it's exactly what we wanted?"*

All I hear is: Cha-Ching.

It takes nearly two hours to tour the decoy homes. When I'm spending a large chunk of time with clients, years of practice has taught me how to engage. I painstakingly research everyone's background from news articles to social media posts. This way, my banter is never too personal or controversial. Rather than yammer on about their wealth or fame, my goal is to make them feel comfortable.

Reading body language is another super power. It always has been. I can generally tell how someone feels by watching them.

It's helped me adapt my own interactions. Instinctively I know when to lean in with interest and when to pull back or even disappear. Don't ever rush and don't overstay your welcome. Chitchat is fine but don't make it about you. It's almost like a game. Watching people's eyes light up as they let their guard down like I'm a trusted friend.

Anyway, the day is going as planned. The four diversionary houses have been viewed and rejected. We're now on our way to the property I'm sure will be Connor and Ronni's new home.

"Hunts Point is a tiny municipality, and extraordinarily private. It's like living in an urban forest, yet every house has waterfront access to Lake Washington." I turn down the two-lane winding road into the quaint neighborhood, passing mansion after mansion. "It's arguably the most exclusive location in the Pacific Northwest. After we see the house, I'll drive you through the commercial area. Lots of cafes and little shops. You're also near a beautiful nature preserve. Many local celebrities call it home."

Ronni's face is practically pressed to the window. "What are the schools here like?"

"The best in the state. Whether you want your kids to go to public or private, one of my services is to help jump you to the top of the waiting list. If this place suits you, I'll send some materials for the two of you to look over later tonight." I turn down the long, paved driveway.

Connor looks up at the thirty-foot-high trees surrounding us. I hear him whisper to Ronni, "This neighborhood is *class*."

Yep. It is.

At the end of the drive is a clearing where a sprawling, modern prairie-style home takes center stage. It sits on two acres and the juxtaposition is incredible. The road to the house feels like you're in the middle of the wilderness but as we emerge, everything opens up. Full waterfront access lined with manicured lawns and sleek stone walkways.

We get out and I lead them up the intricate chevron-patterned driveway and glance over at Connor, who used to run his family's construction company before he was a rockstar. Sure enough, he's impressed.

"*Jaysus*, this is something else." Connor runs his hands along the heavy steel panels embedded into the old-growth wood front door. It's twice as tall as he is, and he's a *giant*. "I've never seen workmanship so beautiful."

"Everything you'll see is custom. From the finishes to the paint. There's nothing in this house you could buy off the shelf." I unlock the door and step aside so they can get the whole effect.

The second Ronni crosses the threshold, I know it's a done deal. "Astrid, this place is incredible," she gushes, her eyes wide with excitement. "I can't wait to see the rest."

"Let's do it." I launch into my practiced spiel, guiding them through the house.

It takes about an hour to show the entire place and point out all the incredible features. The foyer leads into a sun-drenched living area, with floor-to-ceiling windows and a front-row view of the lake. I make sure to emphasize the modern, open-concept design, the custom stone fireplace and the chef's kitchen with state-of-the-art appliances.

Connor stays a few steps behind me, he scans the space with a critical eye. I'm unbothered, though. I expected a high-level scrutiny from a prior professional.

Ronni, on the other hand, wears her emotions on her sleeve. Her delight is infectious and I find myself unexpectedly warming to her. She's down-to-earth in a surprising way, given her uber-celebrity status.

It's easy to see how she and Connor make such a terrific pair. Her sweetness balances his intensity. They move in synchronicity and you can tell they're deeply in love.

They're #relationshipgoals for sure.

"Astrid, tell me this. Will the owners sell the furniture and art with the property?" We're at the end of the tour and Connor glances around the impressive "whiskey" room, which is more like an old-time gentleman's lounge.

I pretend to type a text into my phone. "Let me check. Do you have any other questions for them about this property?"

Connor and Ronni give each other "the look" and he takes her hand. "Nah. Astrid, love. I think this might be the place for us."

"Spectacular." I finish my pretend text without looking at him.

"As we mentioned, we're all-cash buyers," Ronni jumps in nervously.

Now's the time to secure the sale. Operation "make it seem unattainable."

"There's one thing to discuss. As you may have heard from Jason Deveraux, I pride myself on my ability to be discreet." I lean forward on my elbows and deliberately make eye contact with both of them as I name-drop Seattle's biggest tech billionaire, who happens to be the father of Connor's bandmate—and the man who referred them to me.

Ronni leans back in her chair. So does Connor.

He glances between us. "Go on."

"How do you intend on purchasing this property?" I look directly at Ronni, who's been in the news quite a bit lately.

Ronni, clearly uncomfortable, tucks her hair behind her ears. "Why do you ask?"

"Privacy. The residents in Hunts Point are scandal-averse." Occasionally I look at Connor, but I know Ronni's the most vulnerable on this subject. "You're both well-known in your own professions and have rabid fan bases. The residents here shy away from, well, controversy. If you were to look up property records, most of the homeowners here hold their property in an undetectable LLC or a family trust. If you haven't set up one yet, we likely won't get through the Homeowners Association approval before this place sells."

Of course, I already know they have a property trust set up, but my purpose for bringing it up was to make sure they realize their neighbors share their dedication to privacy. This little tidbit is going to seal the sale.

Visibly, Ronni relaxes. "We do, and it's a relief to hear our potential neighbors feel the same way. We want to raise our kids in a quiet, secure location."

"Aye." Connor nods. "This place is perfect. I'm excited for us to have a water view again. It helps us escape from the madness of our lives."

I can't contain my smile and pretend to glance at my phone. "Oh, cool! I heard back from the owners. They're willing to sell the furniture. Should we write up an offer?"

Half hour later, over lunch at John Howie Steak, we celebrate the sale. As we finish up, I decide to broach a topic which might cross a "discreet" boundary I religiously live by.

"Would you mind if I asked you a somewhat personal question, Connor?" I pull out my black AMEX to pay the bill.

His eyebrows raise. "Uh, I'm not making any statements about the status of my band."

Shit. I totally forgot Connor's in the middle of some band drama. Rookie fucking mistake.

"No, no. Of course not, I'm sorry." I wave my hand in the air to try to erase what I said. "I'd never ask you about..." I stumble over my words. "Uh, this is completely on a different topic. I was actually wondering about your brother Brennan."

Connor squints at me. "May I ask how you know my brother?"

"I went to high school with him." I feel my cheeks redden as I try to regain my professional composure. "I have something of his I'd like to return. How about this. If I give you my card will you pass it on to him? Let him decide?"

He leans back and crosses his arms. "Surely you have alternative ways of getting ahold of him?"

Goddammit. I'm losing all semblance of credibility. I've got to abort the mission.

"Forget I said anything. It's stupid. Of course I can figure it out..." I tuck my business card back in my purse.

"It's fine." Ronni grips my wrist lightly. "Give it to me, we'll get it to Brennan." She tilts her head at Connor. "It's not like she couldn't have asked Jason."

Connor's toothy smile creeps over his face. "Ah, you've piqued my interest, Miss Astrid. I was feckin' with you and all your 'pride yourself on being discreet' shite. Of course we'll put you in touch. Hopefully he'll tear himself away from his computer to respond, but no promises."

"Brennan's such a genius, but he's so focused on his company, he doesn't make time for a social life." Ronni winks at me.

Connor chuckles, shaking his head. "Brennan's single by choice. Don't get any bright ideas, wife."

I keep my expression neutral, but inside, I'm piecing together the picture of the Brennan I vaguely remember with the guy they describe. It makes sense. He was always on the periphery, observing but never quite participating. And now, he's channeled his focus into building a company into one of the biggest brands in the world.

What catches my attention, though, is Ronni's comment about him not dating much. Considering how successful he's become, it's oddly reassuring to consider he hasn't gone to the dark side. Many of my tech clients are the opposite. Self-important know-it-alls with a chip on their shoulder. I've seen some treat women like accessories, or worse.

I'm not interested in romance with Brennan though, so I need to shut the idea down. "I appreciate you putting me back in touch. I promise I'm not trying to date him."

We make our way back to the office and finalize the closing items. Once they're on their way, I stare out of my office window at Mt. Rainier and think back to high school.

I envied families like the McGloughlins and how close they were. Six brothers who had each other's backs through thick and thin. They went through tough times together. Though I didn't tell him this, Connor was somewhat of a hero in our school, and not because he's a rockstar. My research confirmed my recollection. After his father's accident, he sacrificed a football scholarship and his own college degree to make sure his brothers could finish their own schooling.

Talk about selfless. He's a fucking legend.

My family is the complete opposite, with parents who worked themselves to the bone and scraped by to make ends meet. Me and my two older sisters were mostly unsupervised, and while I was the responsible one, they ran wild. Nora's been in and out of rehab at least four times. Lark doesn't feel compelled to hold down a job, but has three kids with three different men.

I broke the poverty cycle, thank God. The one daughter who made something of herself. But my success has come with a price. I'm essentially estranged from all of them because they resent me. Though guilt gnaws at me, especially when I send money to help out, being around them isn't conducive for my mental health. So I stay away.

On my way home, my phone pings. I glance down and see it's from Connor—texting Brennan's number.

My stomach flutters nervously at the thought of contacting him for some strange reason. I'm not even sure we spoke to each other in high school, as far as I can remember. It's entirely possible he'll have no idea who I am.

It doesn't matter. This is something I have to do.

I owe it to him.

It's time to right a wrong.

Two

BRENNAN

A Few Days Later

WTF could Astrid Gustafsson possibly want with me?

For the past few days this thought has whirled around in my head on an endless loop.

I couldn't believe it when my brother, Connor, casually mentioned she was his realtor. Then he told me she asked for my number. Something about having something of mine from back in high school.

Oh, I was obsessed with her, but I can't recall ever speaking to her.

Believe me, I *would* remember.

Astrid had me hooked from day one, the way she seemed so flawless, like she'd been born for the spotlight. I memorized her schedule, her classes, her cheer practice—everything. And while everyone thought she lived like a queen, I caught the details: the thrifted designer clothes, the way she'd sneak out alone after school to catch the city bus.

Once, I even followed her, thinking she lived somewhere glamorous. Nope. She got off at a rundown house in the Central District. Hid her real life from her so-called besties, but I saw it all. Learned everything I could. Wrote it all down in my journal.

It made me want to know her for real.

My brother Cillian got wind of how engrossed I became in her life and gave me some tough love. Warned me of how it might look if she—or anyone else-- ever caught me basically stalking her. To be fair, I wasn't a creeper. My concentration on Astrid—or anything else that catches my attention—is how my brain works.

Anyway, he helped redirect my energy into computer programming and I thank God for him every day. If he hadn't, I wouldn't be sitting behind my desk in my company's Belltown office.

I'm in between meetings, staring at my phone. Every so often the screen lights up with a new What's App text or Slack message. Most of them will go unread for days, but I can't help but pull up Astrid's text and look at it for the umpteenth time.

> **Unknown:** *Brennan, it's Astrid Gustafsson from Garfield High. I'd love to catch up. Can you give me a call?*

Innocuous. Bland. Formal.

Fucking intriguing.

Should I call her? Or reply to her text? I mean, initially I was intentionally ignoring her. Now, the prospect of "catching up," whatever that means, is never far from my mind. The problem is, something always pulls me away—juggling product development deadlines, managing investor expectations, trying to keep my best engineers from burning out. Blah. Blah. Blah.

The pressure to innovate while staying ahead of the competition is relentless. One wrong move could cost my company everything. The fires never stop, and lately, it feels like I'm holding a damn extinguisher 24/7.

During my freshman year at University of Washington, I founded CognifyAI when artificial intelligence was still a hazy, futuristic concept people couldn't quite grasp. While most students were busy coding simple apps or dreaming up the next social network, I was neck-deep in algorithms, trying to figure out how to make machines think like us.

Well, actually, how to make them think *for* us.

I come from a big, complicated family with some fucked-up problems and a whole lotta love. My natural tendency is to isolate and find a solution to the problem. It's how my mind works. I can't stand to see the people I love struggle—and for a long time my family was in free fall.

Connor, my oldest brother, became head of our household after Da was injured in a car wreck and couldn't run the family business, McGloughlin Construction, anymore. Cillian, my Irish twin and savior, took it over when Connor became a bona fide rockstar. The twins, Liam and Padraig, followed in Connor's musical footsteps with their band, Fireball. Finally, there's Seamus, the youngest. He's deep into his surgical career.

Anyway, my road to entrepreneurship was inadvertent. All I wanted was to earn a few bucks to pay my own way. To take some pressure off Connor. Turns out concentrating on technology development changed my life. I was bitten by the entrepreneurial bug and I've never looked back.

Fast forward to now and CognifyAI is truly changing the world. We employ ten thousand people throughout the US and Europe. My AI platform has revolutionized the realty industry and we're on track to do the same in travel and transportation by the end of next year.

As most founders will tell you, the road to success is not a straight line. It's full of twists, turns, and pivots and requires singular focus—which is perfect for me. I've learned how to navigate a million different moving parts at any given time. Investors are hungry for results, and I'm expected to deliver quarter after quarter.

The stress is unbelievable. We can't hire executives fast enough. Coders are burning out and the AI market is as volatile as ever. Every other week, I'm back and forth between Seattle and Silicon Valley, not to mention the international trips. My purpose in life, at this point, is convincing the world we're the next global powerhouse.

Truth be told, some days I'm barely holding it together.

I don't tell my family any of this, though. No need to worry them. Besides, as Cillian always tells me when I start to spin a bit, I need to get laid.

He's not wrong. I'm horny as fucking hell with no outlet other than my hand. Lately, the only women I come in contact with work for me. There's no way I'll risk the future of CognifyAI on a potential sexual harassment lawsuit.

As it's been drilled into me by the board, I can't be too careful. Especially because, as one of the world's experts on AI capabilities, I know the risks too well.

So, I'm back to staring at the text from Astrid, sipping on my third caramel macchiato since lunch. Contemplating. Weighing my options.

Fuck it.

I get up and lock the door to my office.

A quick search conjures up a few images of Astrid, mostly her professional real estate pictures. She's beyond stunning now. Long, shiny blonde hair. Legs that go on for miles. Plump, juicy lips. Sexy curves perfectly encased in a sleek, form-fitting dress. A subtle hint of cleavage. I find myself fantasizing again about the color of her nipples. Are they pink? Brown? Rosy red?

My dick fills at the thought of pinching them. Licking them into peaked points.

It's like high school all over again, but so fucking be it.

Scrolling through the pictures, I find it's her eyes that shred me to the bone. Emerald-green orbs bore into my soul through the screen, daring me to... *Fuck*. It's like she's challenging me without saying a word. Damn if my cock isn't now hard as a pole.

Before I can stop myself, I've unzipped my jeans and my dick's in my fist. I pump slowly. Shut my eyes and visualize.

My sex-deprived mind conjures up a scene where Astrid, wearing skimpy black lingerie, is kneeling before me. I can practically feel the silk of her hair when I fist it at her nape and push her mouth toward my shaft. She utters a needy whimper when my crown breaches her lips and a guttural moan when I thrust to the back of her throat.

Ahhh, my hand glides up and down my swollen cock. Soon, I'm jacking myself hard, imagining her laving my balls. Swirling her tongue along my dick like a lollipop.

Using my thighs as leverage, Astrid stands, pulls her panties down and steps out of them. She keeps on her sky-high black pumps and straddles me. Runs a finger along her pussy. Sinks down until I'm buried into her velvety heat and pulls the cups of her bra to the side so her breasts spill out.

Ohhhhh. Pale-pink nipples, puckered *sooooo* tight.

Jesus Christ. I spurt a gallon of come all over my hand and make a mess of my shirt.

Thank God for my private executive bathroom. I clean myself up. Change into a new shirt from the stash of clothes I keep on hand for all-nighters. Contemplate my situation. Feel a bit foolish and not at all satiated.

The thing is, Astrid's name alone brings back shitty memories of high school. Years filled with loneliness. Isolation. Tension. I thought I'd done a pretty decent job of putting everything behind me. The bullying. The insecurities. The longing to find people who understood me.

It never fully goes away, though, does it? No matter how many covers of tech magazines I'm on or how much money I have, the guy who'll never fit in lives inside me. Taunting me. Telling me I'll never be enough.

I mean, look at me. What a loser. Instead of manning up, texting her, taking her out and fucking her for real, I'm in my office, jacking off to a picture of her on my phone like a *real* loser.

Who am I kidding? Astrid has no romantic interest in me. She's the kind of woman every guy notices and every girl wants to be. Born to be admired. Coveted. Cherished. She's also very successful. She sold Connor a fifty-million-dollar house, for fuck's sake.

Aha.

Yep. I figured it out. Chances are, she has some ulterior motive related to my technology. She's a realtor, after all.

"Brennan? You should head out if you're going to make dinner." Brenda, my assistant, knocks on the door. She's a fifty-something dynamo who knows a thing or two.

Sheepishly, I unlock it and brush past her. "Thanks for the reminder. I was changing my clothes. You're welcome to go, I'm heading out."

It's rare I leave work before ten p.m., but I always make an exception for my family. Tonight everyone's in town to celebrate Connor and Ronni's permanent move to Seattle. It's a beautiful evening. I'm not used to being done at the office in time to feel the warm glow of the sun.

The second I open the front door to my parents' Craftsman mansion on Capitol Hill, Connor and Ronni pounce, each holding a twin nephew. Toran and Tristan are their names. I can never tell who is who.

"Did you text her?" Ronni hugs me tightly. "I've been dying to find out what it is she has of yours."

Connor ambles up behind her, rockstar swagger embedded in every fiber of his being. "Aye, please put me out of my misery. She won't stop bugging me about it."

"Who?" Cillian walks up to the three of us and slings his arm around my neck. "If you've got a date, shouldn't I be the first to know? Irish twin rights and all?"

Cillian is a year older than me and we've always been close, though we're as opposite as two brothers can be. Despite our differences, he and I get each other in a way none of our other brothers do. He looks out for me and I look out for him.

I swear, if I hadn't relied on Cillian's sloppy seconds for the past decade or so, I'd be celibate. He's never content for me to be a wingman. If we're out and he has the opportunity to get laid, so do I. A couple of my hookups have even become "girlfriends," so to speak, though I'm the absolute worst at maintaining any sort of relationship.

Regular sex is great and all. The wooing and dating stuff...isn't. I guess it's not my jam, I don't see the point. Consequently, nobody sticks around for long.

"Astrid Gustafsson. You remember her. She was in my class." I shoot him a look and attempt to appear unbothered. Cillian doesn't need to know she was my inspiration to rub one out less than an hour ago. For many reasons.

His eyebrows shoot up. "The girl you were fixated on for a while? Blonde? Cheerleader? Class President? All the guys wanted to fuck her?"

"Yeah, she's the one," I mutter. Hearing my brother say it out loud annoys me.

Cillian scrubs his beard. "Ah, yeah. She dated the douchey basketball player who cheated on her all the time. What's she want with you now?"

Connor's and Ronni's heads comically ping-pong between us.

"She's their big-time realtor." I gesture toward them with my thumb. "Dunno what she wants. Anyone from Garfield who's reached out in the past few years always has an ulterior motive. Somehow they seem to forget they treated me like shit and I'm not interested."

Before my brothers and sister-in-law can reply to my bitter statement, Ma shouts from the dining room, "It's time to eat; can you move your arses to the dining room please?"

Herding the growing McGloughlin clan to the dinner table is no small feat. Once we're eating, it's a controlled chaos of animated voices and laughter. Tonight, as we pass plates of my ma's roast ham, scalloped potatoes, and beans with bacon, it's quiet except for the clatter of silverware and chairs scraping against the floor.

Soon, though, we're shoveling food into our mouths. Padraig cracks jokes with Seamus. Liam rolls his eyes like the broody rockstar he is. Cillian's already on his second plate. Connor and Ronni try to feed their kids and themselves without getting food all over their clothes. Ma attempts to keep all of us in line while Da, who's still recovering from his stroke, watches with a quiet smile.

It's loud and it's messy, but it's where I feel most comfortable. I'm able to be unabashedly myself with my family and they still love me for it.

Despite the deep-rooted problems my da's alcoholism and gambling addiction caused many years ago, we're gradually healing and moving forward. Sure, I harbor a bit of old resentment—which is probably the reason I'm so driven—but these meals together are sacred. My family keeps me grounded.

After dinner we visit for a while but eventually Cillian and I depart at the same time. As I retrieve my car keys from my pocket, Cillian claps my back. "So, you're going to text Astrid back, aren't you?"

"Uh...dunno," I admit. "I'm curious, of course. My mind is going in a million directions. I'd like to..."

"You should." Cillian nods vigorously. "It's not every day the hottest woman from school pops back into your life." He waggles his eyebrows. "You've got shit under control now. It could be interesting."

I shake my head, knowing he won't let up until I agree. "Fine. I'll shoot her a text."

"You fucking better." He points at me and peels off into the night.

Ten minutes later, I'm in bed staring at my phone.

Tapping into it. Deleting. Tapping into it. Deleting.

Finally, I stop overthinking something so stupid and hit "send" to get the whole thing over with.

> **Me:** Hey Astrid. My schedule is nuts but I'm free Wednesday and Friday for lunch if you're available.

I stare at the screen for easily five minutes and finally three pulsing dots appear. My heart thunders in my chest.

> **Astrid:** Wednesday is perfect. It's a date. I'll ping you Tuesday for details.

Holy fucking shit.

How am I going to pull this off?

Three

ASTRID

Three Days Later

THIS SHOULD BE...INTERESTING.

Weird. But interesting. I still can't believe I got roped into planning this stupid event.

Ordinarily, Wednesday is my sacred day. My weekend. The one day I'm able to drop the polished, professional version of myself, and I'm not about to make an exception. Not for a guy from high school.

Not even if the guy's Seattle's next "Jeff Bezos," the person every tech magazine compares Brennan to.

Truth is, I've had it up to my eyeballs with the entitled, rich tech executives I sell houses to.

Today's lunch is one stop in my day of errands so I'm dressed down in black leggings, a loose, flowing tank top, and wedge sandals. Far cry from the tailored suits and six-inch heels I usually wear for showings. My hair is pulled back in a ponytail and I've dabbed on enough makeup to feel human. The Metropolitan Grill isn't normally a spot for a casual lunch, but Brennan suggested it and I wasn't about to say no.

The dim lighting and dark-wood panels create an old-school, sophisticated atmosphere. It's the kind of place where people with real power and wealth seal deals over a lunchtime steak. When I started my career, the Met was intimidating. I didn't ever feel like I fit in. Now, I'm used to it. In fact, I'll probably run into at least one client when I'm here.

The hostess leads me to the two-seater booth. As we approach, Brennan stands up. The chivalrous gesture surprises me. It's a bit old-fashioned, but sweetly considerate. From what I've read, he claims to be painfully shy so I wouldn't have thought he'd be overtly polite.

Then again, he's the one who invited me to lunch without knowing my angle, so who knows. Looks like his mama raised him right, so thumbs up.

I've learned as much about Brennan as I can, of course. Per my usual M.O., I've done a fair bit of research. In fact, I'm up to speed on the entire McGloughlin clan at this point. Close families intrigue me and this group of brothers is fascinating. Each of them is successful in their own right, and seem to be thick as thieves.

In person, Brennan is taller than I remember, at just over six feet. He's stocky with broad shoulders, and while he definitely doesn't give off athletic vibes, he's not overweight. His thick, brown hair flops around his face like he's made a half-hearted attempt at styling it. Like me, he's also dressed casually in a simple black T-shirt and jeans.

Generally, Brennan McGloughlin is not the kind of guy I'd pick out in a crowd. Maybe I should reconsider, considering how shitty my track record is with men. *Hmm.* We'll see how this goes. Perhaps I'll expand my horizons.

"Hi, Brennan." I hold out my hand and he takes it awkwardly.

We manage some sort of weird handshake. It goes on far too long until, thankfully, he steps aside to let me slide into my side of the green, leather booth.

Up close, he's boyishly handsome with kind, brown eyes and dimples that deepen when his lips curve into a tentative smile. Hmmm. Yeah. He's handsome. With a nice jaw line—definitely resembles his more-famous brothers.

The slight awkwardness in the way he flicks his eyes to mine and back to his hands, which are clasped tightly on top of the table, is somewhat endearing. Almost like he's not entirely comfortable in his own skin. Seattle's full of these guys—book-smart dudes with brains buzzing on overdrive. Full of brilliant ideas—but, when it comes to women, they have no game.

Like putty in my hands.

I reach into my purse to retrieve Brennan's belongings, only to find I've left it sitting on my kitchen counter.

Whoops.

"So, Astrid." Brennan's demeanor abruptly shifts and I'm shocked when he leans forward and cuts to the chase. "What exactly do you need from me?"

Well, then. I stand corrected. I've underestimated him.

"Well, sure, let's get into it." Effortlessly, I plaster on my work smile. "As you might have realized, our class completely missed the ten-year reunion and, because I was class president, the administration roped me into planning our fifteen-year. I'd like to pick your brain for some ideas on how to make it more...engaging. More inclusive."

"Huh." He looks back down at his hands. His brow furrows and he nods slightly. Could I be watching said genius shift into problem-solving mode? I hope so. Because I'm fresh out of ideas.

A server interrupts us. We order lunch and I study Brennan, still waiting for his reply.

"How do you see AI fitting into this?" He cocks his head and looks directly into my eyes. Like he's trying to figure out if I've summoned him here for a bunch of nonsense.

I take a sip of water before I answer, because he's spot-on. The reunion is stupid. As I told the committee, this is my one and done. "I was thinking we could create something interactive, like a virtual yearbook or an AI-driven experience to match people with classmates they've lost touch with."

Brennan watches me intently when I speak, triggering a long-forgotten memory from classes we had together. It's his eyes. Soulful. Gentle. I remember him intensely staring at me in class, almost like he *knew* me. Maybe he's always been focused in this way. Giving his full attention to people. Making them feel like they matter.

Sitting across from him, he certainly seems interested. What a rare gift in this day and age when most conversations are carried on as an afterthought while being distracted by a screen.

"I remember you from high school, you know." I find myself abruptly shifting topic when another vivid memory resurfaces. "You were such a nice guy. One time I overheard you talking to your friends in computer lab sticking up for me."

His face pinkens and he blinks rapidly as he tries to piece together what the hell I'm talking about. "Computer lab?"

"Yeah." I rest my cheek in my palm as I recall the event. "Some of the kids were going off. Making fun of cheerleaders. One of them said something mean about me—how I was all looks and no brains. You defended me. Told them, 'Just because Astrid is popular doesn't mean she's shallow.'"

He's silent for a moment, clearly taken aback. "You heard me? I didn't know you were there."

"I did and I was, I reply softly. "It meant a lot to me. The day had been rough. Afterward, I noticed you had such a cool way of paying attention to everyone. It didn't matter if they were jocks or academics, you didn't seem to hold on to stupid stereotypes."

Brennan's expression changes from skepticism to relief. "I've never understood why people can't be more accepting, you know? High school is hard enough without dealing with such harsh judgments."

"I *do* know." I nod with unexpected enthusiasm. "At least we survived, right?"

He chuckles and the tension between us eases a bit. "Yeah, we did."

I try to process this side of Brennan. Personality is impossible to discern through news articles. I already know he's a genius who's singularly focused on his company. This man is also thoughtful and kind. Motivated by something deeper than money and power.

I'm the one who clings to preconceived judgements about people. Maybe I should take a page out of his book.

"We could use AI to create personalized experiences." Brennan drums his fingers on the table. "Maybe I could build an app or something to highlight key moments with an augmented reality twist. Depending on what you're thinking, we could find a way to 'revisit' prom, graduation, or even old classrooms with a modern, interactive element."

I feel a spark of excitement. He's brilliant. "Wait, you created this concept out of the blue? What a cool idea. Our classmates would feel connected to the past but they'll also see how far they've come. Having access to something like this would definitely draw a crowd."

We bounce ideas back and forth, finding an easy rhythm as we talk through the technical and creative possibilities. In minutes I realize Brennan is the smartest person I've ever spoken with. No doubt about it. There's also a genuine passion in the way he's able to conjure up innovative features and functionality from thin air.

I mean, wow. It's not hard to figure out why Brennan's such an enigma. He cares. Not only about the technology, but about how it impacts people's lives. Another rare characteristic, especially in his AI world.

"You know," a boyish smile plays on his lips, "it's kind of funny. No one would ever expect us to work together on something like this. The popular high-school goddess and the nerdy tech geek."

"Goddess?" I laugh as though it's a compliment, though his endearment makes me feel a bit foolish. "As *if*. Anyway, we're still the same people, aren't we? Maybe a bit more evolved."

Brennan tilts his head slightly as he considers my words. "Evolved, yeah. Social ostracization doesn't affect us the same way now, does it?"

"No, it doesn't. Hopefully, we've all learned to let go of high-school baggage." I meet his gaze. "It's nice, though, to see how far we've both come."

Vulnerability permeates Brennan's expression for a fleeting moment. "You remind me a lot of my older brothers. They thrive in the spotlight. I've always been prone to keep my head down and fade into the background."

"I *don't* feel comfortable in the spotlight, though." Impulsively, I place my hand over the top of his. "It's a front I put on because I have to. I used to make myself sick trying to prove I belonged."

He nods thoughtfully, almost like he already knows this about me. "Huh. I guess, in our own ways, we've found ways to navigate through our own perceived shortcomings. You felt pressure to keep up a certain image and I was trying not to get bullied on a day-to-day basis. Different experiences, sure, but the same powder keg of emotions underneath it all."

"Ohmygod. Brennan. You've nailed it." I can barely contain my awe. "If we create something to go beyond the surface, to show how much we've all grown as people, it could be a chance for everyone to see past who we once were and get to know each other without old, tired barriers."

For the next twenty minutes, our conversation flows easily as we map out the possibilities. It's the most refreshing exchange of ideas I've ever had.

He runs a billion-dollar company yet never makes me feel rushed or like he has something better to do. Plus, Brennan's laugh is surprisingly warm and genuine. I'm actually enjoying hanging out with him and wish we could spend the entire afternoon together.

By the time we finish eating, I'm exceedingly intrigued by Brennan McGloughlin. He's not at all what I expected. Plus, he never once asked about his belongings, though that's the reason he showed up today.

Maybe he enjoyed himself as much as I did.

There's something about the way he looks at me with those thoughtful brown eyes. He makes me feel seen and heard in a way I don't think I've ever experienced.

As we leave the restaurant, I can't help but think this might be the start of an unexpected friendship.

Maybe it's exactly what I need.

Four

BRENNAN

Six Months later

My life is fucking out of control.

Time slips away like sand through my fingers—no matter how tightly I try to hold on, it escapes, leaving me with nothing but the unsettling sense my life is unfolding faster than I can live it.

Days blur into nights. Weeks into months. The quiet existence I used to have is a distant memory.

CognifyAI is at a tipping point. My Board of Directors are pushing hard for us to expand into new markets.

They see untapped potential and dollar signs. They're also spooked by how fast AI is being adapted for everyday use.

They want results

Yesterday.

The problem is, the milestones they expect change with the weather. It's no way to run a business—but it's not all up to me. I may be the CEO, but I report to the board, which is made up of our investors who seem to think they know more about the values of my company than I do. So I fight them. They fight back. We compromise.

It's a vicious fucking cycle that has me reeling. Makes me rue the day I ever took VC money.

They're not happy with me these days because I've been increasingly vocal at the stupid things they want me to do. All I see are irreparable cracks forming by trying to expand too fast. Rushing innovation has the potential to backfire spectacularly, which I can't allow. My entire life has been dedicated to building my company and I'm not about to fail.

So I work. All the fucking time.

Last night I returned home from my eighth trip in four weeks to Silicon Valley. I've barely slept all month because I'm constantly fighting fires. This week's crisis is our Chief Technology Officer is threatening to quit if she doesn't get a massive raise and additional equity. I don't blame her, next to me she's taking the brunt of the investor bullshit.

Ah, fuck. I'm rat-holing. *Again.*

Tonight, I'm out with my brother, Cillian at my favorite place, the Metropolitan Grill. I'm nursing the same beer I ordered three hours ago. He's drinking heavily—more than I've ever seen him—and it worries me. I can't watch another family member fuck up his life with alcohol.

When I'm in town, I try to keep a close eye on him, but I've not been here much this year. It sucks, he's my best friend and he's been through a terrible breakup and started a lucrative but complicated job. The personal toll is obvious, even if he refuses to acknowledge it.

Jesus. We're two brothers with successful, booming companies who are so stressed out we're barely able to exchange two words.

Cillian downs another whiskey, his words slurring as he turns to me. "Y'ever think we're all chasin' our tails, Brennan? We put s'much into this life, into these *people*, and...it all blows up in our faces."

"Yeah." I nod, swirling the warm beer I have no intention of finishing.

The noise of the bar fades as I, once again, get lost in my thoughts without really responding. I'm snapped back to the present when my phone buzzes. Like a trained monkey, I check my messages. It's from my brother Connor.

Connor: *Ran into Astrid. She mentioned she hasn't heard from you in a while. Everything okay?*

Suppressing a groan, I add another task to my list. Astrid and I were supposed to get together a couple weeks after our lunch—apparently, she forgot to return this mysterious item of mine she's had since high school. For me, I can't imagine what it could be.

Time fucking flies. It's been six months since I sat across from her in this very restaurant. Despite my initial misgivings—considering my old fixation on her, part of me wanted to keep my fantasy girl a fantasy—she was easy to talk to, which was unexpected. I don't always connect well one-on-one. The idea of working on this stupid reunion project kind of blew my mind.

It also reminded me of when I started CognifyAI. The brainstorming. Strategizing. Solving problems. God, I've missed it.

"Wassup?" Cillian watches me study my screen.

"It's Connor." I pocket my phone. "He ran into a girl from my class. She was asking about me."

Cillian stares at me, his cynical expression on full display. "So, wait. Are you tellin' me you haven't pulled the trigger with her? Y'should definitely go after her. She'd be a hot fuck."

"Nah, it's not like that." I stab my fork into the table in frustration because—let's be honest—while there's no hope of any sort of romance with her, it's not like I haven't jacked off to her a dozen times since the time in my office.

Cillian laughs bitterly and shakes his head. "Not *like* that? I'm telling youse to go have some fun. Get your dick wet. Fuck her but don't fuckin' *love* her."

I'm taken aback by his tone, but I know it's the hurt talking. He fell hard for a woman who wasn't who she seemed. It broke something inside him. Now he's channeling his bitterness into warnings he'd never have given me before. And whiskey. Lots of fucking whiskey.

"I get it, Kill. You're going through hell. Remember, though, unlike you I'm not cool with casual sex. You know I get too attached." I lean back in the booth. I love my brother, but he's not the nicest to be around when he's drunk.

His head lolls a bit. "Ah, fuck it. The minute y'start thinkin' somethin's real, it goes to shite. 'Tis true. Yer not cut out for no-strings pussy, ma wee brother."

His words sting but I can't entirely dismiss them. Besides, I've seen what he's gone through when he fell hard. The toll it's taken on him. I've never gotten *close* to someone loving me before I do something to fuck it up.

We fall into a heavy silence, Cillian finishes off yet another whiskey while I give up all pretense of finishing my beer. I watch him get drunker. Worry about how far he's sinking. Unsure of how to pull him back, though.

It's troubling because during the workday, he's functional. His business is booming but the nighttime boozing is fucking with his attitude. Cillian's bitterness is cracking the carefree façade he's built and it seems like he's heading for disaster.

Maybe I'll talk to my other brothers about what we can do to support him. I'll see everyone tomorrow at my da's sixtieth birthday party. For now, though, it's close to ten and I'm itching to get home.

"Cillian." I tap him on the shoulder cautiously as we wait for our Ubers. "Maybe you should take a step back from the drinking for a bit. Focus on your work. Take care of yourself."

He belches loudly, causing the couple waiting next to us to stare in disgust. "What's there to take care of? Work's fine. The company's better than ever. I've got everything under control."

"Yeah, okay." I sigh as I try to help him stay upright. Memories of my da stumbling home wasted throughout my teenage years fill me with low-level terror. Cillian is not, in fact, okay. Until he realizes it, though, there's nothing I'll be able to do. "I don't want to see you burn out."

"Don't worry 'bout me. Focus on yerself. Fuck Astrid, if y'want." He shrugs, stumbling a bit.

Our Ubers arrive at the same time and I help him inside, making sure he's settled. "See you tomorrow at the party?"

He nods incoherently, waves me off and shuts the door. I watch as the car speeds off into the night. The tension in my shoulders intensifies as I get into my own vehicle. The odds of me sleeping tonight are zero.

Half hour later, I get home to my townhouse—my parents built a compound years ago and gifted me and each of my brothers our own homes-- pull out my phone and scroll through the messages from Astrid I've been ignoring. God, I feel guilty about, essentially, ghosting her.

I've got to get better.

Little does she know, I wireframed our idea the day after we met but it's been pushed to the side as CognifyAI dominates every waking hour.

Or am I making excuses?

Fuck.

I'm trying not to hyper-focus on her but the truth is, I think Astrid might be someone I could care about. It's hard for me to tell, with so little experience, but I think this situation is *very* different. What started out as a strange reconnection could be, at least, a friendship. One I didn't expect.

The truth is, I like her.

I looked forward to getting together after our lunch. Then I got nervous. Aside from an apologetic text a few months ago, I haven't made any effort.

Let's be honest, it's not because she's done anything wrong. I'm fucking terrified of rejection. Petrified of misconstruing Astrid's kindness as meaning something else.

It's happened to me so many times.

"Brennan, you're so awesome but..."

"Brennan, you're so intense..."

"I'm so sorry, Brennan. I don't think of you in a romantic way..."

I can't hear those words from her. I can't.

It'd be torture to be around her and, once again, pine like a loser when she friend-zones me. Or, worse, face the humiliation of her recoiling with horror if I had the guts to make a move.

Overthink much?

Have you met me?

On the other hand, she deserves basic courtesy. It's fucking embarrassing she's resorted to messaging me through my famous brother. Who the fuck do I think I am? I told her I'd help her with this project, and I'm a man of my word.

Before I can second-guess myself, I send her a text.

Me: Hey, Astrid. Sorry I've been MIA. Things have been crazy busy on my end. Can we set up another meeting? I'd like to pick up where we left off.

I hear nothing for the next ten minutes so I pull out my laptop and try to distract myself by firing off emails. It works. Until my phone pings an hour later.

Astrid: *I appreciate the apology, but I'm not in the habit of being blown off. Are you sure you have the time for this?*

Wow. I like her directness at calling me out. Very few people, other than my family and my board, have the balls to confront me these days.

Me: *You're right and no excuses. I won't waste your time again. Thursday happy hour? I've got some ideas I think you'll like.*

Astrid: *Let me guess, the Met Grill?*

Me: *Nah, you pick, I'll come to you. Text me the place.*

Astrid: *Living on the edge, McGloughlin?*

Me: *I'll take my chances.*

Astrid: *Challenge accepted, nite!*

Me: *Goodnight!*

Huh. That was pretty easy.

After returning to my email logjam, hours later I collapse into bed. Exhaustion permeates every cell of my body, but my thoughts keep circling away from my work problems and back to Astrid.

Our text exchange surprised me and makes me feel certain the pleasant conversation we had was real. I close my eyes and concentrate on being fully present. Try to access what I'm feeling. Pinpoint moments of clarity.

It works.

Real connections for someone like me are rare.

This is one I shouldn't let slip away.

Five

ASTRID

A Few Days Later

TONIGHT, I'M PUTTING THIS guy Brennan to the test.

I'm not used to being ignored for such a long period of time. Six fucking months. So much for being able to read people. Or thinking he was a nice person. Seems like he's a dick.

God, he pissed me off and I wrote *him* off. Until I ran into his brother at a coffee shop near Hunts Point, where I have another listing. One snarky comment later and somehow Brennan McGloughlin resurfaced.

Tonight, I thought about standing him up to give him a taste of his own medicine. Unfortunately, I'm intrigued Mr. Second Coming of Tech Jesus is gracing me with his presence.

My words, not his.

It's a chilly evening but since I've arranged to meet him a short distance away from my place, I decide to walk. *Slowly.* When I'm a block away, I take a minute to powder my nose and reapply lipstick.

As I approach the Zoo Tavern on Eastlake, a dive bar with the charm of a place that hasn't changed since the '80s, I have to suppress a giggle. Dim lighting, check. Neon beer signs, check. Pool tables with worn felt, check. The stale stench of fifty years of beer soaked and dried into the carpet? Check. Check. Check.

This place is perfect.

If Brennan's serious about not wasting my time, he'll have to meet me on my turf. No fancy restaurants, no business casual. It's time to see if Mr. Technology can relax and be real.

The second I push through the front door, I spot Brennan immediately. He stands stiffly near the bar, though he's dressed casually in his uniform of dark jeans and a simple black T-shirt. His hair seems to still be doing its own thing and he's sporting a couple of days' worth of stubble.

Good God. The man still exudes a nervous energy. It's incredibly endearing for some reason.

I stifle a smile. He's definitely out of his element, but he showed up and stayed when I was deliberately fifteen minutes late. His first test has been passed. In my book, that's worth a lot.

"Hey," I call out as I make my way over. "Look who actually made it this time."

Brennan smiles sheepishly when he sees me. "Yeah, I figured I owed you. Sorry about before. Things got crazy."

"Yeah, crazy enough to disappear for six months," I tease, raising an eyebrow as I lean next to him against the bar. "I was starting to think I should have put a digital tracker on you."

He chuckles and runs a hand through his hair, which makes it messier. "Fine, I deserved that. I'm here now, ready to make it up to you. How about I buy the first round?"

"Duh." I roll my eyes and playfully hip check him.

His eyes widen in surprise but he manages to place an order for a pitcher of Heineken. As we stand side by side waiting for it, I glance at Brennan to gauge how he feels about being here. He's got a boyish-charm thing going for him for sure. Except, the man exudes a subtle tension. His smile is a tiny bit too controlled. His movements a touch too deliberate.

"You sure this is your scene?" I ask as we make our way to the pool table. "This place is the polar opposite of the Metropolitan Grill."

He pours us each a pint of beer and looks around appreciatively. "Oh, this is the type of place my brothers and I used to hang out in before they got famous. It's actually a nice change of pace from the fancy restaurants I seem to spend my life in these days."

"Cool." I put my glass down and rack the pool balls. "You're in my hood now. I come here to unwind every so often. No pretenses, no pressure. Just cheap beer, bad lighting, and pool tables with shitty cue sticks."

I set up my break shot and feel Brennan watching me, like he's trying to figure me out. The truth is, I'm trying to figure him out too. He's not wrong about being crazy busy, I've been following his progress in the tech world. CognifyAI seems to be at a real tipping point.

It's ridiculous, really—becoming invested in a guy who essentially ghosted me. Something about Brennan draws me in, even though I hate to admit it to myself.

"Nice break. You're defo a ringer." He claps loudly when I scatter the balls across the table and sink both a solid and a stripe.

"You're *defo* right." I wink at him after I sink all but three of the solids. "You play much?"

Brennan lines up his shot. "No, maybe you can teach me a thing or two."

He takes his turn, managing to sink a stripe, but doesn't set himself up for success. When he misses wildly on the next one, Brennan shakes his head glumly. Then winks at me with a self-deprecating smile.

I can't help but laugh. "Well, at least you're honest about your skills."

"Honesty's important." He shrugs.

I chalk my cue and pocket my final three solids in rapid succession, followed by a behind my back, eight ball in the corner, shot for the win.

We play another round and the conversation once again flows easily—light and playful. We chat about stupid, innocuous stuff with, surprisingly, enough subtle flirting to keep things interesting. Like a really good first date.

Which is weird, isn't it?

Over the course of the evening, Brennan loosens up quite a bit. He astutely observes how I line up shots and learns shockingly fast. He even manages to get close to winning a game or two. His competitiveness shows me a different side of him—confident, witty, and a bit mischievous.

"So," he asks as I lean over the table, "how'd you end up in high-end real estate?"

I pause, not expecting the question. It's not like I'm going to give him my whole back sob-story, but he seems genuinely curious.

"It's the kind of career I have control of, to be honest." I look up at him. "College wasn't an option for me so I needed a job where I could use my people skills to make decent money. Real estate fit the bill. Turns out I'm skilled at selling people their dream homes."

He folds his arms across his chest. "Yeah. It seems to have worked out well for you."

"It has." I sink the shot and move around the table. "As of last year, I'm officially one of the top-selling agents in the country."

Brennan nods approvingly. "Congratulations. What a wonderful accomplishment."

"So, I've been following you in the tech news. I get why you're spread thin—you seem to be pulled in a lot of directions." I chalk my cue.

He looks a bit surprised. "You've been keeping tabs on me?"

"It's not hard." I decide to play it cool. "Your name keeps popping up on my feed."

"Yeah, the past couple of years have been pretty intense." Brennan's smile constricts and he looks away.

Catching the tension, I decide to give the man a break. No more tests, the guy's wound tight. "So much pressure. I hope you find better ways to release it than a game of pool."

He looks at me quizzically and hesitates. Shit. I realize he thinks I'm asking about his sex life instead of letting him off the hook for leaving me hanging for six months.

Finally, he answers, "Not really. Been too focused on work, I guess."

"Someone as driven as you..." I give him a knowing smile. "It must be hard to find time for anything else. I appreciate you meeting me tonight."

Then, almost casually, he shocks the fuck out of me. "What happened between you and Jake?"

"Jake? My ex from high school?" I miss my shot so wildly, the cue ball clatters off the side and rolls across the floor.

Brennan picks it up and places it back on the table, looking slightly embarrassed. "Um...yeah? I never comprehended what you saw in him. He was kind of a jerk, honestly."

"Ya think?" I sit on the edge of the table and narrow my eyes playfully, deliberately choosing not to be insulted at the personal question. It's almost like it slipped out of his mouth before he could catch himself. "So you *were* paying attention to me back then, Brennan?"

"Uh, maybe. A little. I mean, it was... Um. It was hard not to notice when he was so fucking loud about everything. He didn't treat you well, from what I saw." His entire face turns pink and he fusses with the hem of his T-shirt.

Holy shit. I thought I suffered in silence. Was Jake such an obvious asshole? "Yeah, he wasn't a great boyfriend, but I was young and naive. It was a long time ago. I've moved on."

"Sounds like we've both had our share of bad relationships." Brennan nods, looking thoughtful.

"You too?" I watch him closely wondering if he's actually interested in me as a person. The prospect of someone being attracted to my brain instead of just my tits and ass sends an unexpected jolt to my pussy. "What about now?"

He hesitates, then shakes his head. "No. My only serious relationship was in college. I thought we were exclusive. She was fucking five different guys. I didn't even notice until she got engaged to one of them. I was building CognifyAI, so, uh..." He pours us both a fresh beer and hands me my glass. "Probably for the best. I'm under a lot of pressure and the company is my priority. I tend to let people down." He glances at me and I catch the flicker of guilt flash in his eyes. "Like you, for example."

"Ah, let's forget about it. We've all got baggage. And honestly, I'm not a success story when it comes to relationships either. Life is weird. You get hurt, you learn, and you keep moving forward." I hold my glass up to his and we clink them together.

He seems to appreciate my gesture and there's a moment of easy silence between us. How refreshing we don't need to fill up dead air with meaningless words.

Who knows, maybe we're becoming friends.

As the night goes on, I find myself even more intrigued by Brennan than I was at lunch. There's a depth to him. A quiet, contemplative intensity. It's flattering the way he's genuinely interested in getting to know me—it's not something I'm used to. Most guys see the polished exterior I've perfected over the years and want to fuck me.

Brennan, on the other hand, isn't giving me any of these vibes. He seems to want to dig deeper. To see what's underneath my facade.

"Hey," he says as the night winds down. "Regarding your reunion project. I have a wireframe in progress but I'm going to be honest—I don't know if I'll have the time to manage it day-to-day. I've decided to put up the money to hire a coder to develop the concept. If you're interested, I'd like you to manage the project—with my guidance, of course. We could co-own it, and I'll work out a way to monetize it after the event."

My jaw drops. I'm completely surprised he isn't backing out, which I expected. What he's proposing means this wouldn't only be about the stupid reunion anymore. We'd be tied together.

Tonight wasn't a date, it was an interview.

Maybe he is a player. I certainly haven't had someone try to pick me up by offering to partner up.

On the other hand, he's a straight shooter. How do I turn down the opportunity to partner with the most talented up-and-coming tech executive on the planet? "Are you fucking serious?"

"Yeah, I'm fucking serious." He drains his beer, looking exceedingly confident. He's in his element. "You've got a great business sense, Astrid. An amazing work ethic. I think we could make this into something special. What do you say?"

Truthfully, I'm overwhelmed and nearly start to cry.

In my entire life, no one has ever handed me anything. Especially someone like Brennan. This is a chance of a lifetime. Maybe I can get out of real estate and start a career I'd actually enjoy.

Quit. Real estate. Wow. I wouldn't have to pretend to be someone I'm not. Maybe I could slow down and have my own family one day.

"I'm in." I throw my arms around him. "Let's do this."

Brennan awkwardly pats my back. "Great. I'm glad."

As we leave the bar, I feel a surge of excitement unlike anything I've ever experienced.

I glance over at Brennan, who walks beside me with a determined look on his face. I know it in my gut. We're on the brink of creating something amazing.

If tonight is any indication of the future, I can't wait for what comes next.

Six

BRENNAN

Three Months Later

I'VE BEEN LOOKING FORWARD to this moment all day.

My entire Saturday was spent at the office with my finance team, poring over my company's P&L statements. Three-year and five-year projections. We have a few weeks to make this quarter's target sales goals or it's going to be a long year trying to recover. Ugh, it was excruciating.

I love creating things, not crunching numbers.

At least it's over now. I've parked my car on a hilly side street and I'm entering a quaint little Italian restaurant called Serafina. As always, my mind buzzes with anticipation at seeing her.

Saturday night has become my official "meeting" night with Astrid. At least if I'm in Seattle. When I'm traveling, we FaceTime, though I'd rather see her in person. She smells like peaches. Smiles like she's perpetually on a tropical vacation. Her laugh reminds me of sleigh bells.

So, yeah. It's definitely my favorite day of the week.

Three months ago, Astrid and I signed formation papers and founded Reuniverse. We're now business partners and—I think—friends. It's a new experience for me, being this comfortable around someone who isn't family.

I trust her.

It's exhilarating. And, terrifying.

Tonight she wanted to meet somewhere other than our usual spot, The Zoo. This quaint little restaurant, with candlelit tables and soft jazz playing in the background, is quite the step up. Romantic, even. It wouldn't matter where we met. Honestly, I'd do anything she asks as long as it means hanging out with her.

I spot Astrid immediately, seated at a corner table, effortlessly elegant. Her blonde hair is swept back in some sort of knot, revealing the delicate curve of her neck. God, the woman is so fucking beautiful. She glances up and the second she sees me, her smile takes my breath away. Every ounce of tightness in my body loosens a little.

"Hey." I slide into the seat across from her. "This place is a little fancier than our usual hangout."

Astrid's green eyes sparkle with mischief. "Thought we'd class it up a bit. You clean up well, by the way."

"Meh." I glance down at my clothes, dark jeans and a crisp, white button-down shirt. "Figured I'd try to look like one of the waiters. How'd I do?"

She makes a point of looking me up and down. "Not bad. I'll stick around."

The banter between us is always so easy. Shockingly natural at this point. We've settled into our own rhythm and we talk or text almost every day, whether it's about the latest developments with Reuniverse or sharing random thoughts as they pop into our heads.

She's becoming my best friend. Something I never expected. I'm not entirely sure what to make of it because I'm so wildly attracted to her.

We order a bottle of wine and, as we catch up, I find myself more relaxed than I've been in days. The pressure I'm under is always so intense. But here, with Astrid, it's like I can finally breathe.

"So, how's everything going with our coders?" Astrid swirls her wine. "Are they driving you crazy with their late-night texts?"

I roll my eyes at the mention of the nickname for the guys we hired in India. "Fuck, yeah, mostly because the time difference is killer. They're killer at what they do but *slowwwwww*. We're making progress, though. Still on track."

"That's what I like to hear. We've got a cool thing going, Brennan. I'm glad we're doing this together." She clinks her glass against mine.

"Me too." Working on Reuniverse has been such a pleasant distraction from the chaos of my other company. No one looks over my shoulder. No one questions every fucking thing I do. "It's been great having you handle the day-to-day stuff. I'm not sure how I'd manage without you."

"Don't sell yourself short, you're the brains behind this operation." Astrid winks.

I shake my head, laughing softly. "Seriously, you're the best."

"Awww, did I just get a compliment?" She leans in, lowering her voice. "Truth is, we make a great team."

For a moment, I'm caught off guard by how much her words mean to me.

Because I like being part of a team, for a change.

I like having a copilot.

Reuniverse isn't about building a business, it's about working on a cool project with Astrid. Over late-night texts. Video calls. These Saturday meetings.

In a few short months, Astrid has become my favorite person. It scares the hell out of me, but I'm rolling with it.

The server places our plates in front of us and we fall into a contented silence as we devour our pasta. I overhear the man at the table next to us order a whiskey and tension permeates my body as memories from last night flood back. My eyes flick to him and his glass and Astrid, who's become attuned to my moods, notices.

"You okay?" She touches the top of my hand gently.

I consider how much to share. I trust her. Spilling family secrets feels like a betrayal but it would be nice to have an outside perspective.

"Ah, it's Cillian." I put my fork down and sigh. "He blew me and Seamus off to get wasted again. It brings up a lot of old memories of my da."

Astrid's expression softens and her fingers thread with mine. "I'm sorry, Brennan. That's tough."

"It is..." Her judgment-free words have me choked up. I need to regain my composure. "He's always been the brother I'm closest to. My Irish twin. We've been through everything together and I'm so worried he's slipping away. I can't bear to see him go down the same path as Da."

She squeezes her eyes shut, as if remembering her own trauma. "It sucks watching someone you love make choices you know are bad for them. Unfortunately, sometimes, they have to figure it out and own their decisions."

"I know you're right but he's been there for me and I want to return the favor. I'm MIA so much these days with all the travel." I caress the top of her hand with my thumb.

She squeezes my fingers gently before letting go. "You're an amazing brother, Brennan. He'll come around."

"The fear is overwhelming, don't you think?" I take a sip of my wine. Astrid has her own family issues she keeps battened down, though she rarely shares much.

Her slim fingers tipped in red skim the rim of her glass. "Yeah. It's like watching a car skid on ice. You see the crash coming, but you're helpless to stop it. Nora's back in rehab and I don't even begin to think it'll stick. Lark always has baby-daddy drama. One of the kids' fathers is threatening to sue her for full custody. Another is behind on child support. The third she still sleeps with, so I'm bracing myself for another pregnancy. Somehow, I'm the one they always call for money only to resent me for helping. I support them from afar to protect my own mental health."

"Ah, Astrid. That sucks. I wish there was something I could say to make it easier." Jesus Christ, I'd give anything to take her in my arms. Hold her for hours.

Fuck her until dawn.

Of course, I won't. I know where I stand. She'd freak out if she realized how many times I've fantasized about her giving me head.

We continue talking through several courses. Eventually, the conversation drifts to lighter topics. Astrid recounts the time a car dealership owner took a shit in a house she was showing, stinking up the entire place. I share tales of the pranks my brothers and I played on each other.

Whenever we hang out, time disappears. I'm genuinely sad when I realize we're the only two people left in the place. The staff busy themselves, waiting for us to leave.

Astrid snatches the bill before I can, sliding her Platinum AMEX across the table with a grin. "My treat this time. You can get the next one."

I laugh. "You're too quick for me."

"It's about time I returned the favor." She winks with great exaggeration.

Stepping out into the cool air, I don't want the night to end. Each time we get together, I find it difficult to ignore my deepening feelings for her.

I doubt she reciprocates them. We're business partners. Friends. Better to keep the wall up. The one I've grown comfortable with in my years of hiding behind work.

"Can I walk you home?" I hear myself contradict my inner voice.

Astrid slings her arm through mine. "Sure, it's about time you asked."

Now I feel stupid. Of course I should have offered. All these months, what was I thinking letting a beautiful woman walk twenty minutes alone in the dark? "Shit, Astrid. I'm such a dick..."

"Stop." She presses her finger to my lips. "If there's something I've learned about you, B, it's you're never deliberately obtuse. Once you figure something out, it's ingrained."

My breath stops. Should I tell her...

No. Why spoil things. It'll freak her out.

As we walk toward the water, I feel a definite current between us. A buzzing, hopeful realization. What if Astrid wants to push things further too? Do I dare see where this could go?

Shit. I'm hesitant—afraid, even.

Our friendship is so important to me. As is our partnership. The idea of telling her my true feelings is a risk. From past experience, I know the pain when she rejects me will be paralyzing.

We reach her houseboat and Astrid turns to me. "Brennan, are you okay? You seem...I don't know, like you're in your head more than usual."

"I'm fine, just a lot of processing." I force a smile.

She doesn't press, but I can see the concern in her eyes. "You know you can talk to me? About anything."

"Yeah, I know," I say, though I doubt she'd want to know my true inner thoughts right now. "Thanks, A. I appreciate it."

She slips her hand from my arm and digs out her keys. "Goodnight, B."

Astrid steps closer until we're almost chest to chest. Her hand brushes mine and the contact sends jolts of electricity through my entire body. My cock fills and I have to take a tiny step back or she'll feel it nudge her. Or, I'm gonna lose control and kiss the bejeezus out of her.

"Goodnight," I choke out.

We stand there for a second, the air between us charged with something unspoken. Like whatever is between us is about to change forever. I'm about to throw caution to the wind when Astrid jams her key into the door and gives me a small, regretful smile before going inside.

The door shuts and I feel the tension in my chest return. Stronger than before. Jesus Christ. I've never felt this way about anyone, I'm falling for her and I'm not sure what to do about it.

On the drive home my mind races with thoughts of Astrid. I go straight to bed, but sleep doesn't come. I lie awake, staring at the ceiling, thinking about the way Astrid's hand felt in mine. Analyzing the way she looked at me.

Christ, does Astrid feel something for me too? Is it possible?

What do I do about it? How can I find out?

Maybe it's time to stop holding back. Go after what I want, for a change.

Do I have the courage?

Seven

ASTRID

Three Months Later

I HAVEN'T SEEN BRENNAN in person for nearly three months.

I'm surprised at how badly I've missed him. We're getting together after we both have dinner with our families and I can't wait.

He's been stuck in Silicon Valley, knee-deep in some new acquisition and his communication with me has waned a bit. Oh, we still text or talk on the phone every day or so—and I get it, he's too busy for more. One of the reasons he's so fascinating is his mind is always churning.

It's weird, though. I'm not gonna lie. Until this particular trip, we'd been practically joined at the textual hip, even when he traveled. This time, when my clever messages go unanswered, it bums me out.

It sucks to feel ignored, but I let it slide. It's blatantly apparent the man has no concept of time. He doesn't realize he's being inconsiderate. As frustrating as he can be, time-blindness is a thing. I'm not going to change him, so why try?

Now, let it be known, if we were *dating*, there's no way I'd put up with this shit. My dating life has been filled with disappointment in this regard. Men who prioritize everything over me and I'm sick of it.

But, we're not dating. In fact, he hasn't given me signs he's interested in a romantic relationship, which is for the best. We're friends and business partners and Brennan has been honest from the beginning about his schedule. It's the reason he brought me into Reuniverse. He has enough pressure trying to balance his responsibilities without me piling on.

Anyways, we're meeting at our usual haunt later and I can't wait to see him, drink cheap beer, brainstorm plans for Reuniverse, and beat him at pool.

For now, I push those thoughts aside and head into my parents' house with several bags filled with food. The front door creaks and the house smells like it always does—old wood, dust, and something faintly burnt, probably from my mom's attempt at breakfast.

It's been a while since I visited. Brennan is so close with his family he's inspired me to try to reconnect with mine.

My parents have always worked themselves to the bone, scraping by with low-paying jobs. Mom cleans houses and works at a shipping company. Dad also works maintenance. You'd think the house would be utter perfection with their skill sets, but no, it's the polar opposite.

Most of the walls are yellowed from age and cigarette smoke. The floorboards creak with every step and the furniture is well worn, sagging in places. My mom and dad spend their lives making everyone else's property sparkle, and spend no energy doing it for themselves.

I've tried to buy them new stuff. Offered, even, to buy them a new home—something where the roof doesn't leak and the plumbing doesn't groan every time you turn on the sink.

My dad won't hear of it. He's proud of this house, even if it's falling apart. Saving enough money to buy it is his greatest accomplishment. There's no point in making either of them feel bad for how they choose to live.

Who am I to judge?

My altruism does *not* extend to my sisters, Nora and Lark. Nora's battle with addiction has cast a shadow over our lives for too long. No one's heard from her since she ditched rehab two months ago. Lark, with her aversion to working and propensity for not using birth control, lives here rent free. She's not pregnant again, thank God.

Peeking through the kitchen into the living room, I bear witness to a tornado. Baileigh, my twelve-year-old niece, is sprawled on the couch, phone glued to her hand. Jaxson and Kayleigh chase each other around the living room, screaming bloody murder. Mom screams at them to settle down, to no avail.

"Hey, everyone, I'm here." I wave from the doorway.

"Oh, look. It's Auntie A," Baileigh sneers. "You're late."

God, her tone grates. She's exactly like her mother. Ungrateful A.F. "Nice to see you too, Bay."

"Auntie A." Jax races up, his sticky hands immediately reaching for the bags. "Whatcha bring?"

"Dinner and some snacks." I hold them a little higher. "How about you wait until we all sit down."

"Aw, come on!" He hops up like a rabid bunny, his energy out of control like always. Kayleigh is behind him and snatches one of the bags out of my hand, rummaging through it before I can stop her.

"Kids, sit down!" Mom's voice cracks through the noise, but neither of them listens. Instead, they tear into a bag of Sunchips like wild animals.

Lark ambles in, ignoring the commotion like it's got nothing to do with her. "Wassup?"

"I brought dinner." I try not to sound annoyed. "Baileigh, do you want to help me plate?"

She glances at me with disdain. "Uh, *no*."

On cue, Jax rips open the bag of chips and it explodes, bits scatter all over the floor.

My patience is already worn thin and I haven't been here five minutes. I'm gonna snap, I swear to God. This is how it always is—Lark barely lifts a finger while the rest of us try to corral her feral children and keep the house from falling apart. The kids have no manners and she doesn't bother disciplining them. Trying to instill any sort of order is fighting a losing battle.

Why the fuck do I bother?

"Hey, Dad." I practically tackle him with a hug as he walks into the room. He's not very emotive, but the one of my family who seems to like me.

"Astrid." He embraces me tightly. "You didn't have to bring all this. Having you here is all we need."

I shrug, trying to keep things light. "I don't mind, I thought it would be nice to enjoy a family dinner together once in a while."

"Appreciated." He smiles and wanders over to his place at the table.

I brought a couple of roast chickens, some potatoes, and green beans. Save for a couple of staples, I'm not a great cook but I can plate like a boss. Not that anyone notices. The meal is the usual circus. Kids shouting over each other. Food flying everywhere. Lark ignoring them while Mom tries to restore some order.

I can't help but wonder if Brennan's McGloughlin family dinners are equally chaotic.

Somehow, I doubt it.

Half hour later, everyone is at the couch watching TV except me and Lark, who remain at the table. When I approach to clear the dishes, she drops her fork on her plate like I'm a busser at a restaurant.

"Must be nice, huh? Living on your fancy houseboat while the rest of us deal with reality." She picks her teeth with her nail.

There it is. The healthy dose of resentment bubbling under the surface is about to explode. My sister has a permanent chip on her shoulder when it comes to me. She thinks everything I've worked for was handed to me like a present.

"Listen..."

From his recliner, Dad catches my eye and shakes his head, subtly encouraging me to let it go.

And, you know what, he's right. I want to go. As in leave. Immediately.

I'm trying, but things never change. Why come here to be met with bitterness and resentment? I grit my teeth and swallow the urge to snap back.

My mom gets up from the couch to help me with the dishes. "You know," she looks down at the platter she's scrubbing, "we haven't seen much of you for years. Don't think coming around with a store-bought chicken like you're some savior makes you a good daughter."

Jesus Christ.

"I *am* a good daughter." I try to tamp my frustration down. "My intentions are pure."

She shakes her head. "Bullshit. From the time you started school, you've always been embarrassed by your own family."

"What?" I bite my lip and nearly draw blood in my attempt not to scream. "That's not true."

"It is and you shouldn't bother being fake. None of us want or need your charity." She wipes down the counter. I know she means it and it hurts.

As usual, I find myself wondering why the hell I try. I have no idea why my own family doesn't want anything to do with me. I finish drying the dishes in silence, my mind already at The Zoo, where I'm meeting Brennan soon.

I suck it up for a while but once everyone is in front of the TV, it's like I'm invisible. I slip out without saying goodbye. I'm frustrated. Completely on edge. My heart aches. My head is pounding. I feel like I'm going to throw up my dinner. I've always wanted my family to accept me and I always find myself on my own.

Why am I never enough?

Before I know it, I'm nearly home. I'm going to be late if I park at the slip and walk up to the bar. On the other hand, my mood has turned to shit and all I want to do is curl up in bed and cry. The fresh air will help clear my head and hopefully I'll be in a better frame of mind by the time I meet Brennan.

Twenty minutes later, I'm still worked up when I push through the door to The Zoo. I spot Brennan immediately. He's standing by our usual pool table with a pitcher of beer and two full glasses. The moment he sees me, his face changes—like he knows I'm in distress without me having to say a word.

Brennan rushes to my side and for the first time in months, I don't have to hold everything together.

"Hey." His arms wrap around me and I sob into his shoulder.

It's been months since we've touched and it's never been like this. He holds me tight. One hand strokes my shoulder while the other cups the back of my head. I've never felt safer. More cared for.

"I'm fine." My words come out shaky, though.

Brennan pulls back enough to look at me, his eyes filled with concern. "You don't have to be fine. Not with me, A."

His words are like a release valve. Tears stream down my face and I don't even care we're in public. I've been strong for so long but now, in his arms, I don't want to be.

"I had a rough day," I admit quietly, leaning into his chest. "My family...it's so hard."

Brennan's hand glides soothingly up and down my back. "I get it. I'm here. I've got you."

The moment stretches between us, thick with emotion. Without thinking it through, I gaze up at him. He's already looking down at me, his expression heated, but tentative. For an instant, neither of us moves. The air between us is charged with an energy we've been dancing around for months.

Then he presses his lips against mine.

The kiss is not tentative. Not hesitant. It's like something inside him has snapped into place and any restraint he's been clinging to gives way. His soft, firm lips are warm and urgent against mine and both hands cup my face tenderly.

This is the single most intimate moment of my entire life.

I kiss him back enthusiastically. My fingers clutch his shirt, pulling him closer. Any confusion about my feelings for Brennan melt away. Everything we've been skirting around for all these months is laid bare.

When we pull apart, panting and a little dazed, he rests his forehead against mine. "God, I've missed you."

"I've missed you too," I whisper as my heart pounds in my chest.

Everything shifts in this moment.

Whatever happens next, there's no going back.

Eight

BRENNAN

Rewind the Same Night, Different Perspective

THE SECOND I WALK into The Zoo, it hits me how long I've been away from my happy place.

I mean, it feels like I never left, but it's actually been ages. Three long months of nonstop chaos in Silicon Valley, navigating through a maze of an acquisition, numerous board meetings to prepare for followed by schmoozy investor dinners. Every step forward in my company feels like it's pushing me ten steps back in my daily life.

I don't have bandwidth. Strings of back-to-back, twelve-to-fourteen-hour days deplete me to the point where I can't function. Sometimes, I'll sleep for an entire day or so to recharge my batteries.

And, my God, this new acquisition is a disaster waiting to happen. My board outvoted me and now I'm stuck trying to integrate a company—and entire executive team—with a profit-first vision into my ethics-first infrastructure. The fissures are already evident.

Truth be told, CognifyAI has grown so big, operations have taken a complete 180 from my original vision. Now the deal is done, though, and it's my responsibility to figure out how to make it work. Meanwhile, a potential IPO looms ahead along with another major product launch.

I'm coming to terms with the fact the next eighteen months are going to be busier than the past three.

If we go public, I'll be golden-handcuffed to my company for a long time. Unfortunately, I'm used to being exhausted, stretched thin, and torn between what I want and what the board demands.

Do I keep going? Do I have a choice?

At the moment, my stress is compounded by the shit happening in my family. Cillian is careening toward a self-destructive implosion. He's pulled away from everyone who loves him. None of us can get through. We're all worried sick because it's official. He's following in my da's footsteps and ruining his life with his drinking.

Liam and Padraig, the twins, aren't much better off. Laid-back Padraig's burned out from the rock-star grind, tired of chasing fame. Ambitious Liam's not ready to let go of his dream. The tension in their band is at an all-time high. I hate how their close relationship is strained to the point of breaking.

A year ago, Astrid and I became business partners and friends. Now she's my unexpected and cherished light. I trust her implicitly. She never pressures me about my work schedule. Her endless support and understanding, no matter how many days we go without talking, is refreshing. I can always count on her for a kind, encouraging word. She's the perfect woman.

The only person outside of my family who encourages me to be true to myself.

There's no question in my mind. We have a special bond.

Astrid Gustaffson has become my safe place.

Hopefully I'm hers too.

There's no doubt I'm attracted to her.

I wish so badly…

Ahh, no. I can't. It wouldn't be fair. Astrid deserves a man who can treat her like a queen. Her past relationships, at least how she's explained them, have been with men who don't prioritize her. I don't want to be another man who disappoints her.

It's depressing.

God, it sucks. She's the one thing I love about my life. She's one person I can be real with. Astrid doesn't care about my money or clout or the headlines. She likes me for being me. Unapologetically.

Anyway, I can't wait to see her tonight. I've looked forward to this for weeks. She's not here yet so I've secured our favorite pool table. I have a full pitcher of beer. I'm so fucking ready for a night off with my favorite person, I can barely keep still.

Ten minutes later, she walks through the door and I can tell something's wrong before she even says a word.

Oh, God. My beautiful Astrid's been crying.

Before my brain can catch up, I swiftly close the gap between us and just act. Wrap my arms around her and pull her tightly against me without hesitation. She melts into my chest and I know, without a shadow of doubt, this is where she's meant to be.

This is what I'm meant to do.

Hold her. Comfort her. Take the burden off her shoulders.

Holy shit, feeling her pressed against my body—everything else fades into the background but the two of us.

"Hey," I whisper as her tears soak into my shirt.

She sobs so hard it breaks me. I tighten my grip on her. One hand strokes her back while the other gently cradles her head. I've never seen her lose her composure, let alone fall apart. To know she trusts me this deeply makes me want to shield her from whatever's hurting her.

Forever.

She pulls back slightly, trying to put on a brave face. "I'm fine," she says, but the crack in her voice tells me otherwise.

I tilt my head down, meeting her eyes. "You don't have to be fine. Not with me, A."

Her walls crumble. All of her strength slips away and her tears flow freely, like a dam has broken.

"It's so stupid," she murmurs. "My family...I hate how they make me feel."

My hand glides soothingly up and down her back. "I get it. I'm here. I've got you."

We stand like this way for what feels like forever. Lost in the quiet of our moment in the middle of a crowded bar.

Just us. Here. Now. *Simple.*

Astrid blinks up at me through her tears. Green eyes search mine and suddenly, we're teetering on the edge of something I've wanted—but deliberately avoided—for months. There's no fucking question about it. I can *feel* it. The way her breath catches, the way her hand lingers on my chest.

I lean in.

One second we're standing there, and the next, my lips are on hers. It's not gentle, or tentative. It's raw. Urgent. Like every moment I've held back is pouring out of me all at once. I grip Astrid's face to pull her closer. She grabs my shirt like she's afraid to let me go.

Nothing has ever felt like this. Her lips are pliant and delicious, but there's a fierceness behind the kiss. Like she's been resisting as much as I have. Pure and simple, this is a release. All the tension and uncertainty has unraveled.

When we finally pull apart, both of us are breathless, but our foreheads remain pressed together. My hands are tangled in her hair.

"God, I've missed you," I murmur.

She nuzzles my cheek. "I've missed you too."

In this moment, everything shifts. We've crossed a line and there's no going back now. Somehow, I don't fear what comes next. She's it. My person. There's no question in my mind.

Of course, the reality of my life threatens to creep back in. The acquisition, the board, the IPO. It's all still a shadow. Astrid doesn't realize I'm about to be tied down in ways I've never been before. She has no real concept about the mounting pressure I'm under.

I push the thoughts out of my head. Right now, all I care about is her. Everyone else can fuck off. I'm not going to take this moment for granted.

I kiss her again, softer this time, savoring the way her lips move against mine. Astrid reaches up and brushes her fingers lightly against my cheek. I lean into her touch. The look she gives me—vulnerable, and maybe a little unsure—makes it impossible for me to resist.

"Let's get out of here." I take her free hand and squeeze it gently.

Astrid gives a small nod. "Yeah."

We walk out of the bar together, hand in hand. My car is parked out front. I open the door for her and get into the driver's seat once she's seated. Neither of us says anything as I start the engine, but her hand rests on my thigh. Like I'm hers.

Which is so fucking true.

Astrid's house is minutes away, but each second feels like an eternity. The sexual tension between us is building with every block.

When I pull up to the dock and park, she turns to me. Her voice is low. Inviting. "This might be a stupid question, but would you like to come in?"

"Yeah." I gulp. I cut the engine. Hardly able to believe this is really happening.

She looks at me and tilts her head.

Daring me to take the next step.

How can I resist when she's my destiny?

Nine

ASTRID

A Few Minutes Later

WHAT IS ACTUALLY HAPPENING right now?

Brennan steps behind me as I unlock the door to my houseboat.

I can still feel the heat from his kisses lingering on my lips. *Ohmyfuckinggod.* The overt sexual tension between us has always been just below the surface, though neither of us have ever acknowledged it. Now it's unleashed and there's no going back.

Never, in my entire life have I reacted this way. Now he's here, in my home, and I'm suddenly both sure and unsure of everything. He's turned a key to my heart and I know there's no going back.

When we have sex tonight, I'll be all in.

But will Brennan?

He takes in my houseboat with his patented quiet focus. His eyes skate over the curved wooden staircase, the wide windows opening onto the lake, and the simple, modern lines of the kitchen.

"This place, it's beautiful, A." He gazes out the window at the glimmering lake. "I should have realized it would be stunning and effortlessly cool, like you."

I lean against the counter, watching him. "I might specialize in luxury mansions, but I prefer to live somewhere simple where I can breathe."

"Well, it suits you." His fingers brush the edge of the quartz counter.

This house has always been my escape, but with Brennan here, it seems different. Intimate. Suddenly, I feel shy.

Since we kissed at the bar, there's been a shift in the air between us. We both pretend to be fascinated by the surroundings when all we're thinking about is what happens next.

At least I am.

Feeling the need to do something with my hands, I take a step toward the kitchen. "Do you want something to drink? I've got wine or beer." I open the fridge. "Or, mineral water."

Brennan watches me for a second, then shakes his head. "No, I'm good."

The silence that follows is awkward. With only the sound of water softly lapping at the side of the boat, we're both waiting for the other person to speak. To make sense of what's going on between us.

A line's been crossed.

We're either on the edge of something big or we're going to try to put the genie back in the bottle.

"It's weird, right?" I break the silence. "You and me. *This.*"

Brennan steps closer. "Yeah—but it doesn't feel wrong."

Oh.

My heart thuds in my chest with an anticipation I've never known.

I search his deep, brown eyes for anything to help me understand what he's thinking. What he wants. "I thought we're just friends. Or, at least, I convinced myself you wanted to keep things platonic."

"I convinced myself of the same thing." He meets my gaze and for a split second, I see utter vulnerability. "Don't you think it's more?"

I decide to be honest. "Until we kissed, I wasn't sure."

"And now?" He moves closer until we're practically chest to chest.

"Now, I'm confused." I take his hands in mine. "What I want and what I need might be different."

Brennan nods. "I'm terrible at relationships. It's never been a priority. I don't know how to..."

His words hang in the air and suddenly, everything clicks into place.

We *are* in a relationship. Brennan has confided his fears, ambitions, dreams of the future and the pressure he carries every day. He trusts me with pieces of his life and challenges he faces in his own family. Slowly, deliberately, he's let me in. Shared parts of himself he doesn't give to anyone else, including his brothers.

All along, it's been his way of choosing me, and I almost missed it.

"I've been testing you," I admit quietly. "Because, I do have feelings for you and was waiting to see if you'd make a move. To be sure you wanted this."

He exhales slowly. One hand cups my cheek. "I *do* want you. I've wanted you since high school. More than you know. I'm not a great bet, though. The last thing I want is to disappoint you."

His touch is soft, but there's an intensity in his eyes. It takes my breath away. Makes my heart ache.

"B," my hand covers his on my cheek, "I don't need you to be anyone but yourself. It's not your job to fix everything or have it all figured out. Just be real with me."

For a second, I think he's going to pull away. But, instead, he leans in, pressing his forehead to mine. "We can talk about those things some other time. Tonight, I want to take care of you. Give you pleasure to erase some of the pain you've been carrying."

The ground shifts beneath me.

"I don't need saving." I can't help my voice from trembling, because I do *want* to be saved. Not always. Just sometimes.

His eyes lock on to mine. "Of course you don't. I don't need to *save* you. I need to *worship* you."

Is he for real?

I sure fucking hope so.

Unable to answer but desperate to get to the worshipping, I grip his hand and lead him upstairs. The curving wooden staircase creaks under our feet as we make our way to my bedroom loft. The city lights glint off the water outside the windows, casting a gentle glow. Everything feels soft and quiet, like the world has paused for us.

We sit on the edge of the bed and he wraps his arms around me. There's no urgency like there was at The Zoo. I rest my head against his chest and listen to the steady beat of his heart. Brennan runs his hand through my hair, slow and soothing. I close my eyes. Let the comfort of his touch wash over me.

It's been a long day—an exhausting, emotionally draining day—but somehow, being here with Brennan makes it all bearable.

"You had a rough visit, huh?" His fingers trace small circles on my lower back.

A rough day—a disastrous showing at the luxury condo downtown followed by the tension at dinner with my family.

"I did," I murmur into his shirt. "I'm exhausted from trying so hard."

Brennan doesn't ask for details. He doesn't need to. He holds me tighter and his lips press against the top of my head. "I'm sorry."

His strong arms around me ease my tension and elicit a confession. "Until I saw you tonight, I didn't allow myself to acknowledge how much I've missed our time together. You've become my person."

"I know how you feel." His hand rakes gently through my hair.

We sit wrapped up in each other for what feels like hours. It's strange. Being allowed to let go, even for a little while isn't scary, it's freeing. I'm always the one who takes care of everything. My clients, my business, myself. Here with Brennan, I don't have to be strong.

After a bit, I lift my head to meet his eyes. "I want to be there for you, too, Brennan."

He furrows his brow. "You already are."

Our mouths crash together. I slide my hand under the hem of his shirt and push it up, but he grips my wrist and presses it against the mattress. Showing me he's going to control the pace. Which I like. A lot.

His lips are soft but deliberate, exploring my mouth with expert precision. His hand makes its way to my waist and he pulls me closer, taking his time. Drawing each moment out. Each kiss is deeper than the last and the tension builds deliciously. By relaxing into the moment, I feel every second. Every breath.

"Make me come." The words escape before I can stop them.

Brennan bands one arm around my waist and skims his palm along my inner thigh. "Are you sure? I don't want you to regret anything."

"I won't regret it." I lie back and pat the space next to me. Kick off my ankle booties.

Brennan lies on his side next to me, his thumb traces my lips and I suck it into my mouth. "Jesus, God, A."

I'm pretty sure I'm more experienced than him but, at the same time, not many partners have been able to satisfy me. I take the lead by gripping the back of his neck to bring his face to mine.

The air between us thickens. Brennan's lips move urgently against mine, each kiss hungrier than the last. He no longer holds back. His hands trail down my stomach and down my thighs to the hem of my skirt, which he pulls up to my waist. Every touch, every movement, sends heat spiraling through me, and I lose myself entirely.

Brennan's thumb traces along the edge of my silky thong and he dips it inside, gliding it along my seam. I wonder if he likes my hairless pussy. He must, I can feel his erection burrowing into my thigh.

"Let me take the edge off." Without warning, he lightly pinches my labia with his fore and middle finger, sandwiching my clit between them. I nearly jackknife off the bed when he squeezes them together and his lips latch on to the sensitive space behind my ear.

It's so intense, like a full, deep-clit massage. I'm on the edge in seconds. Holy shit, the man has actual skills. I've misjudged the situation, believing I'd need to show him what to do.

My head lolls back when his thumb finds my slick bud and circles it as he continues to squeeze my lips together. Circles it. Squeezes. Edging me until my thighs are quaking and my body jolts with pleasure. All of my core muscles flex and release as little zings of ecstasy radiate but don't quite explode.

Brennan watches me intently as he experiments with different pressures and movements. Doubling down when I relax. Backing off when I'm about to go over, leaving me insane with desire.

"What are you doing to me? Let me come. I'm so close." I moan and squiggle.

He feathers kisses along my jaw and releases my pussy. "Do you want to take the lead, or let me take care of you? I'm good either way, it's your night."

As he waits for my answer, Brennan unbuttons my blouse and unfastens the front clasp of my bra. Bends down, sucks a nipple into his mouth and nibbles on it.

Holy shit. He's playing my body like a fiddle.

"You do it," I keen. "*You* take the lead."

"It's my pleasure." Brennan slips two fingers deep inside me and locates my G-spot immediately. "Relax, A. I've got you." He strokes me over and over until I'm writhing and clenching around his fingers. My entire core convulses with such an intense release, I'm gushing everywhere.

Oh, he doesn't stop. Every move he makes is precise. Focused. Designed to heighten my every sensation.

"How is this happening?" I arch up against his wrist. My head thrashes from side to side during the most drawn-out, rolling orgasm of my life.

"It's a respectable start." Brennan slows his movements, kissing me deeply until I settle. When I'm a noodle against the pillow, he pulls out his fingers and sucks my juices off them. "You taste better than I ever imagined."

I watch in fascination as he licks every drop. I've underestimated this guy. Brennan owns my body.

He's cracked my sexual code.

I'm ready—aching, to take this to the next level.

Because if he's that skilled with his fingers, imagine what he'll do with his cock.

Ten

BRENNAN

Later That Night

Talk about unexpected.

It wasn't on my bingo card to make Astrid come tonight, but holy hell. I couldn't ask for anything better.

She lies pressed against me, her head rests on my chest. I'm still clothed. Though I'm not looking, the knowledge Astrid's skirt is hiked up to her waist and her hairless, dripping pussy peeps out to the side of her thong is making it hard not to come in my pants.

The room is quiet, except for the gentle sounds of the waves against the houseboat and the distant hum of the city outside. I tighten my arm around her, keeping her close. Astrid combs her fingers gently through my hair.

This is what's missing. Astrid. Us. Together.

For the first time in a long time, everything feels...right. My mind is actually quiet.

God, I need to try to hold on to this moment. Because, if I'm honest, I know we've crossed a line we can't come back from. There's no denying it, I've fallen for her. Completely. Being with her like this solidified what I've been trying to keep at bay for so long.

I don't just *want* her in my life, I *need* her.

As much as I want to believe she feels the same, I can't shake the doubt. She had a bad day. Maybe this was her way to escape. To find comfort. I've got to be careful not to read into this. Careful not to let myself believe this means something to her too.

You've made that mistake before.

I press a kiss on the top of her head, my heart pounding in my chest. "You doing okay?"

"Yeah." Her affirmation comes out soft, almost hesitant.

I don't want to push her or put pressure on what happened. At the same time, we can't ignore we've been intimate. "You know," I try to keep my tone light, "I've thought about us being together like this for a while now."

"You have?" She tilts her head up slightly, meeting my gaze.

There's something so vulnerable in her voice, it makes my chest tighten. Before we have sex, I'd like to define who we are to each other, but instead, I focus on the feel of her next to me. The way her breathing has slowed. The quiet peace between us.

Even though I don't know where we'll go from here, I know one thing for sure—I want to be here with her so I'm going to continue to take the lead. "Yes, this is where I want to be."

I kiss her and find I'm instantly in tune with her every subtle reaction. It's like something's clicked deep in my brain and I'm able to help her unleash her most raw, vulnerable, sexual side. I've never experienced anything like it.

I take off her top and bra, noting how her body responds to each touch. Methodically, I catalog what makes her cry out. Moan. What draws a quiet gasp.

We're both ready. Our bodies are like two puzzle pieces that must snap into place. There's no hesitation left—just a shared need neither of us can ignore.

"B, I want you," Astrid murmurs against my mouth, her hand encasing the bulge in my jeans. "I've wanted this for ages."

Fuck, yeah. I'm going to love her all night long.

"I want to make you feel better than you've ever imagined." I trace her light-pink nipples with my finger until they both pucker. Fascinated they're exactly the color I imagined all these years. "I want to hear those sexy moans you made when I finger-fucked you. I want you to cry out with pleasure when I'm buried balls-deep inside you."

Astrid's eyes are squeezed shut. "I didn't dare hope you were a dirty talker."

"You like it?" I can't help but chuckle.

She shifts to unbuckle my belt. "You have no idea how much it turns me on."

"Take off the rest of your clothes." I roll over onto my back.

Astrid looks at me with surprise. "What?"

"I'd like you to be naked when I hold your legs down and feast on your pussy." I sit up and pull off my T-shirt. "Then, I want to suck on those delicious nipples when I bury my cock into your hot, wet pussy."

Astrid's expression is priceless. Utter confusion. "Um..."

"I like control when I fuck." I shrug and stand up. Kick off my shoes and unbutton and unzip my jeans, but keep on my briefs. Astrid hasn't moved, but I can tell she's into it because her nipples are puckered painfully tight. "Is this okay with you?"

She unzips her skirt and yanks it down. Her voice is raspy with lust. "Jesus, B. Bring it on."

"You got it." I grip her ankles, yank her to the edge of the bed and press her legs up and out.

Astrid watches me kneel before her and kiss across her chest, deliberately avoiding her tight nipples. She moans and tries to shimmy closer, but I shoot her a look and she bites her lip. Hard.

"Good girl." I kiss and nuzzle her belly button as I hook my fingers into her thong and pull it down her hips and legs and throw it to the floor.

Holy shit, she's laid out before me like a feast. Her bare pussy lips are swollen from my fingers and she's glistening with arousal. Her essence is intoxicating. I nestle between her thighs, admire the way her little clit pokes out for me. Initially, Astrid tenses at my inspection, then settles with her hands splayed out to her sides, clutching at the mattress.

"Your clit is magnificent." I trace a circle with my fingertip around the tight little nub.

She gasps and squirms. "God. I'm dying here, seriously."

"Oh, I've got you." I drag my finger down through her folds and push it inside her. Immediately, she clenches around my finger like a vise and my cock lurches, like it knows how perfect it's going to feel when it slides home.

Jesus. I can't take it any longer. I have to taste her. Astrid leans up on her elbows, watching me intently, and I grin up at her before pulling her lower lips into my mouth. I suck and lick them thoroughly and sink my tongue into her tight pussy. Her hips fly off the mattress, canting unabashedly against my face.

Palming her inner thighs, I hold her still while I lick from her entrance to her clit and back again, naughtily swirling my tongue along her back pucker. She moans and keens with every swipe. I press my thumb on her clit and she explodes. Arches her back and screams my name so loud, there's no doubt her neighbors hear.

Astrid's juices flow freely and I drink every drop until she's satiated and calm, kissing up her thighs and her flat belly as I make my way back to her face. Run my fingertips up and down her skin as I go, watching as goose bumps follow in my wake.

She's absolutely beautiful. Her eyes are closed and her blonde hair fans out around her. A satisfied smile paints her lips.

I cup her breasts and pull a sweet nipple into my mouth. Tug it with my teeth. Soothe it with my tongue. Her fingers plunge into my hair and she holds on tight as I worship the breasts I've dreamed about. Whacked off to.

Real life is so much better than fantasy.

Gliding my hands up her arms to her wrists, I move them over her head. "You taste so fucking delicious."

My cock, straining painfully against my briefs, is nestled against her pussy. I rotate my hips a bit, feeling her hot, wet heat soak me. Her eyes blink open and focus on mine. "I want you inside me."

"I'm clean. It's been a couple of years." I climb onto the bed and hold myself above her, waiting for her reaction.

She breaks free of my grip and pulls me down for a kiss. My God, can she kiss. Astrid gives me everything she has and more, like it's her job before she mutters against my lips, "I'm clean and have an IUD."

I love the way her pelvis cradles mine. The feel of her toned thighs clenched around my hips. I'm not going to last much longer, so I shimmy out of my briefs and my cock springs free. I settle back down against her with my dick resting against her entrance. "You're sure?"

Astrid reaches between us, grips my shaft and flicks the tip against her clit before guiding it inside her. I swear it's like a revelation.

"You're so big." She lays back as I work my way in.

She's ready for me, but I don't want to hurt her. All of us McGloughlin brothers have been blessed with big dicks, but mine's the biggest in both girth and length. *Trust.* The six of us measured ourselves one night when we'd had too many beers, though I'll never admit this out loud.

When I'm halfway in, I start to see stars. "Astrid, I'm sorry but I'm so close."

"Go for it. Slam into me. I want it hard." She reaches around and grabs my ass to pull me deeper.

I pull my hips back and ram deep. Stop so I don't lose full control. Repeat the motion and slowly increase the pace, hooking her leg around my elbow until she's spread wide.

I watch my thick, hard cock impale her, fascinated I'm actually fucking the woman of my dreams and it's even more incredible than I could have ever imagined.

"You fit me like a fucking glove, A." I gaze into her green eyes, which are nearly rolled back into her head. "How does this feel. Is it too much?"

Her body clenches around me, milking my cock. "You were made for me. Your cock is hitting my...*ahhhhhhhhhh*."

Astrid's pussy clenches tightly around my shaft as she comes and I have no choice but to follow, pulsing streams inside her as I grunt like a caveman.

"Holy shit," she pants, gripping my forearms as I come harder than I've ever done in my life.

I collapse onto my forearms and roll her on top of me so she's draped across my body with my cock still buried deep. I cup her face in my hands and kiss her long and slow before pulling back to look at her. "How do you feel?"

"Utterly, completely, thoroughly fucked." She leans over and kisses me. "You surprised me in the best way."

"Good." I kiss her again and pull away. "Because, I hope you weren't planning on sleeping."

Eleven

ASTRID

The Next Morning

"RELAX. LET YOURSELF BE loved."

Brennan whispered these words to me on round three, or maybe it was round four. Now, it's on a loop in my head.

His face is currently buried in my pussy, soulful eyes peer up at me as he flicks his tongue back and forth over my clit. His fingers pump in and out, persistently stroking my G-spot.

I've come so much over the past twelve hours, I've lost count. Everything I thought I loved about sex is out the window. The things Brennan has done to my body have exceeded anything I've experienced by tenfold. In fact, I can't even remember making love to anyone but him.

"Oh shit. Oh shit. Oh shit." I buck against his mouth. "I'm coming. *Ahhhhhh. *Oh shit. *Ahhhhh.*"

My heels dig into the mattress as, once again, my body gives in. My arm flops over my eyes. I'm spent. Every nerve ending in my pussy is so over-sensitized, but I'm not gonna make him stop. It's too mind-blowing. I'm addicted to this.

Brennan crawls up my body and settles in beside me. His arm slips around my waist as he pulls me close, chin resting lightly on my shoulder. I feel his breath soft against my skin.

He doesn't say a word, but the way his hand traces gentle circles on my back makes me feel like he's holding all the broken parts of me together without even realizing it. In his arms, the world fades away, and I feel whole—safe, cared for, and completely loved.

I've never been with a man who gives more than he takes.

If I'm not careful, I'll get used to this.

His monster cock digs into my hip. There's no way I can fuck him again because I'm sore and stretched and satiated. I want Brennan to feel the same way.

Skimming my hand down his thigh, I grip him, still fascinated at how extraordinarily huge he is. The man has a mythical unicorn cock and he knows precisely how to use it. "I'm not usually into giving head but I want to taste you. Will you show me how you like it?"

"Uh..." His breath catches. "You think I'd say no?"

If it were anyone else, I wouldn't offer. I've never been a fan of sucking cock because past boyfriends expect it. I hate it when guys want to fuck your face and make you gag. It's not for me. With Brennan, though, I think it'll be different.

"Good. Let me taste you." I swear his dick jolts at my offer. I stroke up and down his shaft and bend down and guide his tip to my lips. "Just don't choke me, I'm not a fan."

"I wouldn't." Brennan caresses the back of my head as he rolls onto his back.

My lips stretch around his girth and my tongue swirls around tentatively. He tastes a bit sweet, a bit salty and...clean. There's no funk or unpleasant bitterness. Hmmm. I like this. I hollow my cheeks out and suction all around him.

When he pulls out abruptly, it takes me by surprise. "I'm sorry, I'm not very good at this."

"Are you fucking serious?" He tips my chin up to look at him. "If you suck me again, I'm gonna blow."

"So, you liked it?" I rest my head against his hand, still fondling his gorgeous cock.

He strokes my cheek. "No. I loved it. I'd be embarrassed to tell you the number of times I've fantasized about it."

My pussy clenches. He *fantasized* about me? Multiple times?

All I want to do now is make his fantasy a reality. I guide him back into my mouth, keeping eye contact while I experiment. Sucking. Licking. Swirling. Different pressure. Fast and wet. Slow and gentle. I'm *so* into this. Watching his every reaction. Each sigh. Groan. Wince. We're connected so intently, like nothing I've ever allowed myself to experience.

"I've held back as long as I can, A. I'm gonna come." He taps my shoulder but it's too late. "Sorry. *Aghhhhh.*"

Brennan's hips buck into my mouth and his creamy ejaculation coats my tongue and slides down my throat. I swallow it all and savor every salty-sweet drop. I'm proud. It's me who's made him feel such intense pleasure.

His eyes are slack with happiness as he watches me suck lightly on his crown. One finger twirls a lock of my hair, the other caresses my cheek.

It's clear how much I've pleased him.

God, this is everything I've always wanted.

Stop it. Don't get ahead of yourself.

When he eventually softens, I climb back up and he lifts his arm so I can slip in against his side. His chest rises and falls steadily as his breathing returns to normal. There's something lingering in the air—unspoken, but tangible.

We've been up all night exploring each other's bodies with abandon, not taking time to overthink. The shift from friends to lovers is unfolding in real-time.

It's a lot to process.

"I've wanted you for so long. I don't think you have any idea." Brennan breaks the silence. The vulnerability in his words makes my heart swell.

I lift my head to look at him, surprised by the way his eyes seem to reflect every truth we've danced around for the past year. "I wasn't sure," I admit. My fingers trace small, absent patterns on his chest. "I really thought you wanted to stay friends. Well, and business partners."

"Ah." He laughs softly, although he clearly doesn't believe me. "I do want to stay friends. I've also wanted to see you naked since high school. I didn't think I hid it very well." He pauses, his eyes searching mine. "Truthfully, I wasn't sure how to make a move. Back then, you didn't see me, let alone see me as an option. I'm not very smooth with the ladies as I'm sure you've gleaned."

The admission catches me off guard, and I feel a pang of guilt. He's not wrong. Other than the fleeting memories of him in a general sense, I didn't pay attention to him, let alone consider him as a potential boyfriend. I was too wrapped up in trying to be someone I wasn't.

"I didn't and it's my loss." I run my thumb along his lips. "I spent my energy pretending to be perfect when I was far from it. Hanging out with people who I thought were aspirational. I'm not so naïve these days."

He holds my gaze, the silence between us thick with memories. "You're not pretending with me now?"

"Of course not. I'm not that girl." I shift in his arms, loving the warmth of his body pressed against mine. Also, not loving he had to ask if this was make-believe after my epic blowjob—actions speak louder than words, after all.

He nods slightly. "I never thought you were *that* girl. You had substance *and* beauty."

Something in his expression makes me pause. Brennan is special. Insightful. There's no way I'm going to play with his heart. It's time. There's no point in delaying it one second longer. "When I reached out to you, do you remember I mentioned I have something of yours?"

"Yeah." Curiosity flickers behind Brennan's eyes. "I've wondered if and when you'd get around to telling me what it is." He winks. "Or, if it was a ploy to have sex with me."

"My God, of *course* it was the sex. Why'd you hold out so long?" I flick his nipple and sit up. "It's nothing crazy," I tease, sliding out of bed and opening up a dresser drawer. "But I think you'll appreciate having it back."

Brennan watches me curiously as I rummage through my things. My heart beats a little faster when I locate the small, worn notebook. The cover is battered, the edges are frayed, but it's still intact. I return to bed and climb in and hand it to him, watching as his eyes widen. His fingers trace the worn cover.

"No way." He sucks a breath in as he turns it over in his hands. "I thought I'd lost this years ago."

"You did." I nestle against him. "Jake took it from your desk in class. He thought it would be funny to embarrass you, maybe read something out loud. I couldn't let him be so cruel to a guy who never did anything to deserve it."

Brennan's jaw clenches and he looks a bit strange, but his focus remains on the notebook. Like he doesn't want to look me in the eye. "You kept it? Did you read it?"

"I did." I feel a bit exposed. "I mean, I kept it. No. I've never looked inside. Or read it. Part of me figured there was something private in it. Something important you might not want to share."

He opens the notebook, flipping to the first page, and I see his expression soften. He shows it to me. It's like a journal entry. Personal and, in fact, private. His teenage handwriting fills the page, and for a moment, we both sit in the quiet, letting the weight of the past settle between us as we read the words.

I don't think anyone sees Astrid the way I do. She walks around with this perfect smile, always laughing with everyone, but when no one's paying attention, she pulls away. She sits by the window at lunch sometimes, staring out like she wishes she were somewhere else. Everyone thinks she's got it all together, but I can tell she's pretending. It's like she's hiding something, maybe from herself, too.

Somehow I don't think she's truly the version of herself everyone else sees. She's too smart. Too kind. She's not only beautiful, she's thoughtful. She notices things, reads between the lines, even if no one realizes it. I wish I had the guts to tell her. But someone like her? She'd never look twice at me.

"You wrote about me." I'm blown away. I watch his eyes scan the words again. "You noticed things about me no one else did. Things I didn't even notice about myself, but you were accurate."

Brennan closes the notebook, looking a bit sheepish. "Well, I wrote what I saw. You're so perfect on the outside. The most beautiful woman I've ever known, but your looks aren't why I had a crush on you. It's your heart. The depth to your character you were afraid to show anyone. Unfortunately, I wasn't blessed with the Irish charm my brothers have. I didn't have any confidence to talk to you."

"I can't believe it." I swallow hard to keep from crying. He's touched me to the core. "You saw the real me. The girl I was hiding from everyone else. And I never realized."

He gulps. "Confession time. I watched you a lot. Followed you, even. Not in a weird, stalkery way. Cillian found this notebook and told me I needed to stop. He was worried I'd scare you."

"You followed me? Where?" I guess I should feel a little strange, but somehow his revelation is endearing.

He squeezes his eyes shut and shakes his head. "I know where your parents live. That you slipped through the fence to catch the bus. You worked at a grocery store and thrifted all your clothes." He opens his eyes to catch me staring at him, mouth agape. "Look, really. I was harmless. When I get focused on something, it's hard for me to, um, snap out of it. Kill—that's what we call Cillian--caught on and set me straight. I'd never want you to feel afraid of me."

"I don't, B." I stroke his chin. "I never knew. I think it's sweet."

We sit there in the stillness, the notebook resting between us, and I realize how much we've both changed. Brennan isn't the strange boy from high school anymore, and I'm not the girl pretending to have it all together. We're here now on the brink of something monumental. After all these years. Seeing each other fully for who we are at our core.

He gathers me back into his arms and I feel like I'm where I belong. Whatever happens next, we're not the same people we were before.

Brennan's words from earlier come back to me, "*Let yourself be loved.*"

At the time, I thought he meant to relax, to stop overthinking while he was giving me orgasm after orgasm. Now, after seeing the notebook, I think I misunderstood. Tonight was never about sex. It's about connection. Being real. He already knows my vulnerabilities I thought were carefully kept hidden.

So no, he wasn't asking me to let go physically, he was asking me to let him in. Completely.

I think I can do this.

It feels like fate, being here together.

Like we're right where we belong.

Twelve

BRENNAN

Later That Evening

"You sure you're on board?"

I glance over at Astrid as I turn onto my parents' street. I'm not having second thoughts, but I realize this is a big, bold move.

She might be freaking out. 'Cause I am.

A *wee* bit.

I mean, I didn't exactly *beg* Astrid to come to dinner with me tonight, but bringing her home to meet my family feels like the next step. Why wait?

Besides, there's no way I can afford to slip into my old habits if I want things to work romantically with Astrid—and I do. Even though the timing sucks, with the pressures of the upcoming transaction looming, she's important to me. I've got to figure out how to balance everything for once in my life.

The way I see it, if my family meets her and realizes how much she means to me, they'll help me stay accountable. Besides, Cillian promised my ma he'll be here tonight. We haven't seen each other in months and it'll be helpful to get his take.

Astrid turns to me with a cheeky grin. "Honestly? I didn't expect you to introduce me to your parents the day after we first touched pee-pees, but yeah. I'm strangely okay."

Jesus, she's so fucking sexy. Even in simple black jeans and gray sweater. A few strands of her hair have fallen loose from her ponytail, framing her soft skin. And those lips. God, those lips. My cock stirs when I picture her lips wrapped around it...

"Brennan?" She gently touches my arm. "Watch the road."

Luckily, I'm not going fast and swerve out of the path of the line of parked cars. "Shit, sorry."

"You were thinking dirty thoughts. Maybe we'll have time for a quickie in your childhood bedroom." She cups my junk and waggles her perfectly plucked brows.

Aaaannnd, I'm at full wood. I hadn't even *fathomed* the possibility of fucking her in my old bedroom and now it'll be the only thing on my mind all night.

I move her hand away and clasp her fingers with mine so she doesn't get feistier. "You're a *very* bad girl."

"You like it because you're such a good, good boy." She grins as I park in front of my parents' Craftsman. "Now, think of something unsexy to tame him down a bit."

I squeeze my eyes shut and concentrate. *Wrinkly grannies. Wrinkly grannies. Wrinkly grannies.*

It's Connor's tried and true method for getting rid of unwanted and inappropriately timed erections. He swears by it and passed the wisdom down to all of us younger brothers. I have to concentrate until my erection subsides. When wee Brennan is under control, I breathe a sigh of relief.

Astrid stares at me, bemused. "Impressive mind control, Loki."

"Uh, thanks. Can't have a boner in front of my ma. Besides, I didn't tell them you were coming." I reach for the door handle and get out, dash around to the passenger side to help her out, holding out my hand for leverage. "Wait, did you make a Marvel reference?"

"*Duh*." She rolls her eyes and, anchored by my arm, gracefully exits. "Don't change the subject. You didn't even *text*? Why not?"

"My family's on a need-to-know basis." I lead her to the stone steps.

Astrid laughs nervously. "You think they'll be okay with me being here?"

"Shit, they'll be thrilled. My ma will act like she's known you forever and ask when we're getting married." I pat her hand. "Ready to meet your future mother-in-law?"

Instead of being in on the joke, Astrid freezes, pastes a smile on her face and breathes in deeply. I watch her, fascinated, as she transforms into the public version of herself. Poised look, check. Warm, engaging eyes, check. Shoulders back, spine straight, check. Her movements seem to be subconscious. I doubt she realizes what her own pre-game routine is.

A fleeting thought crosses my mind, though. It's possible my family isn't going to meet the version of Astrid I've gotten to know. I hope she relaxes and allows herself to be loose. Vulnerable. *Authentic*.

Well, even if they get the polished version clients see, they'll love her. She's flawless. Engaging. Polite.

The way I see it, any version of Astrid is perfection and, considering I'm throwing her into a strange situation, whatever makes her feel comfortable is fine by me.

Hand in hand, we climb up to the front porch. Before I have a chance to knock, the door swings open and Ma stands in the doorway. She doesn't visibly act surprised when she sees I've brought a woman home, but her eyes dart back and forth from me to Astrid. "Brennan! And who's this?"

"Astrid Gustafsson..." Before I can finish, Ma pulls her into a warm hug.

A couple of seconds later, Astrid drops my hand and wraps her arms around my mom's shoulders. Almost like she craves the affection. They stay like this for longer than what I consider normal, which I guess is a good thing. Finally, they break apart.

Ma beams. "Well, aren't you such a darling girl. Welcome. Come in, love, come in. I'll set another place at the table."

"Thank you, Mrs. McGloughlin." She looks at me and shrugs as we follow Ma into the house, her face flushed with embarrassment. "She gives a wonderful hug."

"Everybody says so," I reassure her, though I can't recall anyone ever saying those words. I want her to feel at home and if hugging my ma enhances her experience, I'm all for it.

Inside, the entire place smells like garlicky herbaceous goodness. Astrid takes it all in. The warmth of the living room. Family photos lining the walls. Candles flickering on the dining table. It's the definition of coziness, though our family life wasn't always this way.

"Rory!" Ma calls up the stairs. "Brennan's here. He brought a guest. Have you heard from Cillian?"

My hackles go up. Shit. Is Cillian going to be a no-show *again*?

Da trots down the stairs, the only sign of his longstanding health issues these days is a slight limp. Years of sobriety have softened him, but our relationship is still a bit strained. I have a lot of respect for him—he's managed to rebuild himself after nearly destroying our family.

On the other hand, I'm still bitter he was a shitty father-figure for most of my formative life. Cillian, Seamus, and I were still boys when he got into the accident. Throughout our teenage years into our twenties, Da was a drunken asshole with fleeting bouts of sobriety here and there.

Cillian, at least, shared an interest in construction with him, eventually taking over our family's business.

Seamus and I, on the other hand, are academics. We never developed the same strong bond with Da. He didn't relate to either of us and we both were forced to carve our own path.

"Hello." He nods at me before focusing on Astrid. "Who is this lovely lass?"

Astrid takes his rough hand between hers. "It's lovely to meet you, Mr. McGloughlin. I'm Astrid. Your accent is so thick, I love it."

"Ahh, it's Rory, lass. You see, I never wanted to lose it. As they say, no woman is safe from a charmin' Irishman." Da winks at her. Holy shit, he's flirting. I haven't seen this side of him. *Ever.* "My boy didn't tell us he had taken up with a beautiful lady friend." He raises an eyebrow at me. "Mr. Secretive."

"Da," I mutter, slightly annoyed.

"Oh, we're new." Astrid reaches for my hand. "We were friends until...recently."

"Where's Cillian?" I abruptly change the subject back to something a little less intimate as we head into the dining room. "When's he supposed to be here?"

Seamus, looking buff as hell, is setting the table. My quiet, thoughtful wee brother lifts his head to hear the answer.

"Oh, aye." Da looks down at the floor dejectedly. "He sent me a text, so he did. Something's come up. Astrid can take his place at the table."

Seamus peers at Astrid with a slight smirk.

"Astrid, this is my wee brother, Seamus." I nod toward him. "He's the surgeon."

"Nice to meet you." My brother holds up his hand.

"Likewise." Astrid winks.

Ma bursts through the door with a platter of roast pork surrounded by potatoes and vegetables. Classic, simple, and perfect. Dinner kicks off quietly as we fill our plates but, soon enough, the topic of Cillian is dropped and Astrid becomes the main focus.

As soon as they find out she was Connor's realtor, it's game over. Ma leans in, grilling her about the real estate market, Seamus pontificates about different Seattle neighborhoods. Da chimes in with stories of construction projects. Astrid is engaging and animated, making them feel like they've known her for years. Her social skills are flawless.

Though I'm listening, I'm silently fuming. My family is dancing around the problem right in front of us.

Cillian. How can we continue to blow off his behavior? Pretend like everything's fine. It pisses me off. I haven't been in town much over the past several months, but it's clear my Irish twin is in trouble. Are none of them taking it seriously? I take a bite of the pork but it tastes like nothing. I'm too worked up.

Beneath the table, Astrid clutches my hand to remind me she's here with me. She leans in and whispers into my ear, "You okay?"

I turn to her, astonished at how perceptive she is. "Uh...I guess."

"Say what you need to say." She squeezes my fingers and nods toward my family.

That's all I need to hear.

"When's the last time Cillian was here?" I put my fork down and glance around the table.

Ma looks sideways at Da. "He was supposed to be here tonight."

"Yeah, but you know he never shows up these days," Seamus mutters, his eyes flicking to mine.

"We'll talk about it another time." Da fixes me with a look as if to say he's not keen to discuss Cillian's problem with Astrid here. Like it's none of her business.

Astrid hasn't taken her eyes off me during this exchange, but now she looks around the table. "How about we finish dinner and I'll do the dishes while you all have a family chat."

"Ach, no." Ma pats her hand. "There's no need..."

"There is." Seamus points his fork at her before taking a bite. "Thank you, Astrid."

"It's no trouble. I totally understand." Astrid squeezes my fingers before releasing my hand, resuming her meal.

It hits me all at once.

Astrid *meant* to divert attention from the Cillian situation because, unlike me, she knows how to read a room. It didn't even occur to me to exercise discretion about a sensitive and private subject matter. Da wanted to respect his son's privacy. I should have picked up on his cues.

Astrid saved the day and it hits me like a club to the head.

We're not opposites at all.

Maybe we're two halves of the same whole.

Thirteen

ASTRID

A Couple Hours Later

THE QUIET HUM OF Brennan's car nearly lulls me to sleep.

My belly's full. I haven't eaten this much in years. Good God, if I ate Maureen McGloughlin's food every day, I'd be three hundred pounds in no time. I'm content and comfortable.

And *exhausted.*

It's nearly nine p.m. We're driving back to my place as the late-spring sky darkens into deep navy. The city lights twinkle as we cruise down the nearly empty road on the way to my houseboat. Despite a bit of family drama toward the end of the night, I enjoyed my time with Brennan's family immensely. It sure was a far cry from dinner at my house the night before.

I glance at Brennan. His jaw is still tight as he focuses on the road. He hasn't said much since we left. I can tell he's still thinking about what went down after dinner.

"So." I break the silence in an attempt to snap him out of his mood. "You haven't said a word. How'd it go with your dad and Seamus? Your mom told me you guys needed to 'hash things out' when she came in to do the dishes with me."

Brennan shakes his head. "Classic Ma. She always bails when it comes to talking about alcoholism. It's like she wants to bury her head in the sand."

Uh. *No.* She understood what she was doing, leaving him to talk with his dad and Seamus. Sometimes men can be so fucking dense.

"Actually, she told me it was rare for you and Seamus to be the only brothers at dinner. She wanted you both to have time with your dad." I let the words sink in for a second. "She's perceptive, your mom."

Brennan raises an eyebrow, surprised. "What did she say?"

"Well, she mentioned your dad's always been close with Cillian. Told me Connor and the twins were practically grown when he had the accident. She knows you and Seamus were 'caught in the crossfire,' as she put it. Thought it'd be beneficial for the three of you to air things out."

He's quiet for a moment, processing. "Huh. I didn't think she noticed."

"Mothers notice everything when they're interested." I turn slightly in my seat to face him. "Maybe you should start focusing your stellar observation skills on your family instead of holding on to all that resentment."

"Resentment?" Brennan gives me a sideways smirk, half-amused, half-annoyed. "Ya think?"

"I do because I live it with my own family and my mom is about the most uninterested mother on the planet. Yours is amazing." I challenge lightly. "You seem to notice a lot about me—use those superpowers to get to learn about your parents as they are now."

Brennan shuffles his grip on the steering wheel. "I wish it were that simple."

I stay quiet, giving him a little space. I don't want to push too hard. Brennan isn't one to vomit out his feelings without processing them ad nauseum. It's clearly been a heavy night for him.

"Well...we did talk about some heavy shit." He speaks after a few minutes. "Ma's dead-on. I think Seamus and I—" He stops himself.

Rather than insert myself into the narrative, I wait. Not rushing him. He sucks in a breath and blows it out slowly.

"Seamus and I confronted Dad about...well, his own drinking and how similar Cillian's behavior is to his. We remember everything and how scary it was. Connor's come to terms with things; the twins don't really give him the time of day. Ironically, the only brother who hasn't had some sort of beef with Da, is Cillian." Brennan drums his fingers in a steady rhythm on the console—his subconscious habit when he's deep in thought. "Jesus. Seamus *really* laid into him about Cillian."

I tilt my head, curious. "He did? What did he say?"

"He pointed out Cillian's heading down the same road Da did, with the drinking. Missing work and deadlines. Family dinners. Seamus delved into the medical stuff pretty deeply. Talked about how badly this is messing him up. Physically. Mentally." I can feel the frustration radiating off him. "The thing is, we can't blame this behavior on his breakup. He was heading down that path a long time before he met her. It's fucking hereditary. He needs help."

I nod slowly, letting the weight of his words settle between us. "You can't force Cillian to get help or listen to any of you. *Trust*."

"Yeah." Brennan's voice catches. "Da didn't want to hear it. He was so defensive. It's like he doesn't want to admit how all of us were affected by what he put us through. He's sober now. Repentant. Sorry and whatever. He's Irish, though. Doesn't believe in counseling. Or therapy. It's been a long time and we're still dealing with the fallout."

I place my hand on his arm. "None of this is easy to face. For any of you."

"I'm sorry you got dragged into it. I brought you over for dinner because I hoped you could meet Cillian." He turns onto my street. "I'm such a shit brother. When I get absorbed at work, sometimes weeks go by and I don't even realize it. We haven't hung out in months when we used to do everything together. I want to be there for him."

There's a heaviness lingering in the car now. The kind that's attributable to a deep conversation about family. Through every pore of my body I sense his frustration. Feel his fear. See how much self-imposed responsibility he puts on himself to take care of his grown-ass brothers.

I understand it, because I've lived it.

There's nothing he can do to change it.

We pull up to my slip and the soft glow of the exterior lights on my houseboat reflect off the water. Brennan puts the car in park but doesn't make a move to get out. I unbuckle my seatbelt and sit back, watching him. He stares out the windshield, lost in thought.

"I'm going to tell you the truth and you're not going to like it." I face him and rest my hand on his thigh. "You're not responsible for Cillian. I know you *feel* like you are, but he's an adult. He has to recognize his problem and want to get better."

Brennan runs a hand through his hair, clearly torn. "I know, but it's not easy to watch."

"You can't fix everything, Brennan. Not your dad, not your brothers." I stroke his thigh. "Your focus needs to be on yourself while you're in this transaction, otherwise the worry's going to break you."

His eyes bore into mine. "It already feels like I'm breaking."

My heart clenches at the helplessness in his voice. For all his strength and intelligence, Brennan has too much on his plate.

We sit for a moment, just breathing. The lights of the city and the sloshing of the lake water surround us. My plan, before everything happened at dinner, was to come back here, fuck my man all night and maybe have a chat in the morning about how we make things official.

It's not the time, though.

Last night I was in a state of despair and he took care of me. It led to hours upon hours of the best sex of my life—and his, so he says. *But*...and there *is* a huge but. Our timing is fucking awful. I can't—and won't—add to his stress.

I'm crazy about Brennan and I think he feels the same way. We need to let this new phase of our friendship percolate without pressure.

"Look." I reach up and stroke his cheek. "Last night was special. Intense. Beautiful. But, I think you and I both know we're not ready to take the next step."

His face falls, confused. "What? No! I thought... Um, you don't want to see me anymore?"

"No!" I shake my head vigorously. Then swallow, trying to find the words. "I mean, this," I gesture between us, "is worth protecting. You're already stressed about work and your family, I'm not about to add labels on our relationship to put obligations to me on your plate."

He stares at me for a moment. Nods slowly like he thinks I'm letting him down easy. "Okay. I know I suck at all the boyfriend things, but damn."

"Brennan. Please don't misunderstand. I'm not saying I don't want us to pursue things romantically," I quickly clarify. "I *do*. But we both have a lot going on and how we are together makes me happy. Just because we've had sex shouldn't change anything."

He nods again, this time definitively. "Okay, we can go that route. For clarity, though, I want to have a *lot* of sex with you."

Brennan leans in slowly, his hand cups the side of my face and his thumb brushes my cheek, sending warmth straight through me. His lips meet mine softly. Tentatively. Testing the waters. Then the kiss deepens. Grows sure and confident. There's a quiet passion, a promise that lingers in the way his mouth moves against mine. Slow. Deliberate. As if he's savoring this moment but also promising our story is only beginning.

When he pulls back, his forehead rests against mine. I can still feel the heat of his lips. The silence between us isn't uncomfortable. If anything, it feels like a necessary pause—like we're both on board to step back and take stock of where we are and what's happening between us.

"I'm going to head inside." I reach for the door handle. "Thank you for tonight. For bringing me to meet your family. I know there were some tough conversations but I love all of them. They're so different from my people."

He watches me, his expression softening. "Thank you for coming. I didn't expect it to go pear shaped, but I'm glad you were there."

"Me too." I lean over and give him another quick kiss.

We exchange a look and before either of us articulate the unsaid words hanging between us, I step out into salty night air. The familiar sound of water lapping against the dock comforts me as I make my way up the dock to the houseboat. When I reach my front door, I turn back to see Brennan still sitting in the car, watching me until I've unlocked it.

I wave and he lifts a hand in return. A small smile tugs at his lips. I step inside and his car pulls away, leaving me standing in the glow of the deck lights, wondering if I made the correct decision.

Moments later, I sink down onto the couch and stare out at the lake. Grateful for a moment of solitude to reflect on the past twenty-four hours. A sense of comfort settles over me.

It's been a lot. More than I expected.

Not quite enough.

In a strange way, for the first time in a long time, I feel like I'm moving forward.

Even if it means giving myself time to breathe.

Fourteen

BRENNAN

Seven Months Later

I'M A STUPID, STUPID man.

How in fuck have I let this much time go by without seeing her?

Astrid struts toward where I'm waiting for her in the small terminal at San Jose airport. Even from across the room, she looks like she belongs in a film—effortless, beautiful. She hasn't seen me yet, giving me a second to take her in.

She's wearing slim-cut, plaid capri pants with a white tank top showing off her shoulders. Her hair is loose around her shoulders and she wears white-rimmed sunglasses giving her an old-Hollywood look. Almost like she's about to slide into the driver's seat of a vintage convertible.

I can't help but suppress a grin.

She spots me and her face breaks into a smile that lights her up from the inside. I'm done for. Months of sporadic texting, video calls, and phone conversations have kept our situationship alive, but seeing her in person after all these months. *Gah.*

Sure, our schedules have been entirely at odds, but I'm never letting this much time go by again. No fucking way.

"Brennan," she calls out as she approaches, unbothered by everyone around her. Her eyes are focused on me and only me, and it makes me feel like a million bucks.

I don't even bother with words. Instead, I pull her close and hold her tight. Press my face into her hair to breathe in her peaches-and-cream scent. "You have no idea how much I've missed you."

"I missed you too." Her arms wrap around my neck and we cling to each other like we've been apart for years instead of months.

Finally, she takes a step back, plants her hands on my shoulders and scans me from head to toe. "You look...different."

I can't help but feel a bit self-conscious, which isn't a new feeling. My body has never been toned and chiseled like all my brothers. Connor and Seamus are former athletes and gym rats. The twins are naturally lean. Cillian works construction. I've always skewed sedentary, though I usually do the bare minimum to keep up appearances.

Unfortunately, I've been working like a maniac with barely enough time to grab fast food to eat, let alone work out. Months of skipping the gym means my shirt stretches tight across my chest and my pants are snug.

Crap. All I've thought about for the past twenty-four hours is how many ways I'm going to fuck Astrid this week. I didn't factor in whether she'd still be attracted to me.

"I've put on a couple pounds." I look off into the distance, not wanting to see her disappointment in my appearance.

"Hey." Astrid cups my cheek. "That's not what I meant. I was going to say you look happy. The past few FaceTimes worried me. You've been distracted. Stressed out."

I flick my eyes to hers. To be fair, she *is* looking at me like I'm a tasty treat. Inside, though, there's a familiar tug of insecurity. Ever-present my entire dating life. I want to be the guy she deserves—the one who's handsome, confident, and pulled together.

Sexy.

For now, I'll settle for she likes me a little.

"I *am* happy." I take her hand and guide us toward baggage claim. "*You* make me happy."

"God, I hope so. Know this. I'm seven-months' horny and I won't wait much longer to ride your gorgeous cock." She hip checks me. Then her expression softens. "I mean it, B. Whatever's going on with us, you're the man I want."

How can she read my mind? Say exactly the right thing? I grab her giant pink suitcase off the conveyer belt and gesture toward the exit. "Well, let's get going. I've got a surprise waiting for you."

We step out of the terminal toward the parking lot. Right in front is the car I borrowed for the week—a classic, deep-blue 1975 Buick LeSabre convertible, shining like a jewel under the desert sun. It wouldn't usually be my cup of tea, but I wanted to try something different.

Something to make Astrid smile.

And it does.

Her eyes widen as she takes in the perfectly restored muscle car. "No way." She runs her fingers along the smooth curves as she circles around to the passenger side.

"I thought you'd appreciate it." I lean against the hood, arms crossed, watching her reaction with pure satisfaction. "Figured we'd roll into Palm Springs in style."

Astrid turns to me, her eyes practically glowing. "This is so fucking incredible. You '*borrowed*' this?"

"One of my coders has a thing for classic cars." I pop the trunk and hoist her bag inside.

She's still beaming when she slides into the passenger seat. She adjusts her sunglasses in the rearview mirror and settles in, looking every bit like a 1960s movie star. "I knew you had excellent taste, but this is next level."

Confidence boosted, I can't help but whistle when I hop into the driver's seat. I turn on the ignition and the roar of the engine rumbles as I pull out of the airport and head toward the highway. The wind whips around us, pulling at Astrid's hair. She ties on a white scarf and relaxes back into the seat with an ease that makes me feel light and happy.

Somehow, the stress of the last few months—the endless meetings and headaches from trying to integrate the damn company—fades away as we settle into the long drive.

Astrid is here. Next to me. Where she belongs.

We pull onto the wide highway leading into Palm Springs. The mountains loom in the distance as the sun starts to dip lower. Astrid leans back, her arm draped along the seat, fingers brushing through my hair like she's done it a thousand times before. Her scarf catches in the breeze, but she doesn't seem to care.

Her eyes are locked on mine and time stops.

The desert stretches wide and golden around us but it feels distant, like we're in our own world. Every brush of her hand feels electric, grounding me in this moment. Assuring me nothing else matters but us.

"I hate it when you're stressed." Her thumb strokes my cheek. "You're finally relaxing."

I let out a breath I didn't t realize I'd been holding. "The acquisition's a mess. The board promised it would be a smooth transition, but I'm still fighting tooth and nail to keep my vision intact. Honestly? I'm starting to wonder if it's even worth it."

"They can't push you out, can they?" Astrid scoots closer to me and leans her head on my shoulder.

"Feels like they're trying." I hear the bitterness and frustration in my tone. "It's all politics and power plays. They're interested in chasing quick profits not doing anything that actually matters. It's exhausting."

She's silent for a moment, gazing up at me thoughtfully. It makes me feel understood. She always sees through my words to what's in my heart. Her thumb traces a small circle on my arm. "Sounds brutal. No wonder you're burnt out and confused. You need a mental break."

"Yeah," I admit. "Probably."

Her hand glides up and down my thigh. "Don't worry. You'll figure it out," she says softly. "You always do."

"Thanks. I needed to hear something positive." I take my eyes off the road for a sec to kiss the side of her head, grateful my tension is easing.

Astrid's palm creeps up my thigh and cups my half-erect cock. "You've worked too hard for it to end like this."

"Yeah..." I suck in a breath when she unzips my pants. "What are you doing?"

"If you don't know, I'm not doing it correctly." Before I can protest she's pulled out my dick and brushes her thumb over the tip.

I swerve onto the shoulder and screech to a stop. "I'm gonna wreck the car if you blow me when I'm driving."

"Well, I'm going down on you now, B, so it's good you pulled over." She makes short work of my buckle, unzips my pants and grasps my cock in her fist. "You need to come in the worst way."

"What did you say?" I cannot believe this is happening. I've never had such a spontaneous sexual experience in my life. I'm not sure what to do.

Astrid leans over and pushes my briefs down. Locks her gaze with mine as she licks and sucks my balls. I nearly jackknife my hips into her jaw, but manage to hold myself back. Watch as her tongue trails up my shaft to my crown where she engulfs my cock with her hot little mouth. "*Mmmmmm.*"

"Fucking hell, A." I stare down at her working me over. Stroke her hair as she licks and sucks me into oblivion and lightly grazes her teeth along my pulsing vein. Her hand pumps me harder and faster until my breath is choppy and erratic. I'm gyrating and groaning, so close. So incredible. I feel so free. Astrid cups and massages my balls, which immediately tighten.

"I'm going to blow." I tap her shoulder, but she doesn't stop.

Her hand works faster. She sucks harder and it's all over. I explode on her tongue and she drinks down every drop, licking me clean. Gently caressing me until I'm soft and satiated.

She sits up, wipes her mouth with the back of her hand and nonchalantly reapplies her lipstick, giving me a sideways grin.

"For someone who doesn't like to suck cock, you're very talented." I tuck myself back into my pants and buckle my belt.

She lifts my arm and places it around her shoulder, leaning against me. Blinks up at me with those green eyes. "Correction. I like sucking *your* cock. Now you can focus on the drive and we can start our vacation. No work, no stress. Just Palm Springs, this car, tasty food, and lots of naked sexy times."

"Deal." I pull back out onto the road.

An hour later, the city comes into view. It's like a different world here, one filled with sleek, mid-century modern architecture, palm trees swaying in the warm desert breeze, and a peaceful, festive atmosphere.

I've been running myself into the ground. Isolating myself from my family and the woman I see a future with.

And for what?

Somehow, I think this week is going to change everything.

Fifteen

ASTRID

A Few Minutes Later

OH, BOY. I'M WORRIED about him.

Brennan reminds me of a mad scientist wholly out of his element. The man is richer and more influential than his rockstar brother by a mile, but he doesn't act like it. Or live like it.

I'm beginning to think he doesn't even *realize* it.

At the rate he's going, he'll have a stroke by the time he's forty.

So, I have two competing objectives this week. I'm going to keep his heart rate up by fucking him senseless as much as humanly possible. I'm also forcing him to relax and get some sleep.

"Is this where we're staying?" My eyes light up when he pulls into the driveway of The Parker. "You've outdone yourself, B."

Brennan stops at the valet and tosses the attendant the keys. The mid-century hotel is pure retro-vibes and opulence, with fifty-foot palm trees towering overhead and peeps of the mountains beyond. He opens the door for me and holds out his hand. "It's the fanciest hotel in Palm Springs and it's also very private."

We step inside the lobby filled with vintage furniture and modern touches making it feel cozy yet luxurious. This place is perfect. I'm beyond excited to spend focused time with Brennan in this oasis. We head up to our room, stopping to make out every so often. Finally, we arrive at our suite and it's everything I could have imagined. Warm desert tones, plush furniture, and a balcony overlooking the gardens and pool.

"It's perfect." I motion for Brennan to join me on the balcony.

He follows me out and we take in the view of the winding paths we walked on lined with lush greenery and vibrant flowers. The soft glow of fairy lights flickers by the pool area, creating a warm, romantic glow over the property. The cool, evening breeze catches my hair and I feel like I'm in heaven.

"You know, I've been thinking about this trip for weeks." I lean back against him. "I'm regretting how long it's taken to get this organized."

He wraps his arms around my shoulders. "Yeah?"

"*Yeah*." I grip his wrists. "I missed you."

Brennan squeezes me and kisses the back of my head. "I've missed you too, A. More than anything. Video chats aren't enough."

"So...what now?" I look up at him, hoping he can read my mind. All of the nonsense I spewed at him the night we had dinner at his parents—ridiculous. I want us to be an official couple. I hope he still wants the same thing.

His hands skim down to my breasts. He cups them and strums my nipples with his thumbs. "I'm going to enjoy the fuck out of this week. You and me. Naked. No distractions."

"Yes." I gasp when he sucks my ear between his lips. "Sounds perfect."

He slowly turns me toward him, pushes my hair over my shoulder and kisses the side of my neck. "I want to be inside you."

"Where you belong." I slip out of my tank top and toss it on the lounger, undo my pants and step out of them.

"Holy mother of God, you're perfection," he hisses as he scans me from head to toe.

I'm not, but I'll take it.

Brennan's fingertips trace the wispy straps of my white lace bra and skate down to the elastic of the matching panties. His touch ignites me— my entire body is heated. More so when his lips graze my shoulder, back up my neck to my ear.

Sliding my palms up his torso, on either side of the buttons of his white shirt, I take my time undoing them one by one. Push it down his arms and it falls to the floor. For all his insecurities about his weight, Brennan looks amazing. Sure, his body's a little softer, but he's so fucking handsome. A little extra fluff doesn't matter to me. At all.

I'm going to show, not tell him, though. Words won't have the same impact as my lips kissing every inch of his body.

I dip my fingertip into the waist of his pants above the zipper where the tip of his cock peeps out. Brennan groans as he watches me. "Ah, fuck—"

"You make me crazy too." I lean and kiss his chest above his heart, swiping the tip of my tongue on his flat, brown nipple. "You've kept me crazy for too long."

"*Too* long," he repeats, raising a brow before lifting me into his arms and carrying me into the room. "Let's get one thing clear, though. I'm not into giving the other guests a show, I want you all to myself."

He lays me back on the mattress, which is firm yet plush. The cool, high-thread-count sheets feel like silk against my skin. "Oh my God, we're never leaving this room." I waggle my fingers for him to join me.

Like clockwork, Brennan's phone starts buzzing. He glances over to the table where it's plugged in and I take his face in my hands. "No. You are *not* thinking about work when you're about to fuck me. You're not a stupid man."

"You're right, it's habit." Brennan kisses my shoulder, dragging the tip of his tongue up my neck and jaw. He turns my face to meet his and presses his lips to mine. "I'm going to take my time and taste every inch of your body." He tugs on my earlobe with his teeth. "You'll be so wet and ready for me, I'm going to fuck you so hard you see stars."

Oh. My. God. *Yesssss.*

"I'll let you in on a little secret. I've been wet since the second I boarded the plane in Seattle and started daydreaming about this moment." I reach for his belt.

"Good." He grips my hands and presses them to the mattress. "Now, don't get any ideas about taking over. It's my turn. I'm going to lick you until you beg for my cock."

"I don't beg for *anything*," I sass, gasping when he releases one of my hands and cups my breast, pinching my nipple hard.

God, I'm in for the best kind of trouble. All these months of intermittent video sex have primed both of our pumps, so to speak.

Brennan's lips meander down to my chest, leaving a wet trail. He tugs the cups of my bra to the sides and teases both nipples into tight bullets with his lips as he grips the sides of my panties and rips them off.

"More." I writhe under him. "Give me *everything*."

Brennan releases my other hand and flips me over onto my belly and continues his tongue exploration on the backs of my legs, alternating wet kisses and little nips behind my knees and inner thighs.

I nearly lose my mind when he grips my ass with both hands and spreads my butt apart and buries his face down there. Instinctively, I want to move away until he starts lapping my core from my clit, through my folds to my anus and back again. Over and over until I'm shuddering.

He moves away and bites one ass cheek then the other. "You taste like candy." He nibbles up my spine to my neck, sucks my earlobe between his lips. "I want to fuck you. Spank you. Pamper you. Fuck you again."

Jesus, I love how commanding he is in the bedroom. He can't dirty talk and expect me not to want more of this. "So, do it."

"If you want my cock, ask for it." He dips a finger into my soaking channel and wiggles it.

I shrug, unable to move much from this angle, but my nipples are so tight, the friction from the sheets sends extra zings to where he's stroking me. I'm a tight ball of lust, but I won't beg him. Not if I can help it. "I don't."

"I think you do." He bites my earlobe again before kissing his way back down and adding another finger inside me. "And, I think you like it when I tell you what to do."

I moan in agreement and instinctively tip my ass up to give him access. His fingers continue to expertly rub against my G-spot and he strokes through my folds with the digits of his other hand. "Your pussy lips are so pink and puffy." He licks me. "And, oh look. Your clit is making an appearance." He sucks it between his lips.

"Ohmygod!" I shamelessly press my ass against his face, hoping he'll send me over the edge.

But no, he moves away, keeping his fingers working inside me. "You're so tight."

"And *sooooo* horny," I whimper, moving my hips in circles. I need him to go harder. Faster...

Suddenly he pulls out his fingers and I'm on my back again. Brennan kneels between my legs, staring at my flushed skin. At some point, he shed his pants and his monster cock bounces against his belly. I want it in me. Now. I let my thighs fall wider apart, but instead of giving in, he kisses back down my belly and sucks my clit between his lips, nibbling on it enough to make me see stars.

It's so incredible, I nearly launch myself off the bed. Brennan cups both breasts in his hands to hold me down as he continues to lick and suck me until I'm in serious danger of losing my mind. He pinches my nipples hard as he drags his tongue through my lips back up to my clit. Over and over as waves of pleasure radiate from every pore.

But I need something else, and—fuck it—pride has no place in the bedroom.

"*Fine*! I *want* your cock. I want it. Fuck me, B," I beg, mindless with desire. "*Now*. I need your cock inside me."

He chuckles. "*Hmmm*. I don't think you're ready."

"You're wrong, I couldn't be any more ready." I clutch the duvet at my hips, holding my breath as he moves back up my body, kissing the insides of my thighs, my pussy lips, my belly, my nipples and, finally, my lips.

"I'm not sure I heard you. Did you want my cock?" he whispers.

I can smell and taste myself on him and, rather than use words, I pull his mouth back down to mine. Reaching between us, I grip him firmly and guide him to my entrance.

"Say the words." His eyes bore into mine and I realize from his expression he needs to hear them.

Stroking him back and forth against my wetness, I try to convey how I feel about him. "I don't *want* your cock, B, I *need* it. You're the most important person in my life and I'd like us to be as connected as two people can be. When you're inside me, I feel complete."

"Ah, shit." Brennan pauses, his hands framing my face. He's breathing hard, not from exertion. It's from the sheer emotion of our reunion.

He pushes in slightly, burying his tip a few inches in. Thank the Lord. "That's it. Impale me. Do it."

"Fuck," he whispers. "God, A." He watches me intently as he slides in farther, stretching me to my limit until he's nearly balls-deep. Then he stops. "Don't move yet." He kisses me. "Are you okay?"

"Better than okay. Remember, you've been in there before, it doesn't hurt. I feel...full." My fingernails drag lazily up and down his sides to his ass.

Brennan tilts his head questioningly. "Yeah, but it's been a while and I don't want to hurt you. This feels so fucking phenomenal, once I start moving I won't be able to stop."

"It's all good, I want this," I assure him. "Unleash your inner beast if you must."

He chuckles and pushes up on his hands, moving faster. Harder. All the while watching my face to make sure he's not hurting me.

He's not. I'm in heaven. My pussy clenches around him, loving the way the thick, ridge of his crown hits me just right, shooting electrical sparks down my spine with each pass.

I reach above me and push on the headboard, getting the perfect leverage to tip my hips up to meet him. Our tempo quickens. We're sweating. Panting. Moaning. Keening. I'm clenching him so hard he winces, trying to stave off his own release before I go over again.

Resting my feet on his calves, I clench down and shift my angle so his pubic bone hits my clit. *Holymotherfuckinghell.* It's like a magic button has been pressed and I explode in a wonderland of glittery pleasure. *"Ohmyyyyygoddd."*

"Fuck." He grips my hips and pounds into me until he groans long and low, his entire body shuddering as he empties inside me.

Holding himself against the headboard, he manages to catch his breath with his cock embedded inside me. I've never experienced anything like this in my life.

I can deny it to myself all I want, but there's only one thought going through my mind.

I'm in love.

With another unavailable man.

Sixteen

BRENNAN

Two Days Later

I'VE NEVER SPENT AN entire day at a spa.

Hell, I've never even spent an hour in one before today. But here I am, lying face down on a plush massage table, with a therapist working CBD oil into my muscles like she's some kind of magician. Knots I didn't even know existed are unraveling and my mind is tranquil, floating in a sea of ambient spa music.

Astrid booked us for the entire day. We've already had a hydrating facial, a sugar body polish and some hot oil treatment to, apparently, "rejuvenate my scalp," whatever that means.

All I know is I can't remember the last time I felt this relaxed. There's a steady rhythm to the therapist's hands. The pressure is aggressively perfect. She works her way down my back. The faint sound of water trickling from some nearby fountain and the scent of lavender lulls me into a dreamlike state.

So far from my usual day-to-day it feels like I'm hallucinating.

"B?" Astrid's quiet voice breaks through the soft haze.

"Hmm?"

"You okay over there?" I hear the amusement in her voice, though I can't see her.

I manage to mumble, "I think I'm in heaven."

Her laugh is light and playful. It tugs at something deep in my chest. I need to be with her. All the time. Burying myself in work isn't fun without her. Not when everything's going to shit. Astrid and I seem to have weathered a huge separation pretty well, and I don't want to test our boundaries anymore.

My therapist finishes up with one last, satisfying press into my lower back, and I let out a contented sigh. When I sit up, I glance over at Astrid. Her hair's tied up in a towel, her skin glows from whatever magic they worked on her.

"Should we relax before we head back up to the room?" Her lips curl into a smile as she pushes herself off the table.

I rub the back of my neck as I stand. "I'm not sure I can walk. My legs are noodles."

"You'll be fine." She slips her arm through mine as we head down the labyrinth of lush pathways bordered by citrus trees to the lounge area by the pool.

This resort is unlike anything I've ever experienced, Everywhere you look, there's something beautiful—a croquet lawn, fire pits, gardens full of flowering bushes and, of course, the towering palms. I'm beginning to understand Connor and Ronni's lifestyle a little better.

We grab a couple of retro-chic deck chairs by the pool and settle side-by-side. The sunlight filters through the palms, casting long shadows on the ground. When I breathe in, the air smells of eucalyptus, orange, and lemon. The atmosphere is so peaceful and calming, I feel centered and clearheaded. I'm not sure I'll ever want to leave, at this point.

"I could get used to this," I say as I glance at the menu.

"You *should* ." Astrid pokes my side playfully. "Knowing you, if I weren't here, you'd have your laptop fired up after ten minutes."

I roll my eyes, but she's not wrong. "Maybe fifteen."

"You're supposed to relax sometimes, B." She tilts her face up toward the sun. "You're on vacation with a hot woman who likes you a little bit. Gives decent head. Fucks like a porn star. What more do you want?"

"I know, I know." I take her hand.

She's good for me. *Too* good for me. In the back of my mind, I'm waiting for the crash and burn. The moment when Astrid tells me she cares about me but...

So far, it hasn't happened. Our relationship feels natural. Easy. And our chemistry is unlike anything I've ever experienced. I've never had so much sex over a two-day period in my life, and we have five days to go.

The problem is, my mind always drifts back to my company. There's a mess waiting for me back in Silicon Valley. It's not just the power plays, it's the daily grind. Every time I launch Slack, there's some new fire to put out.

The executives from the company we acquired don't care about our vision for CognifyAI. Their objective is to force products to market before they're ready, maximize profit and cut costs. I've spent the past months fighting them on every little thing, from staffing decisions to product rollouts, but realize why the board pushed so hard to acquire them.

I'm totally outnumbered. It's terrifying.

Astrid doesn't know it, but I nearly canceled this trip a dozen times. The reason I'm here is because it's December and there's no board meeting until Q1. It's the only time I'll have off for another year.

Astrid watches me intently. "The acquisition integration is still getting to you, huh?"

"They're pushing me to cut corners." I try to keep the bitterness out of my tone. "And I get it, investors want fast returns, but I've never done things for money and clout. I'm about quality. Reliability. Can you believe they're pressuring me to release a product before it's ready, which will be a total disaster."

She tilts her head slightly. "How?"

"One wrong move will set us back years. The company's reputation could take a hit, causing us to lose trust with our clients. And for what? A temporary bump in revenue?" I shut my eyes and sigh, feeling all the calm give way to anxiousness.

"You feel like you're in a constant battle." She caresses the back of my hand with her thumb.

"Yeah. And the worst part is, they've got the majority on the board now. Every day they're chipping away at my control. Every decision I make is questioned. Every move is scrutinized. I know they're waiting for me to mess up so they have a reason to swoop in and take over." My jaw clenches. I've never voiced any of this to anyone out of fear it will fuck things up.

Somehow, it feels like a relief to get it off my chest.

Astrid's brow furrows. "No wonder you've been so stressed."

I laugh, but there's no humor to it. "Stressed doesn't even begin to cover it. I'm barely holding on some days."

Her fingers thread through mine and Astrid's simple touch brings me back to the present, grounding me. "You've been holding on to this all by yourself," she says empathetically. "Why didn't you tell me sooner?"

"I don't know." I shrug. "I didn't want to burden you with it. Some days I can hardly believe you still want to talk to me."

She moves to my lounger and nestles herself against me, her knees tucked between my legs. "As your business partner and woman who cares about you immensely, I need to say something. You can't let outside forces destroy who you are. Open your eyes, you sweet, stubborn man. You're so much more than

CognifyAI. Your worth is not because of what you've built, it's inside here." She taps on my heart.

I close my eyes for a second and hold her tightly as her words sink in. She's spot-on. For years I've been wrapped up in a fight for survival. First building a life-changing product. Then, building my product into a unicorn tech company. I've achieved both, and somehow I've shifted the focus from growing to "not losing."

It's a no-win mindset. The truth is, outside of my family and Astrid, I've forgotten who I am outside of work. And I don't give either of them nearly enough of my time, leaving me with...what?

"It's hard," I admit. "To come to terms with failure."

Astrid fixes me with a stern look.

"It is," I plead. "I'm starting to wonder if it's even worth it. Maybe I should walk away."

She studies me. "Walk away? Could you?"

"I don't know." I run a hand through my hair. "I'm tired of fighting for something that doesn't feel like it's mine."

Her expression is hard to read. She's quiet again and it's clear she's measuring her words. "Brennan, you're one of the smartest, most driven people I know. And, you're your own worst enemy. I wish you could see yourself the way I do. Somehow, I think you still believe you're the same insecure kid from high school. You're not. You have people who believe in you, who are *with* you. At your company. Your family. Me."

"You think so?" I'm genuinely surprised by the intensity in her eyes.

"Of course I do," she says like it's the most obvious thing in the world. "And so do a lot of other people. Do you even understand how much buzz there's been about you being involved in the reunion? Do you get it? You're a legend in AI. A tech innovator in the same category as Jeff Bezos. And Jason Deveraux. You're so siloed, you don't even comprehend what it means. No matter what you decide to do, you're a powerful man, own it."

Her words hit me harder than I expect. I've spent my entire life carrying around this idea of myself—a nerdy kid who was always in the background, overshadowed by my brothers. Even now, with all the success I've had, my own perception of myself guides how I move in this world.

Why can't I move past it?

"I don't know if I'll ever shake it completely." I kiss each one of her fingertips. "It's weird to let go of my past when it's shaped so much of who I am."

Astrid turns in my arms and lays down some truth. "*Stop* with the woe is me shit. You're not a timid little boy. Just like I'm not a shallow cheerleader. We've both changed. We've moved beyond who we used to be."

"You're so observant." I nuzzle her neck. "I've been holding on to a version of myself that doesn't exist now. It's time to man up."

She reaches under my robe and caresses my cock. "You're man enough, babe. Take it from me. You don't have to answer to anyone but yourself. Do what *you* want."

Astrid is everything. I can't put into words how it feels to have someone like her so firmly behind me. "You always know what to say. And do." I press my lips against hers as she strokes me, my dick now at full attention.

Astrid chuckles softly and releases me. "It's one of my many talents. I've got an urge to ride my cowboy, are you ready to take this inside so you can *show* me how manly you are?"

"You don't need to ask twice." I stand, take her hand.

There's a new energy between us. A shared understanding as we hustle to our room where we'll lose ourselves in each other again. Free from distractions.

At the door, something in the way Astrid looks at me takes my breath away.

She makes me feel like I can do anything.

Be anything.

Huh. I actually believe it.

Seventeen

ASTRID

Two Days Later

W E'VE LEFT THE DEN of debauchery.

For the time being.

Nearly five solid days of sex, food, and relaxation meant it was time to emerge and explore Palm Springs today.

Brennan pulls the car smoothly into a spot along the palm-lined street, the engine rumbles to a stop. When he glances over at me, I know what he's thinking. I can tell by the familiar spark in his eyes. The man is insatiable.

If he weren't such a rule-follower, I have no doubt he'd fuck me in the backseat in two seconds flat.

Good thing he has me to corrupt him.

"I haven't been here since my brother played Coachella, it's been five whole years. I can hardly believe how fast the time goes." Brennan takes my hand as we begin our stroll down Palm Canyon Drive. Swoon. Absentminded signs of affection give me fanny flutters every time.

I've made a grave error. I'm wearing a slip dress and sandals and the breeze is chillier than I expected. Being from Seattle and all. I assumed it would be hot—even in December—and I'm freezing. My nipples are like bullets. "Well, this rookie traveler misjudged the weather."

His eyes widen as he takes in my chest and the goosebumps erupting on my arms and turns his gaze to the storefronts.

"Should we get you something warmer?" Brennan nods toward a window display filled with brightly colored kaftans and oversized sunglasses. "You can see how hard your nips are from here. If we don't cover your gorgeous tits, I'm gonna walk around with a hard-on all day."

I glance at the mannequin and kick up my heel playfully. "Not my style, but it might be a nice change of pace for you from black t-shirts and jeans."

"*Burn*." He smirks, raising an eyebrow. "You just wait. The next time you see me, I'll have fully embraced the retro Palm Springs granny vibe."

I nudge him with my elbow. "I dare you. It'll fit your personality perfectly."

"Seriously. You're freezing, let's get you a sweater or something." He leans down and kisses me and I realize how much I love his public displays of affection.

Whatever this is between us, it's big. I know it in my bones. I can tell by the way he watches me when he thinks I'm not looking. And the way his eyes soften whenever I say something. We've moved way past friends or friends with benefits or whatever the hell we've been for the past several months.

I wonder if either of us will have the courage to address it.

Our banter continues as we weave in and out of the shops looking for something I like. Brennan picks up random clothing items, teasingly asking if I think they'd suit him—a sequined jacket here, a ridiculous sunhat there. Each time, I laugh and swat his hand away, but there's an undercurrent to our interactions.

We're biding time until we can fuck each other to oblivion again.

I lead him into a quaint little woman's designer boutique to hopefully find something suitable. Immediately Brennan fingers the edge of a stunning custom-made oversized scarf. It's one-of-a-kind piece—luxurious silk blended with cashmere. It drapes like liquid and doubles as a wrap.

"Try this." He arranges the impossibly soft fabric around my shoulders and spins me around to the mirror. "It's made for you."

The cream and soft gold tones shimmer under the boutique's lights. He fluffs it around my body and the material unfurls like a delicate cloud. The price tag catches my eye—$6,000—but before I can protest, Brennan's already signaled the clerk and pulled out his card.

He has a way of making quiet, thoughtful gestures which leave me speechless.

Next, he stops in front of a small jewelry store. His eyes flick over the delicate rings as I pretend to study a pair of earrings, giving him a sideways glance. "You know, for someone who claims he's not into shopping, you're surprisingly invested."

"It's fun doing anything with you." His fingers graze the small of my back as we step closer to the window.

My heart melts at the casual way he says it, like it's the most natural thing in the world. Like we've always been this connected.

I don't know why it feels like a revelation—maybe it's because with Brennan, I've never felt like I had to be anyone but myself. We've gotten to know each other without any stupid performative dating routine. None of the sexual pretense so many men have expected from me in the past.

It's refreshing, but also terrifying. What happens when Brennan finally steps into the man he's meant to be? When he fully realizes how successful and brilliant he is. Will he still want me around? Or will I become someone he used to know? It's happened before, so I know it's a possibility.

I shake the thought from my head. My own damage has no place here. Today is easy. Fun. The way it should be when you're falling head over heels.

Shit.

We stop for lunch at a small bistro tucked between two art galleries, with outdoor seating and mismatched furniture. Brennan pulls out my chair for me and sits to my right, his fingers caress my nape as we wait for menus.

"This place is perfect." I glance around at the diners who look equally relaxed, some with their dogs lounging at their feet. "I like it here."

Brennan looks around. "Yeah, it's nice."

"So, tell me." I lean toward him. "What else is on our agenda for today? You've got the car, I've got a warm scarf—where are you taking me next, Mr. Tour Guide?"

He quirks a brow. "You trust me?"

"Do I have a choice?" The truth is, I like letting him take the lead. It gives him a boost to his confidence, which is returning after our talk—and a lot of orgasms. He's visibly sure of himself, which is nice to see. "Besides, you're full of excellent surprises."

He takes a sip of his water. "I try not to disappoint."

We settle into our usual rhythm, light conversation filled with banter flowing easily between us, only interrupted by the arrival of simple, hearty salads.

"You know," he sets his fork down when he's finished, "I actually think you're the one full of surprises."

I'm intrigued. "Oh? How so?"

"You shut down the idea of us as a couple after we first had sex." He shrugs one shoulder like it's no big deal, but there's something behind his words, something profound. Once again, he's in tune with my thoughts. "You let me off the hook, I guess... Over these past months, well, I didn't expect... *Us*. I feel like we've been together all this time."

His words hang in the air. We're definitely not a typical couple. We were classmates. Then business partners and friends. One night we fucked on my houseboat and I refused to allow us to put labels on things.

Yet, for the past several months on our regular video chats, whether we're discussing Reuniverse or just checking in, we always end up masturbating together. Neither of us are dating any other people.

We've never defined what *this* is but he's got a point. Brennan and I have *evolved*.

When he invited me here for the week, it was a given we'd have sex. I wasn't sure if we'd continue dancing around defining our relationship. Our discussions always skirt the edges. Maybe now's the time to have the talk.

"Well," I take his hand, "we're the epitome of slow burn. Maybe too slow. I have feelings for you and I want us to take the next step."

Brennan's thumb brushes over my knuckles. "Me too."

"So, we're together? Officially?" I whisper, blinking up at him.

"Did you think otherwise?" He furrows his brow, confused. "I'll never want anyone but you."

I'm so relieved. "Same."

That was easy. We're a couple.

After lunch, we walk back to the car. The second he takes his place beside me, I can't help but kiss him because I'm so fucking smitten. Happy. As we drive out of town, Brennan's hand finds mine and he pulls it to his thigh, creating a simple, quiet connection. His gestures say more than words ever could.

I'm *his*.

I watch him as he drives. The way his jaw tightens slightly when he's deep in thought. The way his fingers drum against the steering wheel like they're tapping out a code only he knows. He has so many layers, some which he's yet to reveal.

As if reading my mind, he squeezes my hand. His eyes meet mine with a soft, steady gaze and I know I'm exactly where I'm supposed to be. "You make me better."

Brennan parks the car at Coachella Valley Vista Point as the sun dips low, casting the entire area in hues of orange, purple, and pink. The desert below stretches out in a breathtaking expanse, with shadows creeping along the mountains, painting the landscape in gold.

We get out of the car and he wraps his arms around me from behind, watching the last rays of sunlight spill across the valley. Everything feels still—timeless, even—like the world has paused for us.

"I want to make you happy." He rests his chin on my shoulder and tightens his hold. "You deserve it, A."

I lean back against him. "I've never felt this happy. Really."

"I'm not great boyfriend material. I worry you're gonna get sick of my shit, at some point. When we were friends, it felt safe. But now?" He sucks in a huge breath.

"We have something to lose." I turn in his arms and grip his face.

"Yeah." He nods. "I don't want you to go back to Seattle."

We stare into each other's eyes, searching. Waiting.

"I'm in love with you," we say in unison.

At this point, the sightseers have all left and he and I are the only two people up here. It's nearly pitch black, but we're in love. Grinning like fools.

"I need to get your sexy ass back to the hotel so we can spend the next forty-eight hours naked." He scoops me up and turns toward the car.

Giggling, I press my face into his neck, clinging to him. "Why wait?"

Brennan sets my on the hood of the car, which is still blessedly warm, and stands between my legs. He lifts my skirt up to my waist and stares down at my thighs, which I spread to show him a little secret.

"You're not wearing underwear." He sucks in a breath

I shake my head and lift the hem of his T-shirt. Groaning, he leans into me as my hands travel over his torso and back up to his face. Suddenly, Brennan squats before me and I lean back on my elbows to watch him lower his mouth to my pussy.

God, how does he do it? I'm gushing and he's barely swiped his tongue through my lower lips, teasing me. I plunge one hand into his hair and urge him to lick harder. Suck harder.

"Patience." He kisses up to my clit, toying with it on the tip of his tongue. "I love when she pokes out and says hello." He sucks on it and my hips jerk.

His hands travel up my calves to my inner thighs. He presses them apart as he continues to devour me. It's sensory overload. I'm heaving. Panting. Zings of electricity are shooting throughout my body. .

"Your cock. Put it in me," I beg. "I want you to fuck me. Right here. Right now."

He stands, grabs my ankles and yanks me down the hood. Works his cock out of his jeans and pumps it firmly, wiping a bead of pre-come with his thumb and drags it through my folds. "You've got it."

"Hurry." I lean up on my elbows and watch him nudge inside. So. Slow. Too slow.

I try to tilt my hips up to meet him, but he presses me down and resumes his pace of sliding in inch by inch. Torturing me with long, languid strokes. Filling me. Pulling out. Pushing back in. I squeeze around him and it's like a dam bursts, I have to bite my fist to keep my screams from conjuring up every wild animal in the vicinity.

"I love you," I cry out without thinking. It's the truth though.

I plant my feet on his chest and grip his wrists as he thrusts into me, harder and deeper now. He moves my legs and pulls me up so I'm sitting on the edge of the hood, my arms and thighs wrapped around him as he rolls his hips to drive into me deeper. I've never felt so bonded to anyone in my life. "I love you too, A. For so long."

Brennan's hands skim down my back to my ass and we grind against each other, our mouths fused as we chase the next monumental release. He sets an impressive pace, increasing the tempo and pounding me harder, until I'm biting his shoulder in anticipation of what's to come. He reaches between us, finds my clit and rubs it aggressively, knowing it's what I need.

We fall apart at the same time, exploding into the desert night like the stars above us. He clings to me, speechless, his face slack with pleasure.

"Holy orgasm," he wheezes. "I've never come so hard in my life."

I know how he feels. "Do you think you can still walk?"

He pulls back to grin at me. "Can you?"

"I'll manage." I rest my hand lightly on his hip, looking down at our joined bodies. "Besides, we need to get back to the hotel. I want it to be just me and you without interruption until I go back to Seattle."

"Me too, but I meant it. I want you to stay." He gathers me tightly against his chest. "Another day. Week. Month. For as long as possible."

The look on his face tells me he's dead serious

I belong with him. He needs me.

And, I realize, I need him too.

Eighteen

BRENNAN

One Month Later

THE DOOR TO THE new condo Astrid helped me rent clicks behind me.

The entire atmosphere is calm, like the place is holding its breath in the cool evening light.

When she decided to extend her stay for a month, I brought her back to my cramped, studio apartment. The look of horror when she stepped inside gave me a wake-up call. A thirty-two-year-old man living like a fucking college student isn't sexy. Or cool.

It's pathetic.

I guess there's a reason I've never taken her to my townhouse in Seattle, it isn't much better. Needless to say, we stayed in a hotel until it was ready. Because, yeah. I may not be house proud, but I still wanted to get laid.

So, she called in a favor with a realtor friend and I signed a year lease on this amazing new condo. At a rent I didn't even know existed in Palo Alto.

Astrid's touch is everywhere. She guided me through a whirlwind of decisions I didn't know needed making. I've never given my living space much thought before, which was a big mistake. With her impeccable taste, the sleek, modern unit feels like a home.

Our home. Except, it's not.

She'll be leaving soon.

I drop my keys in the key-bowl—an item I didn't realize existed until a week ago—and run my hand along the cool marble surface of the kitchen island. A couple months ago, I would've collapsed into whatever chair was closest with a stack of papers and my laptop.

At least this new condo feels like a reset. Somewhere I can relax and unwind and escape the stress of my daily life. It won't be the same when she goes back, but at least her little touches are everywhere to remind me of how lucky I am.

With her by my side, everything feels different. Lighter.

We've gotten into a rhythm, in the best way. She's filled my life with her boundless energy and steady sense of control. We wake up, make love, have breakfast at the café downstairs together and sometimes take a short walk before I go to the office.

She gives me space during the day, but I'm always home by seven for dinner. We either grab a bite out or she plates takeout. Nights are spent fucking like banshees and afterward, we wrap up together in a blanket and watch episodes of *Below Deck* and *Love Island*.

Then we fuck some more. Like we're making up for lost time.

I've learned a lot about balance from Astrid by living with her. My life is so much better for it. I don't want her to go home. I might slip into old habits.

I scrub my face with my hand, feeling the weight of it all start to creep in. She's been my calm in the storm, but the storm isn't stopping anytime soon. I'm not sure what I'm gonna do without her.

"B?" Astrid's voice cuts through my thoughts as she walks out of the bedroom wearing my t-shirt, her hair loose around her shoulders. "You home?"

"Yep." I give her a little wave.

With one quick assessment, she knows something's weighing on me. "What's wrong?"

"Same old shit." I tilt my head. "Yet, strangely different."

"Ugh." She slides her arms around my waist, leaning her head against my shoulder. "Want to talk about it?"

I kiss her temple and breathe in her peachy shampoo for a second. "The board's officially relocating the company to Palo Alto. The IPO is full steam ahead. And, they've made it clear they don't want me to leave." I pull away and sit at the counter. "Apparently, they want to reshape me. Give me media training so I can travel around the world and make PR appearances. I guess the new plan is to mold me into the CEO they think is publicly presentable, not the one I am. So, it's not about building the technology anymore. I'm supposed to officially transition into a talking head."

"Oh, God." She covers a smile with her hand. "Sounds like your perfect job—not!"

"You have no idea. They've hired a legal and finance team to manage the IPO and I'm supposed to fall in line, do the interviews, smile for the cameras, and be something I'm not." I shake my head woefully.

Astrid strolls to the small wine fridge and grabs two glasses and a bottle of red. Uncorks it and pours us each a glass. She hands it to me. "Well, can you say no?"

"I'm not sure." I shrug and take a sip. "At least they're not forcing me out, which is what I figured today's meeting would be about."

She nods and bites her lip, sussing what to say next. "But...you could say no, couldn't you? Focus on something you like better. Like the creative side?"

"*No.*" My frustration bubbles up and the word comes out harsher than I planned. "It's not that simple. I'm tied to CognifyAI—financially, legally. On paper, I'm essentially a billionaire, but I've never given myself a big salary. Never sold any of my shares. I'm not sitting on a pile of cash and an IPO could be the key to financial freedom. I'll have to suck it up for a bit."

Astrid folds her arms as she leans against the counter. "Have you talked to the financial manager yet?"

"Not yet," I admit, shaking my head. "I need to. I've been putting it off until I go back to Seattle."

"*Brennan*..." Astrid takes out a charcuterie board she must have bought this afternoon and places it in front of me. "Please do. You've built an empire. It's time you figure out your finances so you're not at the mercy of the board."

Her advice is so needed. It's hard to believe this thing I've built has spiraled into something I can't fully control. "I know."

We stand there for a moment, the weight of everything hanging in the air between us. It's been so easy with her here. Just the two of us. She grounds me to the point where pressure of work doesn't gnaw at the back of my mind all day and all night. Astrid's my calm. My balance.

And...she's heading back to Seattle in two weeks and I can't imagine how I'll live my life without her here.

"You've changed things for me." I move behind her and take her in my arms. "Living with you...I'm gonna miss you so much when you go home."

"We'll figure it out. I'm not gone yet." She smooths my hair down with her palms.

I shake my head. "I don't want to go back to the way things were. It's not just the condo. It's everything. You've made me realize how unbalanced my life was."

Astrid brushes an errant strand of hair away from my forehead. "You've balanced me too, you know. I've never had this before, B. Someone who makes me feel like I'm more than what I look like."

I tug her against me. She always says things like this, like she doesn't know how special she is. It kills me every time. We're quite the pair. As opposite as we are, we share one thing in common. A lack of self-awareness of our worth. Together, I think we're healing.

"You're so much more," I murmur into her hair. "You know that, right?"

She nods against my chest, but I can feel the uncertainty in the way she holds on to me. I pull her closer to hopefully reassure her. Astrid has no idea how much she's given me by extending her stay. She's brought a steadiness into my life. Fun. Spontaneity. And, calmness.

No, balance.

We both know when she goes back to Seattle, everything could change. Without our day-to-day routine, I'll likely slip back into CognifyAI tunnel vision.

God, I want to tell her about my diagnosis. Why I struggle with mundane things that seem second nature to her. I swear, I've nearly confessed so many times over the past few weeks.

Except, every time I open my mouth, I stop myself. Even though I know she loves me as I am, part of me worries her perception will change. She'll realize I'm more of a project than a partner.

I couldn't bear it. Not from her.

So I say nothing. Not yet. Instead, I press a kiss to her forehead. Hope I'll find the perfect time to unload my truth someday.

"I wish you didn't have to go," I whisper.

"I know," she sighs. "But, I do…"

"I get it," I cut in, trying to keep the exasperation out of my voice. "We can't lose what we have."

She pulls back and looks into my eyes. "We'll figure it out. I promise."

I want to believe her. But I know how it goes. I know it's a grind to make long-distance relationships work. I've watched my rockstar brothers struggle with it. And their bandmates. Now, we're staring down the same path, knowing no matter how much we want to be together, it's not going to be easy.

"Tomorrow, I'm getting my shit together." I decide to shift the conversation in a positive direction. "I'll call the financial manager and dig out the name of my lawyer. When I started CognifyAI, Connor had Jace's dad—your buddy, Jason Deveraux—recommend someone at Finney Cooper. I'll get in touch with him because it's time to get serious. I've let the board push me around. Trusted what they tell me I'm obligated to do."

"Good. You deserve to take control of this, Brennan. It's *your* company." Astrid's eyes light up with approval.

"Yeah." I nod. "It is."

Maybe if I try hard enough, I'll be worthy of her. Show her that having a bit of neurodivergence doesn't define me.

Because I'm not letting go of Astrid.

Never.

She's inspiration enough to make me want to do better.

Nineteen

ASTRID

One Month Later

BRENNAN RETURNED TO SEATTLE today.

Not under the best of circumstances, unfortunately.

I sit by the window, gazing out at the dark water. Waiting. The gentle movement of the lake usually soothes me. Tonight, not so much. My nerves are utterly on edge.

He was supposed to get here hours ago and, aside from a quick phone call on his way to his parents' house from the airport, I haven't heard a thing.

It's stressful because I know what he's going through. The waiting is hard. I'm worried about him. Worried about the situation. I wish he'd send even a short text though...

Is it wrong to feel this way? Probably. Couples are supposed to be in regular communication about important life events. Yeah, I know this isn't about me. He needs to be with his family, and I get it...

Shit. That's a discussion for another day. Tonight, I'll suck it up because he needs me to be strong and I want to be here for him when he finishes up.

My impatience isn't rooted in the current state of affairs. Truth be told, the past couple weeks have felt surreal without waking up next to him up every day. Two months together in California brought us closer than I ever thought possible. I'm so head over heels in love with him, it's undeniable.

Now I'm back in Seattle and reality's slapped me in the face. For me, there's a nagging question about our future because we've slipped back into separate lives. Sure we talk and text. Have video sex. There's no romance. No teasing. No fun. We've lost our mojo.

Probably because he's always in a bad mood. Grousing about the chaos surrounding his company and whether he'll stay or go. It permeates my disposition too, so I bitch about my latest client nightmares. The negativity gives me the ick.

I know I want this corporate shit to end so we can move on with our relationship. I want the whole shebang. A future. Marriage, kids, and a life spent side by side, not in separate states. It doesn't need to happen tomorrow, but letting the day-to-day sweep us along isn't an option. At least not for me.

We'll need to have a conversation about it to see if we're still on the same page. Today isn't the time with everything else weighing on him. Sooner rather than later, though.

The sound of footsteps on my deck makes me jump and I quickly hightail it toward the entryway. A second later, Brennan knocks and I fling the door open. Oh crap. He looks exhausted. His clothes are rumpled and there's a heaviness in the way he carries himself.

"Oh, B." I wrap my arms around him before he has a chance to say anything.

The smallest flicker of relief crosses his face. "God, you have no idea how good it is to see you."

"Same," I whisper. "How are you holding up?"

Brennan exhales deeply, leaning into me for a moment. "We convinced Cillian to check into rehab. It was...a lot."

"I'm glad you were there for him." I squeeze his arm gently, trying to convey he doesn't need to explain.

"Da and I...we, uh. We had to..." He's clearly drained and fighting back tears. "It wasn't easy." He runs a hand through his hair. It's as though speaking words takes too much effort. "Cillian fought us but he finally broke down. Hopefully he'll stay and get the help he needs."

I don't press. I don't need to know the details of his brother's private business. Brennan's obvious exhaustion tells me everything. Instead, I take his hand and guide him toward the bedroom. His steps are heavy as he follows me.

"You need to rest." I lead him to the bed. The room is dimly lit by the lamp on the nightstand. I help him sit on the edge of the mattress. "You've done enough for today."

He sinks down, slumps over, rests his elbows on his knees and buries his face in his hands. My heart hurts. I can tell he's holding so much inside.

Kneeling in front of him, I help him undress. Take off his shoes and socks. Unbuckle his pants and pull them off. Lift his shirt over his head.

He watches me, silently, and I can feel the weight of this evening pressing down on him. Once he's down to his boxers, I guide him to lie back against the pillows.

He doesn't resist. His eyes are half-closed already, but I know he's still too wound up to sleep.

I'm already in my sleep shorts and tank top, so I climb into bed, kneeling behind his head. Slowly, I begin to massage his scalp. My fingers move gently through his thick hair and down his neck, kneading away the tension I can feel knotted up in him.

Moments later, Brennan lets out a long, quiet sigh and his body relaxes under my touch. "You're incredible,"

"You're the one who's incredible." I smile to myself, continuing to work my fingers along his shoulders and back up again. "You're a great brother for being here for him, B. I'm so proud of you."

He doesn't say anything but I feel his hand reach for mine, squeezing it gently before releasing.

"Thank you," he rasps. "For understanding. I know I don't deserve you."

"You don't need to say that." I lean down to kiss his forehead. "I'm here because I love you."

A soft stillness hangs in the air. His eyes are open now, searching mine. "I love you too." The words slip out so naturally, but there's so much vulnerability beneath them.

Though I've questioned it at times over these past weeks, he means it. Deeply.

My heart swells. Warmth floods through my soul as I lean down and kiss him languidly. Tenderly. Filled with promises of a future.

I shimmy down his body and before he knows what's happening, I pull his briefs down and his cock is securely in my grip. Wrapping my lips around his crown, I suck firmly while giving his balls a little massage.

"Holy fucking hell, A," Brennan croaks.

"Mmm," I hum and pump my hand up and down in sync with my mouth, knowing full well it makes him crazy.

He grips my hair and holds me steady, thrusting in my mouth. "Yeah. Suck it," he groans. His head lolls back against the pillows where he looks down at me, watching. "So fucking sexy."

Pulling off my shorts, I toss them to the ground, straddle him and guide his thick cock to my entrance.

"Ah, yeah," I moan when I sink down as far as I can. He fills me completely.

His hands glide from my hips, pulling up my tank top and flinging it somewhere in the room. He cups my breasts and thumbs my nipples, which are already puckered and tight. "You're so fucking gorgeous."

"You're giving me compliments 'cause I'm fucking you good." I circle my hips in a figure eight.

"It doesn't hurt. Seriously, though. You're the most beautiful woman I've ever known. Inside *and* out." Brennan watches me intently as I begin to roll my hips and ride him. I brace myself with one hand on his chest and flick my clit with my finger, swaying my hips until his eyes glaze over. "Ah, fuck. Yeah. Touch yourself." I squeeze my inner muscles against his cock and he moans, "Oh God, you're clenching me like a fist."

He sucks in a breath and watches me masturbate while riding and squeezing him. Without warning, he grips my wrist and brings it to his mouth where he licks and sucks each finger into his mouth. Then he takes control, sitting up straight and wrapping his arms around me.

"I fucking love you." He holds me still as he rocks up into me, his eyes never leaving mine. "I fucking love your pussy." His fingers circle my clit. "I love your mouth." He nibbles on my lips. "Your tits." He sucks on my nipple. "Most of all, I love your heart."

Just when I think he's going to lose control, Brennan pulls out and flips me over so my ass is barely in the air. He straddles me, presses my thighs together and slides his cock in to the hilt. He and I have fucked many times and holy hell if this isn't the best position ever.

"Oh, my God," I groan. "You're so incredibly deep."

I can't move because he's essentially pressing me into the mattress and holding me in place with is body. I have no complaints. I like him dominating me in the bedroom. Plus, his dick feels huger than it already is and hits my G-spot every time he thrusts.

"Is this okay?" he pants.

"Better than okay." I grip the sheets tightly. "I can feel every ridge of your cock and you keep hitting my spot. Yeah...right there."

"I'm gonna blow soon." He slides his hand up my spine and back into my hair. Grips it at my nape. Pulls. Hard.

"God, yes," I cry out, shocked at how much it turns me on.

"You like to have your hair pulled, A?" Brennan pulls a little harder.

I moan, "I guess I do."

Then he begins to fuck me. Hard. His balls slap against my ass over and over, driving him so deep. My thighs are trembling and zings are flitting through my body.

"I'm gonna come, B. Don't stop," I manage to say.

"Yes. Do it. Cream all over my cock." Brennan leans over and bites my neck near my shoulder, and that's it. Wave after wave of pleasure overtakes my body. I clench tightly around him like I want to suck him into my body.

"Fuck," he roars and follows me over, filling me to capacity. When he settles, Brennan collapses at my side and gathers me in his arms. "Mine."

I flip in his arms to face him.

We stare into each other's eyes for a long time before his lids flicker closed and he falls into a deep sleep.

I stay awake for a while longer. Nestled against him. Feeling whole because the man I love is next to me.

Wondering, though...

Why do I feel such a sense of dread?

Twenty

BRENNAN

Three Days Later

SOMETHING'S OFF.

It's been this way since I arrived in Seattle a few days ago.

Astrid sits on the edge of her bed, brushing her hair. I'm leaning against the bathroom doorway, watching her. There's been a strange sense of unease this weekend. Not quite tension. More like there's something she wants to say to me but doesn't feel she can because she knows I'm stressed about Cillian's situation on top of everything else.

Or, maybe, she's having second thoughts about us.

Either way, I'm avoiding the discussion.

The thing is, I'm pretty sure I know what's bugging her. I have to go back to California tomorrow and she and I haven't fallen back into the pattern we established when she stayed with me down there last month.

Up here, I haven't made time for our walks. Fun chats are few and far between. We've eaten dinner together maybe once. No bad TV watching or even cuddles on the couch.

Mostly, we fuck when we're together. Otherwise, not connecting on an intimate level.

And, it's all my fault.

To be fair, in preparation for this IPO announcement next week, I've been caught up with work nonstop. Long, grueling Zoom meetings with the board, the executive team and lawyers. There's so much to the process, I had no idea.

Astrid's busy too. She has mammoth listings to prepare for and spends countless hours creating marketing materials and arranging for open houses. Researching property values in different neighborhoods and how this corresponds to sales. Figuring out what the latest hot amenities are. Stuff like that.

Sensing me watching her, she looks at me through the mirror. Her eyes scan my face like she's trying to figure out what I'm thinking. It's funny, how easily she can read me. She's broken most of my walls down. From the beginning.

I step tentatively into the room. "You ready?"

She shrugs and sets the brush down on the dresser. "Yeah. I guess."

"I'm glad you're coming." I sit beside her and wrap my arm around her shoulder. Rest my cheek against hers. I meet her eyes in the mirror. "Full house tonight."

Astrid takes a deep breath. "I'm not sure I should go."

"Why not?" I can't disguise my surprise.

Astrid turns to face me. "Because you'll be talking about Cillian's situation and it's none of my business."

"What do you mean?" I freeze for a second, taken aback. It's not what I expected her to say. *At all.*

"I mean," she purses her lips thoughtfully, "I loved meeting your mom, dad, and Seamus. But dinner with your entire family is a big deal. It's a statement. The thing is, we may be at a crossroads in this relationship. You've been on the phone all weekend, working. You're leaving for California tomorrow. I think we need to have a real conversation about us and what this is before I'll feel comfortable being there."

Shit. I've fucked up. I get so caught up in my own shit, forgetting to pay attention to what really matters. I run a hand through my hair, trying to collect my thoughts.

"I thought..." I'm unsure of how to explain myself. "I thought you'd want to be there with me. We're a couple, I mean..."

She crosses her arms and her brows knit together. "I *do* want to be there for you. I can't deny it's been different between us, B."

This is not something I can ignore. Astrid means too much.

I step even closer, unfurl her arms and take her hands in mine. "I'm sorry. I've had a lot on my mind. I don't want there to be any doubt—I'm in this ten thousand percent. I love you, A. I want us to be together."

"Me too, but what does being together mean?" She looks uncertain. "Our time in California was the best time in my life, but you're leaving tomorrow. Back into the abyss of all the shit going on with your company. I'm heading into my busy season in another month. Is this going to work?"

Her words hit me hard. "Whoa."

"You made a real effort before I visited you. Which is *why* I visited you." She looks down at the floor glumly. "I don't want to float through whatever we are. Other than when we're having sex, you and I haven't spent any quality time together this trip. None."

I fucking knew it. She's got a valid point. I've been so focused on the company and my brother's situation, I've ignored her subtle hints about grabbing coffee. Going up to The Zoo to play pool. Watching *Love Island* together.

Maybe they weren't so subtle.

"I fucked up." I shake my head. "I want this. I want us. And I'll do whatever it takes to make this work."

Astrid watches me carefully, searching my face like she's waiting for the real answer. I get it—she's been here before. In her past, she's been with powerful men who took and took from her. Made promises they didn't keep.

But I'm *not* those guys, I'm gonna marry this woman. Have a family with her.

Just as soon as I can get out from under my shit.

"What can I do?" I squeeze her hands. "Tell me, A. I don't have your insight. I'm crap at reading the situation sometimes. You're my everything. What do you need from me?"

She hesitates for a second before meeting my eyes again. "I want us to be in a committed relationship and build our lives together. Not go along with whatever happens. I hate letting other people dictate our moods. When I was in California, you were busy but you made time for me. Every day. If you can't for a day or two—even a week, I get it. But I see the writing on the wall for the foreseeable future, B. I don't like it."

I take her words in and think about how we fell into a glorious rhythm of waking up together, eating breakfast, working side by side. Taking time each day just for us. It felt right, easy, like we were building something real. Fun. Loving. And I want us to have the same experience here. I want it every day.

"I promise I'll do better." I try to keep my voice steady because I feel like I'm going to cry. "I want a future with you. Marriage, kids, all of it. You're not an afterthought—you're *everything* to me."

Her eyes soften. "I believe you want these things."

"I love you." I squeeze her tightly. "Don't ever doubt it."

"I love you too," she says softly.

Holding her close like this is everything. Still, I'm trying to tamp down my panic at her leaving me. I've never wanted anything more than Astrid. At the same time,

I'm between a rock and a hard place. I can't abandon my company.

She isn't asking me to, of course. All she needs is for me to prioritize a little time for her, no matter what. From now on, I'll schedule time on my calendar so I don't get too focused and forget. My tendency to put blinders on to the world around me is a problem I can't seem to overcome. Maybe this is a way I can fix my own shortcomings.

"A." I tip her face up to mine. "Know one thing. You *are* my girlfriend. I want you to be part of my life and part of my family. I want to be part of yours."

She bites her lip, still looking uncertain. "Your family's been through so much lately. Maybe they need time to process everything with Cillian. I don't want to intrude."

"You're not intruding. They know you. They like you. And trust me, my mom's going to be thrilled to see you. Plus, Connor and Ronni will be there—they're excited to catch up," I reassure.

I can still see the hesitation, but she's considering. "As long as I'm not in the way."

"Of course you're not in the way." I shake my head vigorously. "You're the one person I want by my side. You make *everything* better."

She looks at me for a long moment. Finally, she nods, letting out a soft sigh. "Okay. I'll go."

Relief floods through me.

I realize, though, it's time to tell her my situation. Why I am the way I am. Why I struggle with some things that seem easy for everyone else.

Not now, when it will seem like an excuse. Because it's not.

Then again, Astrid knows me better than anyone ever has. She's already seen so much of me—my messy life, my family—and she accepts me for who I am. *Loves* me, even.

She. Loves. Me.

But, there's still the one thing she doesn't know about me yet.

I hope she doesn't hate me for keeping it from her.

Have I waited too long?

Twenty-One

ASTRID

Later That Day

ON THE DRIVE TO Brennan's parents' place, I replay our conversation from earlier.

I needed reassurance, which pisses me off.

Then again, I did something I've never done before. Set boundaries. Asked for what I want out of a relationship rather than going along for the ride and getting burned. And, Brennan promised to make space for us. I know he's trying. Part of me wonders if he's doing it to appease me or because he wants the same things as me.

I hope it's the latter.

We park at his parents' house and I feel a familiar swirl of emotions—anticipation mixed with a hint of unease. Sure, I've been here before, met his folks and his little brother and was welcomed warmly.

Tonight feels different. Everyone but Cillian is here. It's kind of like an audition.

I hope I pass.

Brennan, who's been quiet on the drive over, glances at me. His adorable, quirky smile tugs at the corners of his lips. "Ready?"

"Yeah." I nod, though I'm not sure if I am. With everything happening—Cillian going to rehab, Brennan's stress over CognifyAI—I don't want to be an added responsibility. A burden.

As we walk up to the door, once again, Maureen anticipates our arrival before we even knock. Her face lights up with joy. "There's my precious boy." She throws her arms around Brennan.

They share a special bond, Brennan and his mother. For all his brilliance and tendency to isolate, he finds comfort in the familiar things in his life, like the steady presence of his family.

"Astrid, we're so happy you're here." Maureen turns to me. "It's so lovely to see you, darling girl. Come in, come in."

We step into the house and the tension in my chest eases. Maureen is so welcoming. So genuine. Even though I immediately feel more at home here on my second visit than I do in my own house, I can't help but slip into the polished, put-together version of myself when I see the rest of the McGloughlin clan milling around.

It's automatic. A reflex. I've spent years perfecting this facade.

The living room is buzzing with energy. Connor, holding sleeping baby Teagan, chats with two tall, handsome guys whom I assume are Liam and Padraig. Seamus and Rory are beside them, engaged in their own conversation.

Brennan keeps his hand on the small of my back, quiet but not withdrawn. Something clicks for me—he's actually at peace here. The vibe is the same as when I stayed with him in Palo Alto. When he's surrounded by the familiar, by people who know him, he's comfortable.

Connor spots us and ambles over. "Well, look who it is! Good to see you two all loved up." He wraps a long arm around Brennan before turning to me. "Astrid, keeping busy?"

"Soon. Real estate season is around the corner." I peek at his adorable little girl dozing in the crook of his other arm. "And, who is this gorgeous creature?"

Ronni slides in next to me, looking a little frazzled as one of the twins clings to her leg. "That's miss Teagan, our angel child." She reaches down and musses her son's hair. "Torin, go find your brother."

"I can't believe she's a year old." Brennan peers over at Teagan in wonder.

Connor squeezes Brennan's shoulder. "Well, you haven't been in Seattle much. They grow up fast."

"Yeah." Brennan glances at me. "I've had a lot on my plate."

Out of the blue, Tristan chases Toran and they both smack into Ronni, nearly knocking her down. "Ohmygod. Boys. You're driving me crazy."

"The two of youse. Time out." Connor points to the sofa. "Ten minutes. No talking. No poking. No prodding. Behave yourselves. And, apologize to your mum."

Impressively, they obey Connor immediately.

"You have your hands full." I help her straighten her sweater when the boys are settled. "Three kids under five is no joke."

Ronni nods and takes Teagan from Connor. "We're managing. Barely. Thank God you found us the perfect house. I don't know how we'd survive without the space. I'm going to get her fed before dinner, I'll be fifteen minutes or so."

As Ronni heads to the back bedroom, Brennan's brothers approach and I find myself face-to-face with all four McGloughlins at once—Liam, Padraig, Seamus, and Connor. It's like being surrounded by different versions of Brennan, each with their own quirks, but all with the same unmistakable Irish charm.

Connor, Liam and Padraig are deep in conversation about their respective bands, LTZ and Fireball, talking about upcoming tour schedules and such.

Seamus turns to me. "So, Astrid," he offers me a polite smile, "how was your time in California with Brennan?"

"Magical," I say honestly.

We both glance at Brennan, who is staring at his musical brothers, eyes glazing over as Liam and Padraig dive into technical talk about production on their latest album. It's like he's trying to appear to pay attention, even though he's in his own head. Likely sorting through some algorithm.

Connor nudges him with his elbow. "Bren, you with us?"

"Oh. Yeah. Sorry, just...thinking." Brennan's focus snaps back immediately, though he blinks a bit as if waking up from a nap.

"He's always like this," Liam says fondly. "You're solving the next big AI problem while we're talking about stupid guitar riffs."

It's subtle, the way they do it. Connor, Liam, even Seamus, quietly guiding Brennan back to the present. They know his mind. The way he retreats into his own thoughts when he's overwhelmed. How he likes things just so. No one coddles him. It's like a gentle nudge when he needs it. No awkwardness or frustration—only love.

It's beautiful.

I nearly choke up watching all of this unfold. I'm envious, truth be told. He's a lucky man to have a family who accepts him for who he is. No questions asked.

I wonder how much of this Brennan is aware of.

Does he realize how much his family accepts him for who he is? Or, is there a part of him that feels like he doesn't quite fit, even with them? It's something I've been thinking about more and more lately, especially after spending time with him in California—and the past few days.

I've noticed how much Brennan likes routine. How he finds comfort in structure. It's one of the things I love most about him—he's so different from the men I've dated. Guys who are always looking over their shoulder for the next best thing. Or, chasing excitement and chaos rather than stability. When he's focused on something, he's all in. It's refreshing.

Ohmygod.

Thinking back to our earlier conversation, I realize I may have read things the wrong way. Coming here to deal with Cillian's crisis, when he's so entrenched in his company dynamics, has thrown him off his game. He's struggling to make his world feel manageable after being thrown a major family curveball. It doesn't mean he's not invested in our relationship.

Shit happens, sometimes.

I'm going to apologize when we get back to my place. I don't want to put any additional pressure on him. My own issues have nothing to do with Brennan, and he doesn't need to be anyone other than himself with me.

I love him.

All of him.

I never want him to feel like he has to change for me.

Maureen calls us for dinner and family chatter fills the room as we gather around the table. She's outdone herself. The smell of roasted garlic and rosemary fills the air as she sets down a massive platter of slow-cooked lamb, perfectly tender with a golden crust. Next to it is a giant bowl of her famous buttery colcannon and a boat of gravy. There's also a medley of roasted carrots, parsnips, and sweet potatoes glazed with honey and thyme, and freshly baked loaves of crusty Irish soda bread, still warm from the oven.

As we feast on the most delicious food I've ever eaten, Rory fills us in on the mammoth construction project he's taken over while Cillian's away. He seems fairly Zen about it, though everyone seems to be both frustrated and worried about the situation.

"Brennan, you've been unusually quiet today." Seamus glances at his brother. "Everything okay?"

Part of me feels guilty. I hope the reason he's not speaking isn't because he's worried about us. Stressing he's not doing enough in our relationship. He's not going to lose me, I need to clarify this when we're alone again.

Brennan blinks at him. "Yeah, I'm fine. Just thinking."

He's totally worried about us. *Shit.*

"About work, no doubt," Padraig teases, though there's no malice in his tone.

Brennan smiles, but it doesn't quite reach his eyes. "Yeah..."

I squeeze his knee under the table, trying to give him some comfort. He puts his hand on top of mine and squeezes back, but I can still feel the tension in his body.

After dinner, I help Maureen clear the plates. Brennan stays behind with Rory and Seamus, talking quietly about Cillian.

As we do the dishes, she glances over at me. "You're great for him, you know."

"You think?" I pause and meet her gaze, the soapy dish in my hand forgotten.

She nods, her smile warm and genuine. "He's different around you. More at ease. He needs the balance you give him."

"I hope so." Tears well up in my eyes. I want to believe her. I want to believe I'm making a difference in Brennan's life. That I'm enough.

"He's brilliant, you know," Maureen continues. "He's always been different from my other boys. Not in a bad way, well, I'm sure you know."

"Yeah." I nod, though I've not been able to put my finger on it. He's uniquely Brennan.

"Even as a little boy, he always needed structure. A project. A strict routine. It's how he makes sense of the world. I see how you watch out for him, Astrid. I like you because you don't try to change him. You...accept him." She grips my hand in hers.

Her words hit me in the heart. I've always prided myself on being able to adapt. To fit into any situation. But with Brennan, it's different. I'm not altering my life for him. He's not changing for me. We accept each other. As we are.

It's why we're so special.

He's let me into his world and I'm starting to realize how rare that is.

After we finish the dishes, I return to the living room where Brennan is sitting with his dad and Seamus. He catches my eye and motions me over.

God, I love him.

I love him for all the things he doesn't say. For the way he tries to keep everything under control, even when it's clear he's struggling. He may not realize it yet, but he doesn't have to carry all of this alone. Not anymore.

Never again.

Later, as we drive back to my houseboat, he takes my hand and places it on his thigh. "I'm glad you came tonight." Brennan slips his hand over mine. "It means a lot to me."

"I'm glad I came too." I stroke his cheek. "I'm sorry about before. I guess I was feeling insecure."

"About me?" He looks over, surprised.

I nod. "Yeah. I missed us."

"Don't give up." Brennan's thumb brushes over the back of my hand. "I promise, you're the most important thing to me."

"Never." I kiss his cheek.

I lean back into the seat as the city lights blur past. Closing my eyes, I know two things for certain.

I love having Brennan in my life.

And, I love being part of his world.

Twenty-Two

BRENNAN

Three Months Later

WELL, TONIGHT'S NOT GOING as planned.

I'll roll with it though.

Stepping into the Met Grill, I immediately feel a sense of comfort. The reason I love this place is because it hasn't changed in years—the same dark-wood paneling, the same low hum of conversation, the unmistakable scent of grilled steaks.

Bottom line, familiar places ground me.

I'm back in Seattle to see Cillian. He's out of rehab and I was looking forward to introducing Astrid to him. Unfortunately, an important appointment pulled her away at the last minute and she's not sure if she'll make it.

Even though I'm disappointed, she's one of the top real estate agents in the country and didn't achieve such an elite status without being at the beck and call of her high-stakes clients. I'd also be a hypocrite if I got precious about her being late due to a work commitment. So, I get it.

Besides, it's nice Cillian and will I have some time to ourselves—there's a lot to catch up on.

I spot him in the back, already seated. He looks a hell of a lot better than the last time I saw him. Rehab was tough, but it seems to have worked. He's sober, clearer, and seems like himself again. Other than the seriousness in his eyes. Heartbreak. A weight that lingers.

"Hey, Bren." He stands to give me a quick hug. "Been a while."

"Yeah, it has." I slide into the booth across from him. "You look well."

Cillian motions to the waiter for water. "I feel great. One day at a time, though. You know how it is."

I nod, though I can't pretend to know the depth of what he's gone through.

We order two ribeyes, medium rare, with all the sides, and while we wait, I can't help but reflect on how much things have changed in such a short time. Three months ago, I was being pushed around by the board and feeling suffocated by their plans for CognifyAI.

Things are different now.

Thanks to Astrid, I've been working closely with my financial advisor and lawyer to negotiate my CEO package, ensuring my future legacy with the company. It was a wake-up call. If I hadn't gotten ahead of this when I did, I would have been utterly fucked.

Embracing my role as the public face of the company has been strategic. Now, I have a semblance of control. Public persona Brennan is someone I hated at first but now I've come to accept him. If I'm going to keep my eye on the long-term prize, I need to play the game for the board.

"Media training still got you in knots?" Cillian asks with a smirk as the waiter brings us the dessert menu.

I grin, shaking my head. "Nah, I've gotten the hang of it. It's not as bad as I thought it'd be. Surprisingly, it's worth it. If all goes to plan, and the deal we proposed goes through, I'll stick with CognifyAI and I'll be set for life."

"More than." He quirks an eyebrow. "We're talking 'richest man in the world' territory, aren't we?"

"Yeah, or something close. But, there are strings attached. The golden handcuffs they're offering come with a five-year lock-in. I'll be tied to the company for the next half decade." I swirl the lemon slice around in my glass of water.

Cillian studies me for a moment. "And you're not sure if it's what you want."

It's not a question. He knows me too well.

"I'm not," I admit. "It's tempting. I've worked for years to get CognifyAI where it is. Walking away now would feel like giving up. At the same time, I'm not as excited about it as I used to be."

"Oh?" Cillian leans back in the booth.

I pause, thinking about the project Astrid and I have been working on. "I'm more excited about Reuniverse than CognifyAI these days." The words surprise me as they come out. "Astrid and I are in the final stages of beta testing. It'll be ready for our reunion next year. It's fun to build something from the ground up again. I've gotta be honest, the implementation of this AI has real potential on its own."

Cillian chews a piece of his steak. "So, you're telling me you could be the richest man in the world, but what gets you going is this reunion app?"

I laugh, but it's the truth. "Yeah, it kind of is. It reminds me of why I got into tech in the first place—creating useful innovations to help people. CognifyAI's not the same these days. Once we go public, it'll belong to the shareholders. I've come to terms with the change of status but it's weird. Maybe that's why Reuniverse is so much fun. It's ours."

"You're building it with the woman you love." Cillian leans back in his seat as the waiter refills his water glass. Thankfully he doesn't sound bitter. "Sounds like you've got a choice to make. Stick with the golden handcuffs or go after what actually makes you happy."

Huh. His bluntness makes me realize I do have a choice. "Well, I I'm hoping to do both."

"How's she doing, anyway?" Cillian asks after the waiter leaves. "Seems like things are pretty serious."

"Yeah." I swirl the water in my glass. "Astrid's great. And yeah, we're serious. As you can tell, she's crazy busy with her clients and I'm always buried with shit, but we're making it work. I've even set calendar reminders so I remember to text her throughout the day."

Cillian snorts. "What? You set reminders to text your girlfriend? Jesus, Bren."

I laugh, because it sounds ridiculous. It's the only way I've figured out to remember to check in so she knows I've got my priorities straight. With everything going on—IPO talks, the constant travel between Seattle and Silicon Valley, media training and overseeing the technology, I need a system.

"You thinking about marrying her?" Cillian leans forward.

"Uh…" I glance at him, caught off guard by the question. "You know I try not to get too far ahead of myself."

"Sure …" Cillian purses his lips pensively.

I swallow hard because he knows me so well. "I do think about it. Except, until I sort out CognifyAI, we don't live in the same city. I won't be able to give her what she deserves."

Cillian shakes his head. "You're making excuses. If you're serious about her—and it sounds like you are—take it from me, don't lose her. Once you've met your person, being without them is agony."

"She doesn't know yet." I hang my head. "I have no excuse, other than…"

"Hey." He grabs my wrist. "Don't. The worst thing you could do is keep important things from her. She's probably already picked up on the fact your brain works differently. And you know I don't mean that in a bad way."

"So, you think she notices to the point of wondering about it?" I try to keep my voice casual. Like I'm unbothered.

"Eh—yeah. She probably does." Cillian scrubs his beard with his hand, watching me. Making sure I'm okay.

I take another bite of steak, mulling over his words.

It's a strange thing, keeping this part of myself hidden from the woman who, besides my family, is the person I trust most in this world. Truth be told, Astrid knows more about me than anyone. She's privy to my obsessions. Embraces my quirks. Understands and accepts my routines. Fills in my gaps. She might tease me sometimes, but it's never mean-spirited. It's part of our normal banter.

Bottom line, she always encourages me to be myself.

Withholding my diagnosis has gone on too long. There can't be any secrets between us as we plan our future. Astrid deserves to know everything. Even the parts I'm afraid she might not understand.

Then she'll be able to make an informed choice if I'm the man for her.

"Speaking of Astrid." Cillian's eyes flick toward the door. "Looks like she's here."

Astrid walks toward us in an emerald-green dress cinched at the waist with a gold belt. Her hair is loosely swept up, a few tendrils framing her face, and her dark leather pumps add a polished touch. Even after a long day, she looks effortlessly elegant.

I stand to greet her, kissing her quickly before she slides into the booth next to me.

"Sorry I'm so late." She turns to Cillian. "The showing ran longer than expected. It's so nice to finally meet you. Brennan talks about you all the time."

"All good, I hope—except for the alcoholic thing." Cillian addresses his situation head on, flashing her a toothy smile. "You've been keeping my brother in check, I see."

Astrid laughs. "I try. He's not easy to wrangle, but I manage."

I glance at him. *Yeah*. She's aware.

Like magic, the steak salad I ordered for her arrives and as she eats, the conversation flows easily between the three of us.

Astrid is, as always, amazing. She's so natural. So at ease. I love how she can connect with anyone, even my beloved brother. I've never seen her break a sweat, no matter what the situation. I do want my future to be with her.

Cillian's dead-on. There's no time to waste.

After dinner, the three of us wait for the valet to pull up our cars. When Astrid's Bentley arrives, she says goodbye to my brother and climbs into the driver's seat.

She and I are staying on her houseboat, so before I walk around to the passenger side, Cillian wraps me in a bear hug. Claps me on the back, hard. "Don't wait, Bren. She loves you for you. That woman's a keeper."

"I won't." I squeeze his shoulder.

If I hadn't been sure before, watching her charm my brother sealed the deal.

I'm gonna lock her down. Tell her the truth. Ask her to marry me.

Soon.

I've just gotta make sure everything else falls into place.

Twenty-Three

ASTRID

Two Week Later

THE PAST TWO WEEKS have been incredible.

Brennan's been in Seattle, sorting out his CEO agreement before the IPO. Aside from a couple of long meetings, for once he's had real time off.

On the other hand, I've never been busier.

My hard work over the past decade has paid off, though I'm increasingly disillusioned with my chosen profession. A couple of months ago, my biggest rival retired, leaving me with a corner on the market listings ten mil and above. I'm juggling dozens of high-net-worth clients, and they're getting more entitled and demanding.

It takes a special skill to deal with the level of service they expect. The prospect of focusing on Reuniverse has me rethinking my future. It's gratifying putting my time into something where I don't have to kiss ass to make a sale. Hopefully one day I'll be able to work on it full time.

For the next couple days, though, I'm taking time off so Brennan and I can spend it together. This evening we're at The Zoo relaxing and playing pool, like old times.

"Should we play?" Brennan nods toward the pool table, though we both know neither of us really cares about the game.

God, he's fucking adorable. I've never seen him look more relaxed. He even has two days' worth of scruff. I'm going to toy with him a bit and get him good and worked up. Because, I'm not going to last long. I need my nightly allotment of orgasms.

At least two, hopefully three or four.

"I don't know how." I bat my eyes at him, teasingly. "Will you teach me?"

Brennan's lip quirks when he realizes my secondary game of seduction. "Sure, I'll show you how it's done."

He grabs a couple of cues, looking delicious in his worn jeans and black T-shirt. "This is how you break."

"Ooooh. Interesting." I stand next to him and lean over the table so he can see a flash of side boob in my loose tank top.

"You're not gonna distract me." He takes a shot, scattering the balls. A solid drops into the corner pocket and he addresses me in exaggerated mansplain. "Looks like I'm solids."

"You *are* solid," I purr, running my hand down his arm, feeling the muscle beneath his shirt.

He chuckles, leaning closer. "You gonna behave tonight?"

"I don't know what you mean." I blink at him innocently, gesturing to the table. "Is it still your turn?"

He chalks his cue and scans me from head to toe, the bulge in his jeans hard to miss. I know the feeling, I'm so wet for him it's insane. This man does it for me every time.

Brennan takes his shot, missing the pocket, but doesn't seem to care. He's too busy undressing me with his smoldering eyes.

"My turn," I announce, circling the table with exaggerated grace, pretending to search for the perfect shot. I bend over, knowing exactly how this looks from his vantage point—tits fully visible, hips tilted just so—and take a shot, sinking the ball.

He adjusts himself and shakes his head. "You're *so* bad."

"No, I'm a *good* girl," I say breathily. "Beginner's luck, I guess." I wink, biting my lip when I catch the heat in his gaze.

Brennan leans against the stool, arms crossed, his biceps pulling tight against his shirt, watching me like he's planning his next move—and it's not on the pool table.

I take another shot, this time wiggling my ass in his direction. The ball doesn't make it, but judging by the way he's watching me, it's the last thing on his mind.

"I'm on to you, you know." He comes up behind me.

"Whatever do you mean? I'm playing pool." I hip check him and reach for a fry when the waitress drops off our food.

Brennan grabs his cue and effortlessly sinks three balls in a row. "Winner of three games gets ten minutes of sexual favors."

"Twenty." I blow him a kiss. "I want to come at least twice before you fuck me."

We eat our bar snacks and play, bantering and giving each other teasing looks and touches. Both of us know how the night's gonna end. When a classic Stones song starts playing on the jukebox, I can't resist swaying my hips to the beat as I circle the table.

"You still trying to distract me?" Brennan's eyes lock on mine.

"Of course." I lick my lips and sink the eight ball. "One-nil."

Brennan crosses the space between us in two quick strides. His hand slides to the back of my neck as he pulls me in. His lips crash against mine with an intensity leaving me breathless, and for a moment, everything else fades away.

I'm so fucking in love with this man and everything's perfect at the moment.

After our talk, Brennan listened. When we're apart, he checks in with me and makes sure to prioritize our relationship, even though work is always looming. If he's in Seattle, we stay on my houseboat and spend as much time as possible together—dinners, walks by the water, watching the terrible reality shows he secretly loves and, of course, Sunday dinners at his parents' house.

Tomorrow, though, he's meeting my folks who, shockingly, agreed to have brunch with us. Truth be told, I'm dreading it.

Brennan pulls back from our kiss, his breath ragged, eyes dark with familiar heat. "You win." He runs his palm down my arm. "Let's finish this quick and get back home. I'm starving for your sweet little pussy."

I try to keep my cool, but why? "I like winning. Pussy licking is the ultimate win so let's go."

On the way home, we hold hands and hurry down the streets toward the dock. "So, are your lawyer and financial advisor confident they'll accept your terms?"

"Yeah." Brennan chalks up his cue. "Having them involved has been a game-changer."

I lean my head on his shoulder. "Do you feel better about things? You seem less stressed."

"I had no idea how excellent my lawyer is until now." He wraps an arm around my shoulder. "He's kicking ass."

"See?" I kiss his chin. "I thought you'd figure it out. You only needed a little push."

We arrive at my dock and hurry toward my door. He waits for me to fish out my keys. "Guess I owe you one."

I unlock the door. "You owe me *more* than one, McGloughlin."

"Do you enjoy torturing me, A?" Brennan chokes out when I whip off my top the second I'm through the entryway as I strut toward the bedroom.

"Like what?" I peek over my shoulder and beckon him with my finger.

"Christ." He follows close behind. "Swaying your hips. Bending over the table to show me your tits. I'm permanently hard here."

Brennan wraps both arms around me and pulls my back to his chest. He cups my breasts with his hands and thumbs my nipples through my lace bra. His lips fasten to my neck and he grinds his enormous hard-on into my ass.

I turn and our lips smash together. One hand roams under his t-shirt up his chest, shoulders, and arms. The other glides down his back to his ass, where I grab a handful. Loving the way his muscles clench and move under my hand as he rocks his pelvis into mine.

He walks me back toward the bed until my knees hit the mattress. I sit and kick off my shoes. Brennan tugs off my jeans and tosses them to the floor, growling, "Holy fuck, A. you're soaking. I need a taste."

"Oh yeah?" I yank at the hem of his shirt until he tugs it over his head and tosses it to the floor. I skim my hands over his stomach to the button of his jeans. "Take your pants off. We can suck on each other."

"Not yet." He cups my mound with his entire palm and I hiss in a breath when he yanks my panties down my hips and off. "Spread your legs and show me how wet you are."

I do as he asks and one-up him by unclasping my bra to free my tits. "Okay, you can see all the goods. I'm ready to collect my winnings."

"*Gah*. Do you know how gorgeous your pussy is?" Brennan scoots down to my belly and runs a finger through my folds. "It's beautiful. Pink. Puffy. Slick." He flicks my clit with his thumb and I can feel it engorge. "You smell delicious and you're so fucking responsive to my touch."

"B," I can't help but whimper. I want him so bad.

He leans down and licks me from my clit to my opening and back again. "This is mine."

He pushes two fingers inside me and presses the flat of his tongue to my clit, barely moving it. I find myself pulsing against his heat and bucking to get some friction.

"Ohmygod." I grip his hair and hold him in place.

"Whose pussy is this, A?" His fingertips graze over the sweet spot inside me and I tighten around him like a fist. "Tell me."

"*Yours*," I moan and move my hips. I'm desperate to get more pressure where I need it.

He pulls back. "Say it."

"My pussy is yours," I repeat, stronger now.

Brennan wraps his lips around my clit and pulls it gently as his fingers increase speed. "Say it again."

"I'm *yours*. My pussy is fucking *yours*," I cry out when he rubs my spot harder and intensifies the swirls of his tongue on my clit.

With a guttural growl, Brennan sucks my clit hard until I come so violently, I see stars. I'm bucking. Trembling. Panting. Chanting his name. I don't even notice him standing up to take off his clothes until he pulls me off the bed into his arms.

"Wrap your legs around me," he demands as he reaches under my thighs and lifts me up.

I kiss him for all I'm worth, tasting myself on his lips. He turns and pushes me against the wall, pulls his hips back and impales himself inside me.

"Yes!" I scream against his mouth.

With his eyes level with mine, he stares into my soul. "You are *mine*, A. Do you hear me? Mine."

"Yes," I sob as he begins to move in hard, quick strokes. "And you're mine."

He fucks me hard. Urgent. Claims me. His cock is like a steel rod, pulsing and throbbing. Every time he pulls back and rams back inside, I can't help but whimper because I want his cock to live there.

"Is my cock hitting your sweet spot?" he pants as my pussy clenches around him.

"God, yes!" My legs tighten on Brennan's hips as I begin to spasm.

He stops. "Don't come yet."

My eyes burst open with surprise. He's never edged me with his cock inside me before and I fucking love it.

"Not yet." He spreads my ass cheeks with his palms. "Hold on, baby."

"Please, I'm so close. Almost there." I beg and circle my hips against him frantically.

Brennan thrusts deep inside and stops, pinning me against the wall with his body. Filling me with his huge cock. Inserts the tip of his finger into my ass and watches as I desperately press my hard nipples against his chest. He grins devilishly. "Do you want to come? Or do you *need* to come?"

"I need to fucking come!" I curl my hand into a fist and rap it on his shoulder in frustration. "Move. *Please.*"

He hooks his arm under my knee and cups my ass to open me wider. He presses his finger in deeper. "I love the way you feel wrapped around me. I love the way you taste. I can smell how fucking turned on you are. Do you have any idea what you do to me?"

I can't speak. I can only shake my head.

He pulls back and slams home, causing me to cry out in exquisite ecstasy. "Your sex sounds make me fucking *crazy*. I want to fuck you all night long. Do you want me to, A?"

"Yes!" I find my voice as he pounds me. I'm so fucking aroused, my cream gushes over his cock and balls. My entire body is clenched around him like a vise. "God, *please*. B. I can't..."

There's no way to hold back a moment longer and my body is wracked with shudders as I pulse and contract around him.

"That's it, baby. Come on my cock." Brennan buries his face in my neck as he spurts his hot release. *"Ahhhhhghrhhrghh."*

After long moments of us clinging to each other, supported by the wall, I start to giggle.

Brennan brushes a few strands of hair back from my face. "You're mine, A."

"Yeah, Mr. Caveman. I get it." I kiss him softly.

He grins from ear to ear. "Damn right."

Twenty-Four

The Next Morning

TODAY IS A MONUMENTAL milestone.

Yep. At thirty-two years old, it's the first and only time I've ever met a girlfriend's parents.

I'm not sure how it's gonna go. Astrid's been acting weird all morning. I can't tell if she's nervous about what her parents will think about me or what I'll think of her parents. Either way, she's been quiet on the drive over to West Seattle.

We arrive at Salty's on Alki a bit earlier than our reservation and take a moment to enjoy the incredible view of Seattle's skyline shimmering across the water like something on a postcard. This place is a Seattle institution.

"Have you been here before?" I take Astrid's hand as we walk up the concrete steps to the front door.

She shakes her head. "Strangely, no. But my mom always wanted to eat here. I've invited them a few times and they've always said no. Today, I'm guessing you're the draw."

I hold the door open for her and we step inside. She looks around nervously, which kills me. Astrid is the most confident, put-together person I know and to see her being skittish freaks me out a bit. She's shared stories of her family ever since we became friends, but I'm reconsidering whether this introduction should be in a public setting.

Well, we're here. Seated by a large window with a panoramic view of the city. I place my hand over hers, give it a squeeze and look around the place. It's nice, but definitely geared toward tourists rather than locals. It has a chain-restaurant vibe. A quick glance at the menu makes me realize we're paying mostly for the location.

"They'll be fine," she mutters to herself a couple of times.

I brush a hair from her forehead and clear my throat. "So, uh… How should I act around them? Are there any topics I should avoid?"

"You're not prepping for a board meeting, B." Astrid raises her eyebrows and swats me lightly.

"Yeah…" I hesitate because I don't want to screw this up. "But, I want to make a good impression."

She sighs softly. "Just be you. Don't overthink it. Trust me, they're the ones who should be trying to make an impression on you."

"Oh-kay." There's something in her tone that puts me on edge. "Hopefully they like me."

"They don't like anyone. It's how they are." Astrid gazes at me sadly.

I decide not to push. If there's anything gleaned, Astrid's family dynamics are complicated. Today's brunch will be a real test for her, maybe for us.

I kiss her, sensing she needs some reassurance. "I've got you. I love you."

"I love you too." She wipes the lipstick off my lips and smiles, though it doesn't quite reach her eyes.

Jens and Brigitte arrive a little late. Her father's tall and lanky, with a bit of a hunch, his thick, gray hair is slicked back. Brigitte is short and birdlike with long, silver hair and wire-rimmed glasses. They walk briskly toward us but seem like they'd rather be anywhere else but here. We stand as they approach.

"Hi, Mom, Dad," Astrid greets them and hugs her father.

Jens pats her back awkwardly. When Astrid leans over to hug her mother, Brigitte stiffens. Like Astrid has a contagious disease. Hmm. Maybe she doesn't do affection.

I extend my hand to her parents. "Mr. and Mrs. Gustaffson. Nice to meet you."

Jens takes my hand and shakes it firmly but Brigitte barely looks at me. She turns to Astrid. "Brunch on the waterfront. I should have guessed."

Astrid's smile tightens, but she doesn't say anything. Her eyes flick to mine for a moment, an apology buried in their depths. She knew this was coming.

We sit down and a waitress comes over with menus. As soon as Brigitte sees the prices, her face pinches with disdain. "Twenty-four dollars for avocado toast?" she mutters to herself but loud enough for everyone to hear. "Absurd."

I watch Astrid closely as she skims the menu. Her fingers absently trace the edges of the paper, but she doesn't seem to be reading it. She's tense, almost like she's bracing herself for whatever's coming.

It hits me wrong. I hate she can't be herself around her parents. This version of her is different—guarded, like she's shielding herself from something I can't quite comprehend. *Yet.*

The conversation starts slowly. After some—eh—pleasantries, Jens asks about my work. Before I can dive into anything about CognifyAI, Brigitte jumps in. "Technology," she says with a dismissive wave of her hand. "I don't get the obsession. Everyone glued to their phones, chasing after the next shiny thing."

"I've told you about Brennan's company CognifyAI." Astrid takes a sip of water. "What I haven't mentioned is when we first reconnected he agreed to help me with our high-school reunion. We came up with a cool idea and now we're business partners in a new start-up we named Reuniverse. Brennan's developed some cool AI technology with real market potential."

I'm shocked to hear her talk about our project this way. Are they really only learning about it now? It's been nearly two years since we had lunch at the Met. Why wouldn't they know?

Brigitte rolls her eyes. "Billionaire tech people are the reason this country is going to hell, and AI? It's ruining everything. What a waste."

Ah, that's why.

It's funny, I have pretty thick skin when it comes to what I do. I don't give a shit what anyone thinks, but when I glance at Astrid, who's trying so hard to stay composed, she's a shell of the woman I know. My girlfriend, who has more drive than anyone I've ever met, is quietly listening to her mother dismiss our work like it's nothing.

And Jens stares out the window like a zombie.

"Well, it's actually the opposite." Astrid swallows. "We wanted to do something to help people reconnect with people who matter to them."

"Unnecessary. More hiding behind computers. Sounds like another way to flaunt your money and buy big houses. For what?" She sniffs dismissively and takes a bite of her forty-dollar omelet.

Astrid looks down at her napkin and I can see her mentally withdraw from the conversation. I want to jump in, defend her, but I know it's not my place—not here. Not yet.

I glance between Astrid and her parents, feeling like I've stepped into a conversation I wasn't prepared for.

I decide to change topics. To hopefully smooth things over.

Leaning forward in my chair, I gaze at my girlfriend lovingly before focusing on her parents. "Brigitte. Jens. It's so great to meet you. *Finally*. My family adores Astrid. She's a fixture at our Sunday night dinners when I'm in town—it's like she's known them forever."

Astrid shifts slightly next to me, her smile tight, and I notice she avoids eye contact. Huh.

"She's great with my nephews too. My oldest brother Connor has four-year-old twins," I press on. "Torin and Tristan won't leave her alone. They might both be in love with her."

I expect her parents to respond, maybe smile or laugh, but instead, Brigitte sets her napkin down and shakes her head. Jens snorts, covering his mouth with a fist. I glance over at Astrid, trying to figure out what I said wrong, but she's hunched over like she's shrinking.

"Really, it's no big deal." She stares at her plate, her tone almost dismissive. "Brennan's family's great, I'm not there often."

Wait, what? My heart sinks a little. She's there a lot. And, no big deal? My family's a big deal to me.

Brigitte looks at me directly and narrows her eyes. Her lips are pressed together in a thin line. "Every Sunday, huh?"

"Well, it's interesting you're spending time with someone's family." Jens clears his throat and gets a faraway look in his eyes.

Whoops. Way to read the room wrong. Whatever I said has added to the tension. The air is thick and uncomfortable. Astrid shrinks even further into herself, she's closing off in a way that breaks my heart.

I'm missing something important and I'm not sure what it is.

As we leave Salty's after brunch, her parents can't get away from us fast enough. They don't even give their daughter a hug on their way to the car.

I can't help feeling unsettled. The awkwardness between Astrid and her parents gnaws at me. Their family dynamic is so different from my family—where even if we're mad or disagreeing, there's no question of the love between us. Astrid's family, though... It's like there's this invisible wall, and I feel helpless trying to understand it.

"Let's take a walk." I motion for Astrid to join me as I head toward the waterfront path.

We stroll past the Seattle skyline bathed in the early afternoon light. The air is a bit cool, but the sun is warm. I glance over at Astrid, her hands are buried in the pockets of her jacket and her brow is furrowed in thought.

I hate it when she isn't comfortable with herself and feel an overwhelming urge to ease the tension. "That was...uh, something. I don't think I made a great impression. I'm getting an idea of why you're always stressed after you spend time with them."

"They don't get me. I don't get them either, to be honest." With a heavy sigh, she stops to stare out at the water.

"Why ?" I'm genuinely curious. "Have you ever thought about looking into your family's history? Seeing if there's something to explain it?"

Astrid's expression is hard to read. "What would I be looking for?"

"I don't know." I shrug. "I guess if you've always felt this disconnect, maybe there's something else going on. Could you have a heart-to-heart with your folks and tell them you've always felt like the odd one out?"

"Oh, jeez. That would go over like a lead balloon." She narrows her eyes and her lips tighten. "And, no. I don't need to dig up my family's past to understand we're different."

"I get it, but what if there's something they're keeping from you?" I find myself unwilling to drop it because I want her to have some peace.

Astrid, however, is clearly frustrated. "Why are you being so pushy? You press too hard sometimes, you know?"

"I'm sorry." I raise my hands in defense. "I know how much you love your family. I also know how much this hurts you. Maybe finding out what the story is could help."

She's quiet for a second, staring at me like she's deciding on whether to say something. Or not. Then, she tilts her head and fires back, "Have you ever looked into your own tendencies? You get so focused on one thing sometimes and you don't know when to stop."

Shit.

As much as I'm taken aback by her retort and I'm not sure how to answer, she's scored a direct hit. It's so past time to tell her. I'm going to address it once and for all. Nevertheless, I glance away for a second to collect my thoughts before turning back to her.

She might never look at me the same way, so I'm nervous. I love Astrid. She's my everything. I hope this doesn't make her look at me differently.

"Actually," I swallow the knot in my throat, "I *have* looked into it. When I was in college, I was diagnosed with something called hyperfocus. It's a form of neurodivergence. When I get fixated on something, I can't seem to stop. It's worked well for me—my company, for instance, has thrived because it's been my world. But, it also causes issues. As you probably realize. It's a constant learning curve for me."

Astrid's eyes widen, flicker with surprise and a touch of hurt. "And you've never mentioned this to me before, why?"

"Well..." I look away, feeling the weight of everything I've left unsaid. "I guess...it never felt like something I should have to explain." I try to tread carefully because I'm teetering on a tightrope. "It's nothing to be ashamed of. Everyone thinks and works differently."

She nods, clearly waiting for me to continue.

I search her face for clues as to what she's feeling. It's nearly impossible to explain what's so complicated in my mind. "A, I didn't hide it because I thought you couldn't handle it. I just... I didn't want it to be something that changed how you see me."

Astrid's face is blank. She just stares at me.

Of course, I feel an uncontrollable urge to fill the silence. To make her understand. "It's never been something I broadcast. Even in my own family, we barely talk about it. Not because we're avoiding it—it's because...well, it's part of me, but not all of me."

"Oh." Astrid searches my eyes and I can tell she's not satisfied with my explanation.

"I promise I wasn't deliberately keeping it from you, I don't want it to be a thing." I take her hand. "I've learned how to adapt over the years, but I know I can be intense. I know when I'm focused I forget things..."

"Uh-huh. Like forgetting to tell me about something so critically unimportant in your life that you deliberately hid it?" Astrid pulls her hand away and looks at the ground. Kicks a clump of grass.

Fuck. I don't want her to be upset. I scramble to explain. "No! I work around it. Like, when you were upset with me about not being in touch as often as I should have been, I set calendar reminders to make sure I didn't forget."

She looks at me so incredulously, her mouth drops open. "Wait, what?"

"Calendar reminders." I smile proudly. "It worked."

Astrid's face contorts with pain. "Let me get this straight. You had to set calendar reminders in order to remember to call me. So, all along it wasn't because you *wanted* to call me."

"No, of *course* I wanted to call you. Why would you think otherwise?" I'm confused at what she's not understanding.

"You know, Brennan. I postponed a lucrative showing to do brunch today. Why? Because I wanted to introduce my boyfriend, whom I love very much, to my parents who don't give a shit about anything I do. Now I find out said boyfriend, after years of friendship, being business partners and lovers and—whatever the fuck we are—hasn't trusted me enough to confide a critical part of his personality that he clearly is extremely bothered by." A tear rolls down her cheek. "What is *wrong* with me? Why am I not enough for people who matter most to me?"

She turns and storms back toward the car, tapping furiously into her phone.

That's when I know how badly I've botched it. I've had years of opportunities to fill Astrid in about my situation, but no. I was a coward. Afraid the woman I hope to marry would reject me for something out of my control.

Damn. My stupid fucking insecurity may cost me the person who matters the most.

Even worse? I've made her feel like shit. Unworthy of my trust. It's the last thing I'd ever want to do. Not when she's the best person I know.

"Astrid. Wait! The truth is, I was scared to tell you," I shout as I run to catch up to her.

"Yeah, because you thought I was so shallow I couldn't handle it." Astrid whirls around. Her face is stony now. A wall is up.

I step toward her. "A, I would never... No..."

"*Yes*." Astrid strides purposefully back toward the car. "I'm so pissed, I can't even see straight. Pissed *and* hurt."

I catch up to her. "A. *C'mon*. Please let's talk about all of this."

"I thought you were different. I never thought you, of all people, would fucking lie to me. Treat me like I'm gum on your shoe." Astrid's jaw is set. "I don't want to talk to you . I need to be on my own."

"Let's drive back to your place," I plead.

"*No*. You go back to your townhouse. Or to your family dinner. *Whatever*. I don't care. All I know is I won't be there tonight." She holds up her phone. "My Uber will be here in a minute. Give me some fucking space. We can talk when you come back in two weeks."

"Wait! Astrid. I love you. Please, don't leave like this." I stop in my tracks as a Lincoln Navigator pulls up and she gets in.

She doesn't answer.

The door slams shut.

And the love of my life drives off without another word.

Twenty-Five

Two Weeks Later

ANOTHER LONG, EXHAUSTING AFTERNOON is in the books.

As I approach my houseboat, I already feel the weight of the day ease off my shoulders. It's been a long two weeks. Endless showings. Difficult clients.

The woman I was working with today couldn't decide whether they wanted a glass penthouse with a view of Puget Sound or a Craftsman mansion within the heart of Madrona. She chose the mansion, naturally, at my prompting.

Normally, I'd be buzzing with adrenaline after closing a deal where I'll get a five-hundred-k commission check, but now all I want is to see Brennan.

I've cooled off substantially since our argument after brunch. Once I had some time to sort out my feelings, I realized my anger wasn't about his hyperfocus revelation. I mean, c'mon. It wasn't like I hadn't thought he might be neurodivergent. So what? I love him for who he is.

No. It hurt me to feel left out of such an important part of his life. We've been close for years, now. Why didn't he trust me?

I'm used to it when it comes to my parents and sisters. Men I've dated. With Brennan, though, I guess I thought we told each other everything. I mean, I've shared all my secrets. It's devastating to think he was scared to tell me. My emotions went haywire. I overreacted.

Did some research. Realized it wasn't about me.

Admittedly, I was blindsided. Neurodivergence is a big word. A big concept. At first, I reacted the way I always do when I'm hurt. I pulled away and made it about how he didn't trust me.

It stung, knowing I'd missed something this important about the man I love so deeply. Especially when I take pride in reading people so well.

Once I had some distance, I dug deeper. Read everything I could find. Tried to come to an understanding about why he kept such a big part of his life from me.

I realized it wasn't about trust at all.

For someone like Brennan, hyperfocus isn't just a quirk; it's something he's worked around his whole life. Managing it in silence, without expecting anyone to understand. I can see things from his perspective. Opening up to the person he loves so deeply might've felt like exposing his biggest weakness.

I'm not gonna lie. Even with all my research and newfound understanding, it's complicated. Part of me is still hurt he didn't let me in sooner.

Still, I realize if you love someone fully, you don't just take in their easy parts. You work to understand the ones they keep hidden, too.

We've talked every day since. Resumed our usual long-distance pattern. He's back in town for a week to, hopefully, finalize his deal with CognifyAI. While he's here, we're doing a demo of Reuniverse for Jason Deveraux. Brennan believes the technology is more lucrative than CognifyAI.

He's on the late flight from Palo Alto, so I have enough time to shower and change before driving to SeaTac.

I can't wait to see him. Make up in person. Reconnect mentally and physically. Get our groove back.

I park the car and notice lights glowing warmly inside the houseboat and the silhouette of someone moving around. My heart skips a beat and I'm about to dial 9-1-1 when I recognize the person inside.

Brennan.

I throw my car in park and burst through the door. Sure enough, he's placing a stunning arrangement of flowers in a crystal vase on the table, which is beautifully set up with candles, white linen napkins, and a spread of food we'll never be able to finish.

He looks up as I walk in. The moment he sees me, his whole face lights up. Brennan's lopsided, boyish grin melts me every time.

"Hey." He strides to me and wraps his arms around my waist. "Surprise."

I can't help but feel overwhelmed by how thoughtful he is. I cup his face in my hands, brushing my thumb over his cheek. "You did all this? I thought I was picking you up at the airport."

"Ah, no big deal." He leans down to kiss me. Our lips meet. It's a gentle, lingering kiss which melts the distance between us away. "I figured it was a better way to spend our night than a rushed car ride home from the airport. Plus, we haven't had a proper date in a while."

Relief and joy wash over me in waves. He planned all this? After the way I acted the last time I saw him and the things I said? The way I blew him off? "I love it."

"I've missed you," he whispers into my hair. "Let's eat. Then we can talk. There's...a lot I want to say."

We pull back and he brushes a thumb over my cheek, wiping away the tears escaping from the corners of my eyes. "Go get comfortable," he says softly. "I'll pour the wine."

I nod and slip away to the bedroom, changing out of my work clothes into my favorite soft joggers and t-shirt. As I smooth my hair back, I catch a glimpse of myself in the mirror and take a deep breath.

Whatever this night is, it feels important. Like a chance to start fresh.

When I return, the wine glasses are filled and he's lit candles. My dining room is a cocoon of warmth and light. Brennan pulls out my chair and we settle in for our date.

"This is amazing," I look at the spread. "Did you plan all this to woo me? Tell the truth."

I'm not kidding. The food smells incredible — roasted duck, a delicate salad with beets and goat cheese, and a perfectly crusty baguette with French butter.

"Maybe." His expression softens. "I wanted us to have a night where we could be together. Talk. Away from everything else."

I sip the wine and let the soothing warmth spread through me. "This is perfect. Do you want to start?"

Brennan hesitates and looks down at his glass. Flicks his eyes back up at me. "I've thought a lot about what happened at brunch with your parents. And, well, a lot of other things too. I want to make sure we're okay."

I wince at the memory of the awful, tense meal flashing through my mind. I haven't seen or spoken to my parents since. "We're fine. I was upset, but I think I understand why you didn't tell me."

"I still should have. Even if I was afraid it would change things between us, I don't want you to feel left out of my life." He reaches across the table and takes my hand. "I try not to let stupid labels bring me down. On the other hand, I should have connected the dots better. You thought I didn't trust you and it's never been the case. I'm ready to tell you everything, if you're willing to listen."

I set my fork down to give him my full attention. "Please."

Brennan takes a deep breath, like he's gathering the courage to say whatever's been weighing on him.

"When I was in undergrad, I may have mentioned this before in passing, but I thought I was in love with a girl in my programming class. We started sleeping together. I lost my virginity and...uh, well, I *thought* we were a couple. Later, I found out she was fucking other dudes too, so I broke it off." Brennan scrunches his lips. "Suddenly, all her friends wanted to fuck me. I thought I'd hit the jackpot, honestly. It was such a change from high school. It was great for a while. I had a lot of sex. Then, I found out it was all some kind of fucking joke. I was 'the retard with a big, thick...'"

"Dick." I huff out a breath.

Brennan's eyes widen. "Well, cock or eggplant emoji, but same difference. It hurt me to the core. I always recognized I was different. I'd heard 'nerd' and 'geek' a million times but, to my knowledge, no one ever overtly implied there was something *wrong* with me."

"Oh, B." I squeeze his fingers because I remember how Jake would talk about Brennan and his friends. "I hope you didn't take that shit to heart. What dumb-asses."

"Sadly, I did. I was depressed and didn't want to tell anyone what went down. Least of all Connor, who was busting his ass to pay for my college. Eventually, when my thoughts turned a bit...dark, I went to the counseling center to find a therapist." He nods to himself. "I was diagnosed with a form of neurodivergence called hyperfocus. There's more sensitivity around it now, but at the time it was characterized as being on the 'spectrum.'" He sighs heavily. "I was devastated because it felt like they confirmed there was something wrong with my brain. It seemed like such a stigma, I didn't want *anyone* to know."

I look into Brennan's beautiful, brown eyes and want to take every ounce of pain he's ever felt away from him. "I did some research. It sounds like when you get absorbed in something, you lose track of everything else."

"Time, hunger, even people. It's why I'm able to code for hours on end without stopping, but it's also why I sometimes forget to check in, or why I get so fixated on things I can't let them go." Brennan sounds as if he's reassuring himself.

I try to process how it must feel. "So, it's like you disappear into it?"

"Kind of." He quirks his lip. "It's more like tunnel vision. I can be so deep into a project, everything else fades away. When I'm in that headspace, I'm truly not ignoring you. I do *care.* I lose track and sometimes can't break free. My brain works in mysterious ways. I'm sorry if I need a reminder to get in touch, it's not personal. I don't want you to think it's because I don't love you. I do. More than anything."

I gesture to the fully catered dinner spread out over my dining room and the ice bucket with a bottle of wine chilling next to us. The vase of fresh flowers. "B, look at what you've done. Of course I know you love me. I was having a bad moment because of my own situation and took things out on you without thinking. I'm sorry."

"I'm the one who's sorry. I never wanted to hurt you," he murmurs. "I only want you to feel special."

I close my eyes for a moment, letting myself melt into my love for him. He *always* makes me feel special. Tonight is a reminder. No matter how complicated things get, we're still us. "Well, you succeeded. I love it. I love you. Thank you."

"Good." He leans across the table to give me a sweet, lingering kiss. "I don't ever want you to feel like I'm keeping things from you. I want to be better at sharing things, even if they're hard to talk about."

"How were you as a little kid?" I take a bite of the to-die-for duck.

He laughs. "I'd get entirely lost in things. My family used to call it my 'rabbit hole,' because once I got working on something—Legos, sandcastles, I had a thing with matchbox cars for a while—I'd be lost for hours. Threw fits if I was dragged away to do stupid things like take a bath or eat dinner."

"So funny, I was the opposite. Always so eager to please. I'd do what anyone asked so they'd like me." I tilt my head, fascinated by how we're so different but so perfect for each other.

"I wish I knew little Astrid…" He takes a sip of wine. "I know your relationship with your family is tough. Mine wasn't always as good as it is now. My da, in particular, would get frustrated with me in ways he never did with my brothers. Ma had so many little boys running around I'm not sure how she kept things together. My brothers always accepted me and included me, but they all had their own interests. When my da had his accident, we were in crisis mode and getting lost in coding helped me cope."

"I love hearing about all of this." I hold up my wine to clink glasses with him. "You're safe with me. Cheers to us."

He touches his glass to mine. "Yeah, cheers. Do you understand now why I set those calendar reminders to call you? Not because I don't think about you, it's because when I'm in that headspace, I might forget to reach out even if I don't mean to."

"I get it now." I feel a pang in my chest, remembering how hurt I felt. Now, hearing it like this, I realize it was never about me not being important enough. "Thank you for explaining it because I didn't fully understand before. What's done is done. We're moving onward and upward."

He looks relieved. "Thanks for saying that. I've never told anyone outside my family about this stuff. If we're going to have a future, I want you to know me. All of me. Now you do."

We finish our meal and I clear the plates, setting them by the sink. Brennan pours us another glass of wine and we sit on the couch overlooking the lake. I nestle into the crook of his arm, feeling a surge of affection.

"I've been thinking a lot about your family," he breaks the comfortable silence. "I know I was pushy after brunch and I'm sorry. I have to be honest, I still think there might be something to find out to help you understand why things are so tough."

I'm about to brush it off, but he's been so honest about his past and he's looking at me so intently, I can't. "I don't know. I don't see what we'd find."

"Maybe nothing," he agrees, "but maybe it would help you understand why things are the way they are. Maybe it would give you some peace, like I've found."

I look down and swirl the wine in my glass. "No. Not now. I don't want to dig things up. It'll make it worse."

"Okay. I get it." He kisses my temple. "I'll try not to push. Whatever you decide, I'll support you. I'm here, okay? No matter what."

My heart is full of warmth. I'm glad he made the effort to surprise me tonight. "Thank you. I appreciate you."

We relax and unwind for a long while, wrapped together watching the reflection of the moon ripple on the water outside the window. It feels good finding our way through the messiness of life together. I have a partner.

"Come here," he whispers. "I want you. I'd like to focus on orgasms this entire weekend. Any objections?"

I close my eyes as his hands roam my body. Let myself get lost in his touch. "None."

Twenty-Six

BRENNAN

The Next Morning

GOD, SHE'S INCREDIBLE.

Astrid has no idea I'm watching her.

In the year we've been seeing each other, other than heating up leftovers, I've never actually seen her cook. So, when I woke up this morning, I didn't expect to find her dancing to a Taylor Swift song wearing my oversized T-shirt and pulling out bacon from the oven.

"I've never seen anything so sexy in all my life." I make my presence known as I pad down the stairs.

She turns and smiles as at me in a way that makes my heart stand still. "That's disappointing, considering the sexiest thing *I've* ever seen is you eating me out for an hour straight."

"To be fair." I laugh as I saunter over to her and kiss her forehead. "I meant *you* generally, not the cooking part. Do I have time for a quick shower?"

"Sure." Astrid kisses my cheek and makes a point of leaning over to retrieve a pan from the cupboard.

Fuck. I see a flash of bare pussy. Immediately, my dick is standing at full attention.

I move behind her, grip her hips and grind my erection against her ass. "I see what you're up to. I'm game for a quick appetizer fuck."

"Stop it. Go shower!" She laughs and deftly moves away. "I'm getting the eggs ready, so I need to concentrate."

I do, in fact make it quick. I'm seated at her counter ten minutes later wearing nothing but a pair of boxer briefs, which showcase how hard I am for her.

"Sexiest thing *I've* ever seen." She glances down at my protruding package. "I'll have him for dessert."

"You didn't have to do all this." I pull her against me and slant my mouth over hers to kiss her thoroughly.

She pulls back and pats my cheek lightly. "One track mind, B. Let's eat then we can fuck."

Astrid sets bacon, eggs, and coffee in front of me and takes the seat next to mine. "How are you feeling this morning? Ready for your big meeting?"

"Yeah. I'm alright. I think this is going to wrap up soon." I take a bite of the eggs, which aren't terrible. "Maybe the worst of this CognifyAI situation is over."

"I hope so." She licks a piece of bacon suggestively and I swear it makes me harder.

"Now who has a one-track mind?" I devour the rest of my breakfast so we can get to the sex stuff. "Maybe cooking is one of your hidden talents."

She rolls her eyes. "Hardly. I watched a YouTube video. I'm definitely not hiding any culinary skills, I don't have any."

"Well, I'm all for you practicing. As long as you do it without panties." I take the last bite. "I'll bend you over the counter next time."

She throws her head back and laughs heartily. My God, Astrid's happiness is my drug. I want to have moments like this every day of my life. It's time to make our relationship permanent. I've known she's the one for me for—well, since the first time we fucked, but I've never told her this.

I was afraid I wouldn't be enough for her. Thank God our relationship's evolved. Especially with my CognifyAI situation coming to fruition.

"Are you finished?" I twirl a lock of her hair around my finger.

She nods. "Yep."

"Good. It's time to fuck." I stand and scoop her out of the stool and head straight for the stairs to her bedroom.

She buries her face in my neck. "Hey, aren't we supposed to wait ten minutes after eating or something?"

"Uh, *no*. I think we'll be fine. My cock needs you. Stat." I kiss Astrid's temple and set her down on the edge of her bed.

I position myself between her knees and run my knuckles down her cheek. Her hands settle on my waist and she strokes the sides of my hips, nuzzling my soft belly, which I've long since stopped worrying about.

"I love the way you touch me," I whisper and lean in to kiss her forehead. I feather kisses down her cheeks and across her nose. Tilt her chin up to take her lips.

God, she's beautiful. Her long, disheveled hair cascades around her shoulders. Pale-pink nipples pucker like little bullets. She's long and slim with creamy skin and tiny freckles I love to lick and kiss. Perfection.

Mine.

Astrid slides my boxer briefs down my hips and my erection springs free. She wraps her hands around my length, leans over and sucks the tip into her mouth.

"Fuck," I grit out. My butt clenches and I plunge my fingers into her hair to keep her in place, but not so rigidly to push myself into her. I've learned she doesn't like it rough when it comes to blow jobs. For all those years of whacking off to the image of her blowing me, real life is way better than fantasy.

She licks up and down my length, down to the patch of dark hair at the base and back up again, tracing the thick vein running up the underside of my shaft. "I love your cock." Her eyes catch mine as she takes me fully into her mouth and swirls her tongue around my tip. Widens her mouth until I touch the back of her throat, which is something she's worked up to over the past several months.

In and out, I guide myself unhurriedly and steadily until we find a nice, easy rhythm. My head falls back and my hands massage her scalp. She grips my ass with both hands and squeezes with each pass. I'm in a trance. Lost in the ecstasy of her hot, talented mouth. Until she swallows against my tip, giving it a massage nearly sending me over the edge.

"Christ!" I pull out abruptly.

She pouts up at me with swollen lips. "I wanted to make you come."

"Oh, I want to come, but not in your mouth." I sit next to her and pull her flat down on the bed. "I want to come in your pussy."

"Well do it." She scoots up on the bed and flashes me a naughty grin when she spreads her legs.

She's gushing with arousal. I cover her body with mine. "I will." I glide the underside of my cock against her pussy lips. "Eventually."

"You're mean." Astrid's stomach muscles tighten and she rotates her hips, pushing her wet pussy against my cock.

I narrow my eyes playfully. "You're something else."

"Me?" She sighs when my tip pushes against her entrance. "Because I want you inside me?"

The thing is, this is our game. She knows I like to take control so I reverse our position by rolling us across the bed so she's straddling me. I grip her hands in mind to link our fingers and pull them down on the either side of my head. "Good. I'm ready for you to fuck me, A."

Astrid leans down and kisses me deeply. "Oh, I'll fuck you senseless, B. You know I will." She lifts her hips and swivels until my tip nudges her entrance and she sinks down until I'm buried to the hilt.

"God, you feel like heaven." I pull my hands out of hers and grip her hips to raise and lower her on my cock until she adjusts to my girth.

When she's ready, Astrid leans back and plants her palms on my thighs and begins to ride me hard and fast. I'm in complete rapture. My cock is in hot, velvet heaven as I thrust up to meet each one of her movements. I'm clutching her hips so tight, I'm probably going to leave bruises.

And, God, the visual of her riding me. Her face is slack with pleasure. Flat stomach quivering. Tits bouncing to the rhythm of her gyrations with little pink nipples puckered so tight. I can't help it, I sit up and wrap my arms around her waist and take one of those little buds into my mouth and suck it hard. Pulling her against me, I thrust harder and deeper.

"Come," I demand before sucking her other nipple. "Now."

Astrid pushes against me and grinds her clit on my pelvic bone and I adjust the angle so my crown hits her sweet spot. She wails when she goes over, clamping down on me to ride the wave of her orgasm. I'm not done, so I lift her off me and crawl off the bed, turning her so her legs are dangling off the side and she's facedown against the sheets.

"Hey," she cries out.

I plant myself behind her between her legs and grip her hips again and slam back inside. "You can take it, trust me."

I take one delicate wrist and pull it behind her back for leverage as I fuck her blind. It's the roughest I've ever been with her, but judging by her juices running down the length of my cock and her keening moans, she's not only *taking* it but *loving* it. After a few thrusts, I'm done for. I lodge myself to the hilt and still as I come so hard I nearly lose consciousness.

"Oh, God, B..." Astrid groans as she squeezes me through her own release, milking me until I'm empty.

I release her wrist, brush the hair from her neck and bend over to plant wet kisses across her shoulders and nape. "You're *mine*."

"Yes," she whispers when I pull out and help her back up onto the bed.

I wrap myself around her, leaning up on my elbow to look down at her. "I love you and want to marry you. This isn't an official proposal. It's letting you know how I feel."

Tears fill her eyes and she nods, seemingly unable to speak. I glide my hand down her gorgeous face and keep going. From her neck to her breast, where I thumb her puckered nipple. My hand moves farther, over her stomach to her pussy. I kiss the side of her face as I drag my fingers through our combined release and circle her clit with my thumb.

My cock is full again. Only she could ever do this to me. I pull her thigh up over mine and slip back inside where I belong. With my body filling hers, and our eyes locked, I grip her hand and hold it between us. "I love you, Astrid. More than I ever thought was possible."

"I don't remember what my life was like without you." She nudges her nose against my cheek and rests her forehead on mine. "Of course I want to marry you."

Whoa. I'm blown away. She really is mine. Forever mine. This time we go slow. I rock my hips into her in long, languid strokes. "You're so beautiful." I kiss her deeply. "I'm so lucky." I kiss all around her face.

What's happening between us now is bigger than any company. Any IPO. Any stupid reunion. This is the most important merger of my life.

Our bodies move together at the same pace but, somehow, the intensity is amped up by many notches. While I'm on the precipice of another amazing, teeth-numbing orgasm, I want to come together. I hold myself still, reach between us and press on her pubic bone while circling her clit. Immediately, Astrid's inner walls clench around me.

I let go and pulse inside her.

Afterward, our fingertips trace each other's shoulders, backs, arms. I stay wedged inside her as we gaze deeply in to each other's eyes.

Knowing this is where we belong. With each other.

She's officially my person. And, I'm hers.

It's the most perfect moment of my entire life.

Twenty-Seven

ASTRID

A Few Days Later

ANOTHER LONG DAY OF difficult, entitled clients has me reconsidering my profession.

For the millionth time.

I mean, is it me or are people super assholey these days? My entire day was spent listening to a pharmaceutical multimillionaire client and his enlightened-my-ass wife talk about vibes and cleansing spells. They expected me to have memorized every single chemical used in the finishes of all five new-construction homes I walked them through.

Oh, I remembered each and every stat. Peter Vander, Seattle's award-winning green architect built them so I had the specs. But, seriously? The woman was drinking vodka in her forty-ounce, personalized Stanley Quencher H2.0 Flowstate Tumbler and, by the end of the day, could barely stand. Give me a fucking break.

I'm looking forward to being home with Brennan. He signed his contracts today and our plan is to celebrate by playing pool at The Zoo and eating shitty, fried food.

Except, the moment I walk through the front door of my houseboat, I can tell immediately something's off.

Way, way off.

Brennan sits on the couch, staring at his phone. His shoulders are slumped and there's a heaviness surrounding him. Tears well up in my eyes because I can tell he's hurting. Normally, if he's not working, he'll greet me with an enthusiastic kiss. Or, at least a lopsided smile. Tonight, he barely looks up. My stomach falls to the floor. I hope his brother hasn't relapsed or something.

Slipping off my shoes, I place my purse and keys on the counter. "Hey." I walk over to him and run my fingers gently through his messy hair. "Rough day?"

"Yeah." He glances up. There's a combination of frustration and defeat in his eyes. "You could say that."

I sit next to him. Close enough so our legs are touching and he leans into me, like he's trying to find some comfort. "What's going on?"

"Well." He takes a deep breath and looks down at his clasped hands. "Apparently, the board found out about Reuniverse. I guess word travels fast. Somehow, they found out about our meeting with Jason Deveraux and claim Reuniverse is a CognifyAI asset."

"*What?*" I can't keep the shock out of my voice. "It was a last-minute dinner. How did they even find out? More importantly, why do they care?"

He shakes his head, rubbing the back of his neck. "I don't fucking know. Their position is, because I'm the CEO of CognifyAI, anything I develop—even outside of the company—is the company's intellectual property. As such, they want me to sign over Reuniverse."

Holy fuck. I feel a flash of anger on Brennan's behalf, but on mine too. Reuniverse is our company. It's not a side project; it's something we've poured our hearts into. It never occurred to me CognifyAI could swoop in and take it. I feel a knot of frustration tightening in my chest.

"How ridiculous," I spit out. "We built this on our own. It's not like you used any of CognifyAI's resources. They *can't* take it."

"They can try." Brennan shakes his head. "They're saying my brain is one of CognifyAI's resources. Also, because I have a fiduciary duty to CognifyAI they're citing a clause in my current contract they claim forces me to transfer Reuniverse to CognifyAI's control. They say if I don't play ball, they'll sue me. If they follow through on their threat, it'll tie up everything for years. And, make it impossible for Jason's group to invest in Reuniverse."

"So, you're damned if you do damned if you don't?" I lean back, trying to wrap my head around what he's saying.

He snorts out, "Essentially, yes."

"Wait. Maybe we should call Jason. His team seemed to be quite serious. They want this to happen." I think back to our discussion at dinner.

"I know." Brennan sighs. "Jason's kicking himself for not investing in CognifyAI when he had the chance and seemed to be practically foaming at the mouth to get a piece of Reuniverse. I'm realistic, though. If this turns into a legal battle, he's not going to touch it. No one wants to buy into a lawsuit of this magnitude."

I can see the devastation on Brennan's face and I hate it. I take his hand and squeeze it gently. "There has to be a way around this. Your lawyer is great. Let's try to calm down a bit. We can't let the stupid, greedy board steamroll over you."

"They seem to think they have the upper hand." Brennan lets out a bitter laugh, shaking his head. "By the tone of the meeting we had today, they're playing hardball. They've torn up the agreement we were supposed to sign and are making new demands. All because they want me to assign Reuniverse to them."

"No way. They're tying Reuniverse to your new contract?" I ask, incredulous. "As in, you don't get to stay on as CEO unless you give them our company?"

"Pretty much." Brennan's jaw tightens. "We went round and round on it for six solid hours today. No compromises. They're calling it a 'best and final offer,' but it feels like blackmail. If I agree, I'm locked in for five years. Golden handcuffs. They own Reuniverse. And now they want me to warrant I won't work on anything AI-related outside of CognifyAI for a decade."

I can't help my frustration bubbling up to a boiling level, but I need to keep calm for Brennan's sake. "They can't force anything. Reuniverse is half mine and I don't have to sign over my ownership interest."

"Maybe, but litigation is expensive and you've worked your ass off for every penny you have. " Brennan sounds so defeated. "The last thing I'd ever do is allow you to spend your own money to defend yourself against something that isn't your fault."

His concern touches me, but we're getting married—formal proposal or not—so this is a team effort. "We're together on this, B. It's not up to you to 'allow' me to do anything."

"Okay, fair point, but they don't even know about you yet. At least, I don't think they do. Right now, they have me backed into a corner. At the end of the day, maybe this is their way of pushing me out while trying to control me. I went into the meeting this morning feeling great. Now, it's all falling apart."

I can't stand seeing him like this. "Brennan, listen to me." I turn to face him fully. "You're Brennan fucking McGloughlin. You built CognifyAI from nothing and now you've built Reuniverse, too. *You* can handle them. *We* can figure out a way around this."

For a moment, he doesn't respond. He stares at me, thinking. I can see the conflict in his eyes. I try to communicate telepathically. Let him know I'll back him, no matter what.

"At this point, I don't give a fuck about CognifyAI. On the other hand, I can't lose Reuniverse. It's the first thing I've felt excited about in years. It's what I'm good at. Working on it with you brings me such joy. It reminds me of when I started CognifyAI, before all the board politics and legal battles." He grips my hand tightly.

"We're not going to lose it," I state firmly. "Let's set up a meeting and figure it out."

Brennan takes a deep breath and his shoulders relax a bit. "God, I love how feisty you are. So sure of yourself."

"I believe in you." I reach out and cup his face. "And I know how much Reuniverse means to you. To *us*. This isn't over."

His eyes soften. I see a hint of a smile. "Thank you," he murmurs, leaning in to kiss me. "I'm glad we're in this together."

"Yeah. Don't forget, you're not alone anymore." I kiss him back, letting my lips linger on his. Hoping he can feel how much I mean it.

He wraps his arms around me and pulls me closer. For a moment, it feels like we're the only two people in the world who are facing a common challenge together. As a couple. How we manage this will be a testament to a life we're still trying to build.

A fleeting thought takes root. What if he's able to leave CognifyAI behind and I wrap up my real estate career. We keep Reuniverse and grow it. With his creative genius and my focused drive, together we might be unstoppable.

Whoa. Why haven't I thought of this sooner?

"I'm so sorry, A. I should've seen this coming." Brennan strokes my hair softly. "I was so focused on my problems with CognifyAI, I never fathomed they'd come after Reuniverse."

"Let's call Jason tomorrow. See if he's willing to back us." I pull away slightly to look at him.

He quirks a brow. "Sure, but I promise you. He's not going to get into a legal battle with CognifyAI. His team doesn't make investments lightly. They like clean companies with maximum potential. The man is basically retired, for God's sake. All this shit will scare him the fuck away."

"With all due respect, I deal with these guys every day in my own line of work. Most of them are blowhards who have never been challenged because they puff out their entitled chests and get away with being dicks. We're going to find a way to make Reuniverse untouchable. There has to be a loophole or something you can use to protect it." I grip his shoulder and hope my words are encouraging.

His soulful eyes widen with surprise at my tone. "Okay, boss lady. I like seeing this side of you. I'm talking to my lawyer tomorrow. Tonight, his team is digging through all the original contracts and subsequent amendments to find a solution. I'm not inclined to be optimistic because the board has smart lawyers too."

"They don't have me." I feel my body well up with confidence. "We're not going to let them take this from you. Not without a huge motherfucking—but strategic—fight."

Brennan laughs. "I don't know what I did to deserve you."

"When you made me your business partner two years ago, you gave me something to believe in." I run my fingers through his hair. "Now we're life partners too, so let's make sure we don't let anyone steal what's ours."

Something inside me has clicked into place.

I've spent my whole life trying to prove myself. Even when I didn't know who I was proving it to. Maybe I've built up resilience—the need to push back harder every time I'm knocked down because of it.

Because, for me, it's not about showing off. Or winning. It's about survival. Brennan might be wired to focus, but I'm wired to make sure whenever the world says no, I find a way to make it say yes.

I think it's why Brennan and I work. He's the one with big, wild ideas and the ability to create magic. I'm the one who doesn't back down until things happen. When I want something, I don't hope for it—I hunt it down and force it to bend to my will. Hell, it's how Brennan and I even met back up in the first place.

It's how I got to where I am. How I'm going to get us through this.

Maybe it's ruthless. Maybe it's necessary.

Either way, together we're formidable.

Twenty-Eight

BRENNAN

Three Months later

TODAY'S GONNA FUCKING BLOW.

Never, in a million years, did I think I'd be subjected to such utter and complete bullshit.

The past three months have been a whirlwind of legal drama and emotional exhaustion. Once I comprehended the CognifyAI board was serious about owning Reuniverse, we entered into initial mediation proceedings. I flew back to Palo Alto and the drama hasn't stopped.

Lawyers. Lawyers. Fucking lawyers.

First, we fought about where the mediation would happen. CognifyAI wanted to keep everything in Silicon Valley. My lawyers pushed back to keep it in Seattle. Ultimately, we agreed on Palo Alto because CognifyAI's headquarters are there now.

Thirty thousand bucks later, we were on to discovery.

Fights about emails. Documents. Forensic computer diagnosis. Corporate formation. Thousands of files were reviewed, cataloged, and filed. All the while dealing with endless Zoom calls, paperwork, and strategy sessions.

Ninety thousand dollars later, and we're finally at the starting point.

This entire process leaves a bitter fucking taste in my mouth and endless legal bills.

How has it come to this? CognifyAI is my company and I hate it. Hate everything about it. There's no joy in being the CEO. Not when I'm fighting to preserve my integrity each and every day.

I've done nothing wrong.

I swear to God, I've wanted to throw in the towel so many times. Give them both companies to stop the bleeding. Every time I get an email from my legal team, I have to brace myself. There's some new accusation.

Demand. Derogatory comment. My mental health is at an all-time low.

In a perfect world, my ability to hyperfocus would have me overprepared for this mediation. I'd be able to anticipate anything and everything they throw at me and have an answer for it all. Unfortunately, I'm so angry, my mind is a whirlpool of a million fragmented thoughts. Agitated. Spinning. Nonstop mental gymnastics trying to find some order.

That's the downside of how my mind works, sometimes. Which sucks because this mediation is probably the most important milestone in my career. If I can harness my focus on doing well, I'll have choices. If I can't, I may lose two companies I've put my heart and soul into.

Now, what I *am* focused on is Astrid. Right now it feels like the only good thing I've got going is her and her determination to pull us through. When I'm in Seattle on the weekends, she and I spend Friday and Saturday together. Sundays we're at my parents' house.

Astrid's houseboat has become our sanctuary. The one place where we can cuddle, fuck, watch bad TV and pretend everything is normal. Throughout this process, she's been my rock. Nothing about this litigation phases her. She's a goddamn warrior for me, her and Reuniverse.

Not so much with regard to her parents. Astrid decided it's best not to speak to them since the horrific brunch. She says she'll reach out eventually, but needs time to process. Whenever I bring it up, she changes the subject. I get she doesn't like to talk about it so I haven't pushed, but I know the situation weighs on her.

Especially now.

Part of me feels like she's quietly quitting her family. Maybe forever.

Which is why, despite her asking me not to, I'm finding relief from the hellish litigation by researching her background. It's kept me sane on the late nights I can't sleep to try to piece together the situation. I can't understand why they're so cold to her.

I've made progress and, for now, it's giving me an outlet while I'm in limbo about the status of my future.

The plan is, I'll surprise Astrid and give her real peace. She'll see how committed I am to her and her happiness. Ultimately, my hope is her family can heal and she can experience the same sense of belonging and closeness the McGloughlins enjoy. I know it's possible.

But, today we mediate.

The conference room is cold as hell. I can't tell if it's the air-conditioning or the tension in the room. Probably both. I'm on one side of the conference table with my three lawyers and Astrid. We sit across from the CognifyAI legal team, all of whom glower at me like I'm some criminal.

I glare back but Astrid remains composed, steady, and completely unbothered. She's stellar under this type of pressure.

I'm not. They're here to dig. To find anything to paint me into a corner. My best-case scenario is keeping my composure because, though I've been well prepared, my emotions are all over the map.

The mediator, whose name I can't remember, is a fifty-something woman in a no-nonsense black suit. She takes her place at the head of the table and clears her throat, setting the tone for the session. "The sole purpose of why we're here is to clarify certain aspects regarding the development of Reuniverse and to address concerns brought forward by CognifyAI's legal team. I expect both sides to be truthful and forthcoming with information."

Astrid gives me a quick, reassuring glance before focusing back on the mediator. I know she's ready, but it sucks she has to go through this. It's my fight, and yet they're using her as a way to get to me.

CognifyAI's lead lawyer, who I call Blue Suit, leans forward. "Ms. Gustafsson, let's start by discussing your role in Reuniverse. Please describe what you do."

"Certainly." Astrid nods, cool as a goddamn cucumber. "I handle the marketing, business strategy, and user engagement for Reuniverse."

A perfect, succinct answer giving nothing else away. Brilliant.

Blue Suit scribbles something on his notepad. "You're a realtor, why would Mr. McGloughlin partner with you on this project?"

"Because it's my idea and I brought it to him." She smiles contritely.

He scratches his head. "Huh. Interesting. CognifyAI started as a real estate app. Were you aware of its origins?"

"Yes." She stares at him.

Blue Suit flips through some pages. "It's strange he'd partner with you, don't you think? Why did he?"

"My background in real estate has given me a lot of experience understanding how to connect people and build networks, which is central to Reuniverse's vision." She looks at her fingernails, which are painted blood red. "So, not strange considering I brought the idea to him."

"Let me get this straight, *you're* the one who had the idea for Reuniverse?" Blue Suit raises an eyebrow.

She mirrors his eyebrow raise. "Yes."

"So, how did you come to partner with Mr. McGloughlin? Please give me the details." BS is back to scribbling on his notepad.

"Brennan and I went to high school together. I reconnected with him through his brother, Connor, and I pitched the idea of doing something AI-focused for our reunion. I had a basic concept and suddenly we were discussing the idea of creating an app to help people reconnect in a meaningful way. It was meant to be for our reunion, but we both saw potential, so it developed into a business partnership."

BS's eyes narrow, like he's found an fissure in our story. "When you say 'discussing,' Ms. Gustafsson, do you mean these conversations happened during CognifyAI working hours?"

"No. We've always kept our work on Reuniverse separate from Brennan's responsibilities at CognifyAI. Our discussions and planning happened after hours, on weekends, and through private, separate channels." Astrid's face is so serene, it's uncanny. She's killing it.

BS leans back and shoots his colleague a knowing smirk. "*Interesting*. And how would you describe your relationship with Mr. McGloughlin?"

My pulse spikes and I see Astrid's lips tighten slightly. We've prepared for this question and I know where this is going—they want to use our relationship against us. To suggest I've been using Cognify's resources to benefit a personal project.

"We're in a committed relationship." Astrid is clear and steady. "And it's none of your business."

BS's smile is cold and calculating. "Oh, it is CognifyAI board's business. Mr. McGloughlin cannot fraternize with his staff."

"We'll, I'm not his staff," she replies, not missing a beat. "I'm his co-founder. And if you know Brennan so well, you'd realize how hyper-meticulous he's been to ensure there's no overlap."

Madam mediator interjects, "Please keep this focused on the matter at hand. CognifyAI, if you have specific evidence to present, please do so."

BS slides a stack of documents across the table to the mediator. "We've conducted a forensic audit of Mr. McGloughlin's digital activity, and there are still unresolved questions. This is a motion requesting full access to all related documentation, including code, emails, and any internal memos related to Reuniverse. It extends to Ms. Gustafsson as well."

I can't help but stiffen in my chair. "I've provided everything," I grit out. "Reuniverse operates on a completely separate system. I've purchased independent hardware, software, and hired separate personnel. On my own dime. With my own contracts."

"Yet, you can understand our skepticism," BS replies smoothly. "He's the founder of CognifyAI and his fiduciary duty requires disclosure of any projects overlapping with CognifyAI's interests. Given Reuniverse's scope, it's reasonable to investigate whether there's been any misuse of resources."

Astrid leans to Joe Finney, my lead attorney. "Do I need to answer him? Brennan has been transparent, and already shown them everything. Reuniverse was built with separate funding, separate resources, and on our own time."

I can see the CognifyAI team bristle at her words. They're not used to being challenged so directly, especially by someone they're interrogating. But Astrid's spot-on, and they know it. She's been a force, coordinating with our lawyers, gathering documents, and strategizing on how to push back. Without her, I'd be drowning.

BS shifts tactics. "I'll withdraw the question. Let's talk about funding. Who financed the development of Reuniverse?"

"I did." I lean forward. "Out of my own pocket. I hired independent developers, set up a separate LLC, and ensured there was no conflict with CognifyAI."

"Who are the developers?" BS flips through his notes. "We have reason to believe some of your team members might have worked for CognifyAI in the past."

"None of the developers currently working on Reuniverse have been employed by CognifyAI." I shake my head. "Most of them are based in India and have no ties to my work at CognifyAI."

BS doesn't look convinced. "You're telling us none of them used any CognifyAI technology or resources to develop the app?"

"Yes," I say firmly. "We've been extremely careful."

The mediator interjects again, trying to keep things on track. "CognifyAI, please move on."

There's a pause, and I can see BS trying to decide his next move. Astrid's perceptive. This is called "stalling." They've already delayed the IPO because they want me to sign Reuniverse over. They're trying to keep me tied up in this legal dispute to force my hand.

Astrid squeezes my knee under the table, a silent reminder to stay calm.

"We've noticed some connections between Mr. McGloughlin's family and potential investors." BS abruptly shifts topics. "Specifically, we've heard Jason Deveraux is interested in investing. How much money has he given you?"

My heart skips a beat and I feel a flash of anger. I'm still unclear how they found out about our meeting. Astrid doesn't miss a beat. "Mr. Deveraux is a *potential* investor. His connection to Brennan's family is through Connor, who's in the band Less Than Zero with Mr. Deveraux's son Jace. I've known him longer than Brennan as I've been Mr. Deveraux's realtor for years."

"We'd like to issue a request for all documentation regarding Mr. Deveraux," BS insists, his eyes glinting. "And any agreements he's party to regarding Reuniverse."

The mediator cuts in again, sensing the rising tension. "Let's stick to the facts. If CognifyAI has specific concerns, they need to be addressed formally. This is a mediation, not a trial."

On and on it goes. I find myself tuning out. As the session winds down several hours later, I'm drained. Nothing's resolved. I hate this uncertainty. I've spent years building CognifyAI, and now it feels like my ambition and talent is being used against me.

Once they finally leave, I look over at Astrid to see how she is. I've never seen her more sure of herself and it gives me a flicker of hope.

"We'll be fine," she whispers as we gather our things. "They don't have anything. They're trying to make you panic."

I don't feel as confident as she does. "I wish this was over. I'm tired of fighting."

Astrid turns to me, her eyes sharp. "Oh, we'll finish this. We're going to win, B. I know it in my bones."

God, I love her.

Other than my brother Connor, I've never met anyone who doesn't get rattled when faced with such adversity. It makes me believe her.

Maybe we can get through this mess and come out the other side with everything we've built intact.

"Okay." I let out a long breath. "I'll follow your lead."

There's nothing like a strong, self-assured woman. Especially when she's yours.

Twenty-Nine

Two Weeks Later

I LOVE BRENNAN'S FAMILY.

They're so different from mine.

I cut ties with mine after that horrible brunch. I've not made a big deal about it but I'm sick of clinging to hope I'll find a way to fit into my family's world. Witnessing how my mom treated Brennan made me realize a truth I'd been avoiding for years. Something's wrong with them.

They'll never see me for who I am. Only for who I'm not.

I'm tired of the dismissive comments about my work or the cold, passive-aggressive digs about my ambition. It's exhausting tiptoeing across glass during every single interaction. Feeling like I'm one wrong step away from being verbally annihilated.

I've spent years trying to earn approval that's always out of reach. That morning, something snapped inside me.

I realized, I'm done.

Sure, it hurts, more than I want to admit, but there's also a strange sense of relief. Like I've finally put down a heavy weight I've been carrying around for way too long. Being a part of the McGloughlin family dinners made me realize it's time to stop fighting for a place where I'll never truly belong.

Here, I fit in.

There, I never will.

Found family can be infinitely more supportive than your real one.

Tonight, everyone's gathered around the McGloughlin dinner table to celebrate Brennan's birthday. They always make me feel like I'm part of something solid.

They don't break no matter what the world throws at them, and the McGloughlin's have been through a lot.

It's beautiful.

Hopefully Brennan and I will have kids of our own someday and continue the tradition.

As far as tonight goes, Maureen's outdone herself, as usual. The roast beef tenderloin is a perfect medium rare. It practically melts in my mouth. There's buttery colcannon with a hint of cabbage, mashed carrots and parsnips, and fresh dinner rolls, still warm from the oven.

I savor every bite, thrilled that Brennan, who's sitting at the head of the table, looks happier than I've seen him in weeks. Being around his people gives him comfort.

As usual, the conversation is lively, jumping from topic to topic, but inevitably it circles back to the lawsuit. Brennan's still in the trenches, fighting for Reuniverse and I'm supporting him as much as possible. As much as it stresses him out, he seems eager to talk about it. To get his family's take on things. All night he's gushed about how I've been handling everything, his eyes light up when he talks about the strategies I've helped devise for the team.

"You guys have no idea how much Astrid's help has meant," he practically swells with pride. "She's been relentless. I mean, I'm the one with the lawyers, but she can read people like a book—and I put myself in that category. I'd probably be a mess if it wasn't for her."

My cheeks heat up when everyone looks at me, though I can't help but smile. It's nice to be appreciated in front of his family. "I'm doing what I can."

"Thank you for looking out for our Brennan," Connor chimes in. "This whole thing sounds like a nightmare. Good on you, Astrid."

"Nightmare's an understatement." Brennan shakes his head solemnly and takes my hand. "If anyone's going to drag me through it, it's this one. Enough about me. What's the haps with everyone else?"

Cillian leans back in his chair. "While you're wrestling with your tech empire, I'm still knee-deep in the Bright Shipping project. The buildout of the new headquarters is coming along, and I couldn't have done it without Da." He glances over at Rory lovingly. "It's the biggest job I've ever managed, and I'm lucky to have him by my side. Would've been a mess without his help."

Rory's eyes sheen with quiet pride. "You're doing great, son. It's been good to be back on site."

Everyone's been keeping an eye on Cillian, who's been sober for a few months, so the positive update is welcome. I can tell he's trying to keep things light, but there's a lot going on. When he mentions Bright Shipping, I noticed his gaze drift off to the middle of the table. His focus a little too intense, like he's trying to avoid thinking about the woman who shattered his heart.

And, as I watch Rory smile at Cillian, there's a flicker of something bittersweet. It's taken him years to rebuild trust. Each of Brennan's brothers has a complicated relationship with their father, though now there's a kind of unspoken truce. He shows up, is remorseful and does better each and every day. And, that means something.

It makes me wish my own parents would change, though I'm not holding my breath. If they want me back in their lives, they'll have to make the effort for a while. I've tried enough times.

Connor clears his throat, cutting through the thick silence. "So, twins. Everything okay in the band, these days? You two getting ready for the tour?"

Fireball is going on the road with LTZ for a bit, which is exciting in and of itself.

Liam, who is sitting next to me, nods and smiles but there's a glint of something edgy behind it. He glances at Padraig, who looks down at his plate with a neutral expression. "Of course we're gearing up for our show on New Year's Eve."

"You all are expected to come." Padraig's enthusiasm isn't quite the same, but he's clearly trying to appease his brother. Ever since I met them, there's been tension. Mostly about their personal lives, from what I can gather. "It's gonna be huge."

Connor takes his wife Ronni's hand. "It's been a while since we've toured together. With the success of our new album we decided to go big. Logistics with everyone's schedule took a while to figure out, but it'll be fun to be on the road again."

"Count us in." Brennan doesn't hesitate. "We'll be there."

I have to suppress a verbal squee. Less than Zero is legendary and I've never seen them live.

"Seamus, you'll make it, yeah?" Connor nods to his youngest brother.

I notice Seamus's cheeks flush slightly as he looks up. "Uh, yeah, if I'm not on call." There's a flash of something in his eyes and I can't help but wonder what, beside work, is keeping him occupied. "It's not in my control because my boss is in the middle of a malpractice lawsuit."

"Sure, we understand," Liam teases as he waggles his eyebrows at Padraig.

Seamus rolls his eyes, but doesn't play into it. I catch Brennan's knowing look with Cillian and it piques my curiosity. I love witnessing the dynamic between the brothers.

I swear, this family could have its own reality show. They're that entertaining.

Maureen finally brings out the cake, a massive, dark-chocolate confection from Deep Sea Sugar and Salt that I ordered because Brennan adores their cakes. It's rich, decadent, and exactly the kind of thing he loves. But as soon as Maureen slices into it, I see her pause, her nose twitching slightly.

"Is that...beer?" She glances at me with a raised eyebrow.

My stomach drops. Oh *God*. How thoughtless. It didn't even occur to me when I ordered it. The cake's soaked in a porter beer syrup. I'm a moron.

"Oh no." I stand up quickly, my face burning. "I'm so sorry. I didn't think..."

Cillian and Rory exchange a glance, and for a moment I brace myself, expecting a lecture or, at least, a sharp comment. But it doesn't come. Instead, Rory is gracious.

"It's okay, lass," he says softly in his Irish lilt. "You didn't mean it."

I blink, surprised at the warmth in his voice. "Yes, but I can fix it. I'll run out and grab something else."

Maureen stops me, placing a hand on my arm. "No need, love. I've got ice cream in the freezer. It'll be grand. And Brennan and the rest of us will still get to eat this delicious cake."

She winks at me and the tension I hadn't realized I was holding eases.

The rest of the evening passes in a blur of laughter, teasing, and warmth. After dinner, I end up in the living room sprawled on the floor with Ronni and the kids. The boys are trying to teach their little sister some board game that involves a lot of giggling, not much actual strategy.

They're adorable, and I can't help but feel a pang of longing as I watch them. I'm at the age where I better get moving if I want my own family. The lawsuit's put a damper on Brennan and I discussing our future plans. When Teagan crawls into my lap and starts showing me her doll, I'm pretty sure my heart melts on the spot.

"Careful with that little beauty. You're gonna get ideas." Ronni nudges me with her elbow. "Next thing you know, you'll be pregnant with a little McGloughlin of your own."

My laugh comes out a bit shaky. "Would that be so bad? I mean, eventually."

Ronni tilts her head, studying me. "Have you talked to Brennan about it?"

"Yeah. We've talked about getting married," I admit, glancing toward the kitchen where I can hear him laughing with Connor and Seamus. "But with everything going on with his company, everything's essentially on hold."

"He loves you, I see it in the way he can't take his eyes off you." Ronni leans in and whispers, "When the McGloughlin brothers love, there's nothing else like it. Connor was so patient with me and look at us now."

"I love Brennan so much." The words come out easily. "I want a future with him. A real one where we get married and have kids. Truthfully, the longer this drags out, I'm scared but don't want to freak him out. I worry CognifyAI is going to get in the way."

Ronni gives me a sympathetic look. "Have faith, Astrid. You'll both figure it out. We had some serious obstacles and love will find a way."

She would know. Connor and Ronni had a hellish journey to get to their happily ever after. It doesn't loosen the knot in my chest, however.

I know what's at stake. Brennan's been fighting hard to keep Reuniverse separate from CognifyAI, but the lawsuit drags on. He's spent close to three hundred thousand dollars in legal fees. They're trying to break him through his pocketbook and it may be working.

Despite my encouragement, he's wearing down, bit by bit. It's a conundrum. If he signs up for the golden handcuffs they're offering, he'll stay in Palo Alto for at least five years and Reuniverse will be owned by CognifyAI. I'll get a hefty payout, but we won't live in the same city.

Because, I can't exactly start over there. It would take years to build up my clientele in California. No matter what happens, I'll be staying in Seattle.

I want to believe we're strong enough to handle it, but I'm not naive. It's not about distance. It's about what we both want out of life, and whether our paths will still align when all of this is over.

Brennan catches my eye from across the room, and he literally beams at me. Like I'm his entire world.

I know how he feels, and I remember no matter what happens, I'll fight for us.

Sometimes you have to hold on to what matters.

Even when circumstances try to pull it out of your grasp.

Thirty

BRENNAN

New Year's Eve

WHAT A WAY TO spend New Year's Eve.

I'm riding the high from the Less Than Zero concert. I've received great news. And, my beautiful girlfriend is by my side.

The night's been electric and as we return to the houseboat, I can't stop smiling. Astrid's practically glowing. The rush of adrenaline I get seeing her like this—I'm buzzing. Alive. Hopeful.

"Totally insane." Astrid kicks off her shoes and grabs us each a beer from the fridge. "I've never been backstage before. It felt like stepping into another world."

Backstage at a big arena concert *is* a whole different world. Cables and guitar cases are stacked everywhere, people rush around with earpieces, shouting over the music as they make sure everything's running smoothly. It's chaotic, but there's a weird order to it all. Everyone seems to know where they need to be.

I lean against the counter. "You fit right in. Like you've been doing it your whole life."

Astrid knocked it out of the park. She's gorgeous in a fitted black leather jacket worn over a green, silky camisole. Dark, high-waisted jeans and ankle boots complete her edgy outfit. Her hair is in loose waves. She's looks like a fashion model in cool, comfortable clothes.

She rolls her eyes, but there's a genuine, excited smile tugging at her lips. "*Stop*. It was *wild*. Fireball was incredible and finally seeing Less Than Zero? From backstage? It's like, I don't know—a dream."

"They've been at it for fifteen years and bring it every single time." I can't help but beam with pride. "And you got the full experience. VIP treatment, backstage, the whole deal." I set my keys down and take off my jacket.

"Fireball's set was killer, too. I've seen Liam and Padraig play many times, but they've developed this edge. A raw energy that pulls everyone in."

She makes a swooning gesture. "Yeah, I totally agree. I met everyone in LTZ too. Ty and Zoey were so sweet. And their kids are fucking adorable."

"Yeah, all they're mini-rockstars in the making." I laugh. "Little Oliver has Ty's swagger."

"And Jace!" Astrid perks up, her eyes wide. "I've heard so much about him from Jason and seeing him with Alex and their kids. He's incredible. You could see how much he loves them."

"Yeah, he's mellowed out a lot. When he's on stage, though, he's still a monster." I think back to when I met Jace years ago. He's the reason Connor was able to get back into music and pursue his dream again.

"I got to hang out with Jason, too." A sly smile spreads across her lips. "He's got big plans for Reuniverse when the lawsuit shit is finally over. It was kind of surreal. He's talking about our little project like it's going to be massive."

I can't help but feel a flicker of pride. "It *is* going to be massive. I'll make sure of it."

Astrid wraps her arms around me and I pull her close. Our lips meet in a slow, lingering kiss. It starts soft, deepening into something potent because we've been holding back all night. Her hands find their way to my waist and everything else fades as we get lost in the moment.

When we pull apart, she rests her head on my chest. "I'm glad you brought me. It was an unforgettable night."

"I wouldn't have wanted to share it with anyone else." I hold her tightly, brushing a kiss against her hair. "Seeing it all through your eyes reminded me I've missed too many of my brothers' concerts over the years. I'm going to make much more effort going forward."

She tilts her head back to look at me. "I know I say this every time, but your family is amazing. How much love you all have for each other. And, Connor and Ronni. My God, they're so *solid*."

"I love them so much," I say between kisses. "Now you're part of it."

We stand there cuddling for a while in the quiet of the night. My mind drifts to everything that's happened over the past few months. The legal mess with CognifyAI and all the uncertainty has tied me up in knots for months. Tonight, none of it seemed to matter.

"So, you'd officially classify tonight as fun?" I tease.

"*Fun?*" she echoes. "B, I was let into a secret world. Fun can't begin to describe it."

I capture her lips again and kiss her soft and slow. "Good. Do you want me to make the night even better?"

She tilts her head. "How?"

"Sit down." I gesture to the couch. "I've got something to show you."

Astrid raises an eyebrow and plops down.

I reach into my jacket pocket, take out a folded piece of paper and hand it to her. My heart pounds a little harder than usual. "Open it."

She shoots me a playful, suspicious look but takes the envelope. As she unfolds the paper inside, I watch her expression shift from confusion to shock. Her eyes widen, and she looks up at me, mouth slightly agape. "Brennan, is this...?"

"Yep." I nod, feeling the grin stretch across my face. "Cognify's letting go of the claim on Reuniverse. It's over, Astrid. We're free."

She stares at the paper for a second then glances at me, her eyes glistening. "How did you...?"

"You inspired me. It wasn't easy." I sit next to her and run a hand through my hair. "We managed to negotiate a buyout when we found all of the documentation around the acquisition. It wasn't going to go well for them and we all agreed my heart's not in it after all of this bullshit they've put me through over the past couple of years. So, we keep our company. I give up half my equity in CognifyAI and I'll take over as the Chairman of the board. I'm losing some money, but no golden handcuffs. No five-year commitment. I walk away with life-changing money and get to focus on Reuniverse with you."

Astrid's silent for a moment. I can see her trying to process everything. "I don't even know what to say. This is exactly what we wanted. I think we manifested this shit."

I take her hand and squeeze it. "I know. The caveat is, they want to announce after the IPO. I'll stay in my current role through June."

"That's totally doable." She nestles against me.

"And, perfect timing." I play with a lock of her hair. "We can launch Reuniverse at the reunion, work with Jason if we choose, or keep it small and manageable. Either way, I want to build it with you."

Tears well up in her eyes, which she blinks back and replaces with a smile. "I'm so proud of you. I know how hard this has been."

"There's something else." I swallow roughly because my nerves kick in. "Now that things are going to change, we should, you know, resume discussions about our future."

Astrid sinks against me and strokes my cheek. "Oh, yeah?"

"Yeah. I was thinking it's time we found our forever home and moved in together. If you're up for it." I feel a surge of relief at getting the words out. Like everything in my life has been leading to this moment.

Her eyes light up and she actually giggles. "Brennan McGloughlin, are you asking me to shack up with you?"

"Well, I guess so." I chuckle. "First, I'd like to squeeze in a short vacation to celebrate, if you're up for it. Before your busy season kicks in. No matter what, by June I want you with me. Not only on weekends. Not in between business trips. Every. Fucking. Day."

She doesn't hesitate. "Yes. Absolutely yes."

Our lips press together in a deep, persistent kiss and the tension of everything we've been through melts away.

We're moving forward. Our future isn't something I have to fight for anymore. It's there. Waiting for us to step into it.

"Happy New Year, A." I stand and pull her up with me. Lead her to the stairs to her bedroom. "I think it's time for a celebratory night of orgasms, don't you think?"

Astrid slaps my ass. "Abso-fucking-lutely. Lead the way."

Thirty-One

ASTRID

Three Weeks Later

I'VE NEVER HAD A vacation like this.

Not in my entire adult life, and I've been missing out. Big time.

When Brennan surprised me with a week-long trip to Maui, I couldn't believe it. It's the nicest thing anyone has ever done for me. Seriously.

We're back in the hotel room after a long day of splashing in the ocean and lying in the sun. I'm sprawled out on the bed in my bikini, my skin is warm and a little salty from the ocean.

Brennan stands by the sliding glass door, fiddling with the blinds as the sun dips slightly lower on the horizon. A warm, golden light fills the room, illuminating his tan skin. His hair is still damp and the way it curls slightly at the ends makes him look softer. More relaxed.

I've never loved anyone more.

"What do you think?" He glances over at me. "Stay here forever? Get jobs selling overpriced coconuts to tourists?"

I roll onto my stomach and prop myself up on my elbows. "We'd make a killing. You'll be the tech genius who figures out how to turn coconuts into WiFi routers and I'll be the one convincing people they need them."

"Or..." He saunters over to me. "We could skip the coconuts and get a house on the beach here. I don't give a shit about sunburns if it means getting to see you in a bikini every day."

He deftly unties the strings of my top and waggles his eyebrows.

I turn back over and stretch out like a cat. Grab his hand and pull him down on the bed. "Tempting, but we'd go stir crazy in a week. Plus, we have this tiny little company to launch."

"Ah, okay." He flops next to me on the bed and lets out a dramatic sigh. "Real-life responsibilities. I have something better in mind."

Brennan lowers his face to my chest and circles a nipple with his tongue. Then nuzzles the underside of my breast. "Relax and enjoy."

"What are you doing? I thought we had to get ready?" I hold his head in place, because I have no intention of letting him stop now that he's started.

He drags his lips down my belly, over my navel and peels down my bikini bottoms. "What I've wanted to do since you emerged from the ocean like a Bond girl. I'm tasting you."

"Mmmmm," I purr approvingly.

Brennan kneels between my knees and lifts my legs over his shoulders and tilts my pelvis up with a hand on my ass. He traces one finger down my slit from my clit all the way to my ass. "You're always so swollen and wet for me."

He leans in and gently kisses my sensitive nub. Licks it. Sucks it between his lips.

"B." I close my eyes. "Yessss."

He presses the flat of his tongue against my clit, pushes it down into my folds and inside me.

"Oh, God!" I cry out as he sucks my lips into his mouth. Then swooshes his tongue through my pussy lips and repeats.

Even at this angle, my hips writhe and circle against his face. If he stops, I'll fucking kill him. My head thrashes from side to side as the tension in my core coils tighter. I'm certain this orgasm is going to kill me. "I can't even..."

"Oh, yes, you can." He pushes two fingers inside me and continues to lap at my clit and pussy. "It's the week of a thousand orgasms, remember?"

"Yeah....ohhhhhh." I hook my ankles over his shoulders and press my pelvis against his face.

He devours me, sucking my clit so hard I see stars. The world falls away when I come so hard I can't breathe. Through my orgasmic haze, Brennan lowers my torso to the mattress and I watch him tenderly kiss the hollows of my thighs, my pubic bone, and up my stomach. He sucks each nipple into a taut peak as he pushes me up to the headboard and nestles in between my legs.

I realize, at some point, he lost his board shorts and his beautiful cock rocks against my folds. Bracing his elbows on either side of my head, Brennan buries his fingers in my hair and nuzzles my neck. Nibbles on my earlobe.

"Do you have any idea how fucking delicious you are?" he whispers.

I stroke my fingertips down his cheek and lift my head to take his lips. I taste myself and it makes me want him badly. "I need you inside me."

Brennan's lips quirk against mine. Carefully, he moves his hips back until the tip of his cock pushes against my entrance. Slowly, he presses in and fills me. Watching me intently, with a look filled with so much love I nearly start to cry.

"You feel so good," he whispers into my ear and begins to move with long, slow hip rolls. Hits my sweet spot time after time, pushing me higher until I'm on the brink. Then he stops and waits for me to come back down.

"You're a tease." I clutch his ass and hold him where I want him. "We're gonna be late for dinner."

He smirks and licks a trail from my collarbone to my ear. "So what? I wanna make this last."

Brennan sucks my nipple back into his mouth and I feel little zings down to my clit, which feels so engorged I might explode. I squirm a little, trying to get some friction, but he stops.

"Every time you try to control me, I'll stop moving." He lifts one of my legs up onto his shoulder, opening me wide. Rolls his hips sharply, pushing himself in so deep I gasp. "Just enjoy my cock."

So I do. *God*, I do.

He leisurely starts to move again. We've been together so long I've adjusted to his size, but I'm amazed at how deep he is right now. The ridge of his cock rubs precisely where I need it and my muscles seize around him. Brennan clenches his jaw and squeezes his eyes shut, circling his hips to keep me on the edge of nirvana.

When I try to grip his ass he grabs my hand and links our fingers. Pins it to the bed above my head. His face is a grimace of ecstasy. He definitively speeds up and adjusts his thrusts so my clit hits his pubic bone with each pass. My thighs grip his hips and my body arches to meet him.

"Okay, A, now it's time to come." He bites the top of my shoulder and I unravel beneath him, crying out, squeezing his hand. He growls through his own orgasm, filling me with his hot release.

After, Brennan stays buried inside me but releases my leg and hand. He cups my face and we kiss each other thoroughly, tangling our tongues and caressing each other through our aftershocks.

Eventually he softens and flops on his back and my body immediately misses him.

Lying there together, I trail my fingers through his still-damp hair, enjoying the way he leans into my touch. "You know. I think I'm going to sell my houseboat once we find a place. I love it, but it's not a long-term solution for us..."

"Maybe we keep it as our little hideaway. It's nostalgic. Where we first touched pee-pees," he teases, stroking my nipple with his thumb. It cracks me up how much he obsesses over my tits.

"Yeah, it's a thought, but seriously, B. I want our own place." Being around Brennan's niece and nephews has given me baby fever, though. "I'm thinking we need an office. A great master suite. Cool yard. Great kitchen. A lot of en suite bedrooms...maybe even a little garden."

"A garden?" He lifts his head to look at me.

"I like the idea." I nuzzle his cheek. "Besides, you're about to become one of those tech billionaires who buys a dozen properties with infinity pools and wine cellars. Might as well lean into it. Plus, I have a little nest egg to contribute, too."

Brennan gazes at the ceiling like he's actually picturing it. "How about settling down in Madison Park, keeping your houseboat and finding a vacation home somewhere quieter? Like the San Juan Islands? We could have it all."

"Land moguls?" I tickle his scruff.

He shrugs. "Yeah. I've been thinking about it a lot lately. I want to make sure we have a home base to raise our family. That is, if you want to have kids with me."

There's something in the way he questions it that makes my heart do a little flip. He's not asking out of insecurity—it's because he sees the future the same way I do.

"You're sweet when you get all domestic." I lean over to kiss him. "Of course we're going to have kids. Wanna know what I've been thinking?"

"Of course." He shifts to his side, propping himself up on his elbow with his eyes locked on mine.

I take a deep breath. "I'd like this to be my last season as a realtor."

The words tumble out and I watch his face shift from confusion to realization.

"Wait, what? Are you serious?" He sits up.

I nod slowly, feeling the weight of the decision, but also the lightness of it. "C'mon. I've been thinking about it for a while. You know I don't love real estate. I'm sick of it, actually. Now that it's officially ours, I'd like to focus on Reuniverse. Full-time. If we're going to make it what we want it to be, I want to give it my attention."

He blinks like he's processing some new piece of information. "Amazing. I mean, I never wanted to pressure you to actually walk away from it."

"I'll keep my license." I sit up across from him cross-legged. "I've built my reputation and business for many years and I'm happy to make commissions here and there from select clients. I can do all of that in my sleep, though. With Reuniverse, I'm reenergized. The only tech billionaire I want to spend my time with is *you*."

He stares at me for a second like he's trying to comprehend the enormity of how our next chapter could play out. "I don't know what to say other than, wow."

"Wow?" I quirk a brow.

"Yeah. Wow." He leans over for a kiss. "It's all I could hope for. You're sure? You get off on closing deals."

"I do love closing deals. I'll love them more when we launch Reuniverse and I get to close deals to get the technology into everyone's hands." I grip his face and press my forehead to his.

His eyes soften and he leans in. "We've come a long way."

We sit, holding on to each other. Basking in the afterglow of our love. Planning our future. Listening to the easy rhythm of the ocean outside the window filling the silence. Brennan and I are on the edge of our own epic life together and I don't have to stress.

For once, I'm not anxious.

"Okay." I pull back and stroke his leg. "Enough of this smarmy shit. We need to get ready. Our dinner reservations are coming up and if we're late, we're going to miss the last sunset of our vacation."

He groans dramatically and rolls off the bed as he heads toward the shower. "Fine. Only because of the poke. God, I love poke."

We shower together quickly and hurry to get ready.

As I slip into my sundress, I catch a glimpse of us in the mirror.

We're both tanned, relaxed, and our hair a little sun-kissed. We look good together. We're happy.

I'm exactly where I want to be.

Thirty-Two

BRENNAN

A Bit Later

I CAN'T BELIEVE I've held it together for so long.

Tonight's the big night and my heart is thumping so loud, I'm surprised Astrid can't see it through my shirt.

She and I sit on a private lanai at Spago at the Four Seasons in Wailea, where we're staying. The warm Maui breeze drifts through the air carrying the scent of plumeria and sea salt. We made the sunset and it's stunning. The sky is painted in shades of pink and orange. The waves are a gentle, soothing soundtrack in the background.

I can't take my eyes off Astrid.

She sits across from me. Candlelight flickers and highlights the warm glow on her bronze skin. Of course she looks divine in a white, off-the-shoulder sundress, which flows softly over her frame. It hugs her in all the desirable places, showing off her tan and delicate cleavage. Gold jewelry—a dainty necklace and bracelet catch the light. The ocean breeze teases loose a strand of her hair from her low ponytail.

She's radiant underneath the Hawaiian stars.

Tonight, everything should be perfect. I've planned every detail, including the meal. The waiters are discreet yet attentive. The setting is flawless and I've never been this nervous in my life.

But I'm ready.

I'm sure.

The appetizer course arrives, Bigeye Ahi Poke Cones, which are crisp tempura shells filled with a mix of raw tuna marinated in sesame, miso, and a hint of ginger. Astrid picks one up and takes a small, delicate bite. Her eyes light up. "These are almost too pretty to eat, but holy hell are they good."

I feel a sense of relief wash over me. So far, so good.

"Wait for what's next," I say before downing mine in two bites.

We move on to Hotate Scallop Crudo. Thin slices of scallop with a tangy lime vinaigrette, topped with slivers of Fresno chili. Astrid closes her eyes as she tastes it, savoring every bite. Watching her enjoy what I've ordered makes me feel so happy.

It's all I want to do. Make her happy. My new focus. My *forever* focus.

"You're spoiling me." She opens her eyes to catch my gaze. "I could get used to this."

I smile happily. "That's the idea."

Each course feels like a step closer to a moment I've been planning for weeks. The Seafood Red Thai Coconut Curry is next—a fragrant, spicy mix of Kaua'i prawns, Mahi Mahi, and scallops in a rich coconut broth.

Astrid takes a spoonful and her eyes widen with delight. "Brennan, this is amazing. How did you plan this?"

"I've got my ways." I wink at her.

She laughs heartily, filling me with pure happiness. I've missed seeing her this relaxed and joyful. Like all the times we played pool at The Zoo. Over the past year we've had too much stress and now it all seems worth it. Everything is falling into place.

As the evening progresses, the courses keep coming. Broiled Miso Marinated Walu, a tender and flaky white fish balanced with a hint of sesame and fresh cucumber. Next, a glazed Gouchujang Pork Shank melts in our mouths.

Astrid leans back in her chair, content. "I don't think I can eat another bite." She pats her flat stomach. "And, I don't want this night to end."

"Good." I signal to the server. "We're not quite done."

He returns, carrying a tray with one final course. A Chocolate Porter Cake, which is close to what Astrid ordered for my birthday. This version is dark-chocolate cake soaked in porter beer, layered with semi-sweet ganache. It's decadent. Almost sinful.

When Astrid sees it, her eyes light up. I know she felt bad about bringing a similar version to my family gathering, but I've been obsessed with it. So fucking good.

"You're something else, B," she beams. "I don't care how full I am. We're finishing this."

I watch closely as she takes a bite. Her eyes flutter closed in pure bliss. She's everything I ever wanted. More than I dreamed of. When she whispers, "I love you," I know it's time.

"Astrid." My voice catches slightly but I stand up on wobbly legs and reach into my pocket. My hands tremble a bit because never, in a million years, did I hope to meet my person. "There's something I need to ask you tonight."

She blinks up at me with confusion. Then it dawns on her and her entire face lights up. "What are you—"

Before she can finish, I'm down on one knee in front of her. Presenting the seven-carat ring I've had for over a year. A vintage diamond set in platinum with intricate filigree detailing, making it look timeless and unique. Exactly like Astrid. The diamond catches the light from the lanterns around us and sparkles brilliantly.

She gasps, her hands fly to her mouth. *"Brennan."*

"Astrid." I try to keep my voice steady despite the pounding of my heart. "You are the most incredible person I've ever met. You make me better, you make me braver, and you make me want to be the man you deserve. I can't imagine life without you in it, and I don't want to. I want to share everything with you—the good, the bad, the successes, and even the failures. I want to build my future with you. So...will you marry me?"

For a second I think she's going to turn me down because she bursts into tears. I'm terrified—is marrying me so terrible? But, wait. She's nodding and reaching for me. Finally a smile breaks across her face and she eeks out a breathless, "*Yes*. Yes. YES."

Her acceptance is barely out of her mouth before I've wrapped her in my arms and lifted her from the ground and swung her around. She grips my face and kisses me hard. It feels like the world is spinning and standing still all at once.

When we separate and the surroundings come back into focus, we notice the waiters are applauding and whooping. Astrid blushes, burying her face in my shoulder.

I can't stop smiling. I don't think I've ever been this happy.

She holds out her hand and I slip the ring on to her finger. It fits perfectly. Like it was made for her. "It's incredibly beautiful." She's choked up. "Wait, is this...?"

"Yeah, it's the ring you admired last year in Palm Springs. The moment I saw it, I knew it was yours. After you went back to Seattle, I bought it thinking I'd propose last year. But, with all the legal shit happening..." I brush a strand of hair from her face. "I didn't want to propose until we were through it."

Astrid's eyes are filled with so much love. I feel my heart swell. "I can't believe we're engaged. I can't believe this is real."

"Well, it is." I hold her hand up to the light. "Smooth sailing from this point forward."

On cue, a man begins to play a Hawaiian love song on the ukulele. We sway together to the sound with the waves crashing softly in the background. The moon shines down on us. It's perfect. I'm not worried about the future. I'm happy to be in the present with the love of my life, knowing our lives together will be beautiful.

"I love you." She looks up at me, caressing the hair at my nape. "I love you so much."

"I love you too." I lean down to kiss her again. "I promise I'm going to spend the rest of my life proving it to you."

Thirty-Three

ASTRID

One Month Later

It's all coming together.

Our new life. A new outlook. Possibly a new home, if the seller accepts our offer.

Then we can start planning the wedding.

For now, though, we're hopefully finalizing Jason Deveraux's involvement in Reuniverse.

To say he's the epitome of Seattle tech sophistication is an understatement. A quintessential Pacific Northwest fifty-something tech billionaire exuding an approachable, laid-back charisma, but Jason exhibits the kind of authority that comes from building an empire most people could never fathom.

He and his son Jace share the same piercing green eyes and a calm, measured demeanor. Unlike Jace, whose long tresses reach halfway down his back, Jason is clean-cut with neatly trimmed, salt-and-pepper hair. Like most rich Seattleites, he mostly wears golf shirts and jeans instead of blazers and suits.

We sit at a small conference table in his office overlooking Lake Washington. Jason leans back in his executive chair surveying the two of us with a knowing smile. In front of us are sleek black leather portfolios, each embossed with the Deveraux emblem.

A carafe of water and a tray of gorgeous pastries sit untouched in the center. My eyes flick over to them because I'm fucking starving. I'll wait, though. Brennan and I have a lunch date at the Met after this meeting to discuss whatever happens here today.

"Alright, let's cut to it." Jason seems charged with excitement. "I've been thinking a lot about Reuniverse, and honestly, this is one of the most exciting projects I've come across in years. Before we move forward, I want to make sure we're all aligned on where this can go, and more importantly, how we're going to get there."

Brennan tenses beside me, his shoulders stiffen, but he doesn't break eye contact with Jason. I reach under the table and brush my fingers against his hand. He relaxes a little.

He has a little corporate PTSD. The past couple of years have taken it out of him. Between his changing role at CognifyAI and the legal battles over Reuniverse, he's had enough stress and sleepless nights to last a lifetime.

I have a good feeling about this, though. Sitting across from Jason, there's a sense of possibility in the air. Like Brennan and I are standing on the edge of something monumental.

"We're intrigued." I offer Jason a warm smile. "Brennan and I have talked about this endlessly and we both see the potential. We want Reuniverse to change the way people connect. We're also cautious. Neither of us have the tolerance to go through what happened with CognifyAI."

Jason nods. "Completely understandable. Let me be clear. I think you have something special here. Reuniverse isn't another social app, it's a platform with the ability to touch people's lives on a personal level. We're talking about reconnecting with old friends, finding long-lost family members, reigniting forgotten memories—all in a completely new way. That kind of emotional pull? It's not something you see every day. And it's certainly not something we should be cautious about. We should be confident."

Brennan clears his throat. "I'm glad you see the vision. When Astrid brought me the idea, I felt the same way. And, I felt the same kind of excitement, which is why I fought like hell to keep the company. But..." He hesitates, glancing down at the sleek black table before focusing on Jason. "The scale. The growth. I've been there. Astrid was being nice. I don't want to make the same mistakes I made with CognifyAI."

"I'm aware of what you went through." Jason taps a pen to his lip. "What did you learn?"

Brennan nods, his jaw tightening. "I learned the hard way scaling too fast without clear boundaries can be a nightmare. My board was too focused on growth and pleasing investors, in my opinion, we lost sight of what made the company innovative." He takes a breath. "I don't want Reuniverse to become a corporate machine where creativity gets suffocated under layers of bureaucracy. This time, I want to make sure we keep our core vision intact, even if it means a slower, deliberate path. It shouldn't be about numbers or a stock price."

"I see." Jason's face softens but his eyes remain sharply focused. "Exactly why you need to carve out your own space, away from Cognify's shadow. Reuniverse must stand on its own. It needs to be a brand. A movement."

Brennan takes this in. His fingers drum lightly against the edge of the table, a habit I've noticed when he's processing something.

I lean forward to interject my own thoughts, considering I'm Brennan's equal in this venture. "That's where your guidance is so valuable, Jason. We've got it to this point on our own. The reunion is in less than three months and we're fine tuning the tech, but it's ready. Taking it to the next level and scaling is where we would like your help. We'd like to go big but we need to do it properly. We can't afford another situation like CognifyAI where financing technicalities take away our control."

"Exactly why we're here." Jason nods his approval. "Let's get one thing straight, this isn't about avoiding mistakes. It's about building something remarkable. I've seen countless tech startups come and go. The ones who stick around understand it's not selling a product. They're creating an experience. Reuniverse has the potential and I can help knock this out of the park."

"Let's discuss it." Brennan squeezes my hand under the table.

Jason points to his copy of the portfolio. "Read pages three through six."

We do as he asks. Initially, I feel a nervous flutter in my stomach because I've not been to college, let alone business school. I think I comprehend what I'm reading, but I can't be sure. It terrifies me to appear stupid. Especially when Brennan and I have probably overprepared for this moment because we're both scared shitless of overlooking something.

When we both glance up, Jason looks at us through bridged fingers. "Look, I get it. You're both used to handling things yourselves and you can only get so far without help. Scaling means letting others come in and pave the way. People you trust to see the same vision as you. I can offer funding *and* a partnership. I'll personally teach you how to build out a leadership team, refine your strategy, and get the resources you need to go global."

"You're serious?" Brennan looks shocked. Intrigued. I see a flicker of fire in his eyes.

"Absolutely." Jason leans back in his chair. "Your risk is my risk, which means I'll set you up for long-term success, not a quick profit. I'm proposing something out-of-the box. I want to invest in Reuniverse, but I'm really investing in you both. For example, have you heard about what some investment firms are doing now with founder health and wellness programs?"

I'm thoroughly intrigued. "I've read about it, but please explain."

"It's not only about business." Jason leans forward and emphasizes each point by tapping his finger on the desk. "It's about making sure the people behind the business are thriving. Both of you will have leadership coaching, wellness retreats, even stress management counseling. My idea of winning is making sure you're in the best possible shape to lead Reuniverse for years to come. We're talking about building a company culture, which means it starts at the top and radiates outward."

I can see the wheels turning in Brennan's mind. "I've never heard of anything so collaborative," he admits. "I'm not sure why because it makes perfect sense. As founders, we're pulled in so many directions. Engrossed in getting through the day-to-day. We rarely have a true opportunity to focus on the long-term, other than making the numbers and creating some stupid five-year plan."

"Well, I believe that type of thinking is becoming outdated." Jason stands and walks to the window. "I'd like to extend the offer to both of you."

Brennan's hand tightens around mine and I squeeze back, trying to convey my excitement.

"We had a rough few months last year." I join Jason at the window. "Brennan and I have always known this idea is bigger than us. We appreciate your guidance."

The two of us look at Brennan, who is thumbing through the portfolio. A hint of a smile tugs at the corners of his lips. His eyes widen as he flips through the pages and I can see he's reviewing the projections and plans laid out in meticulous detail. "This is so much better than I expected."

"To summarize, we'll provide the funding, help build the infrastructure, the team, and the support network. We want Reuniverse to be a household name and we're willing to put in the time and effort to make it happen." Jason sits next to Brennan and claps him on the shoulder. "I want to be part of your team. I'll personally mentor you both through the challenges ahead. We're going to make Reuniverse bigger than Facebook or TikTok with the right people, and the right mindset."

"What do you think?" He peers up at me. I watch all the uncertainty and doubt literally melt away. Replaced with something stronger. "You and I need to consult with our lawyers, but I'm inclined to say yes."

Jason has a twinkle in his eye. "Great. Take your time going over the proposal. I never want you to feel pressured into making a snap decision. Do your due diligence and I'll eagerly wait for your official response."

We say our goodbyes and Brennan and I walk to the car holding pinkies. Neither of us look at each other. Until we get into my car.

The we turn to each other and scream our excitement at the top of our lungs.

Holy shit!

We've won the lottery.

Thirty-Four

BRENNAN

Two Weeks Later

God, I love being a lame duck CEO.

CognifyAI almost feels like a distant memory. My condo in Palm Alto is cleaned out. I'm rarely in the office. I provide a quote for some press release here. Take a strategic phone call there. In another month, they're announcing my departure and appointment as Chairman of the board.

Going forward, I'll be on deck for board meetings and available for historical knowledge. That's it.

I couldn't be happier.

Well, not true. Momentarily I'll be much happier.

Astrid is half-asleep, flopped on her back with an arm flung over her eyes. I tug the sheet down, exposing her plump breast to the coolish air and her nipple puckers immediately. My cock swells and I lean over and drag my tongue over her pink nub.

"Mmmmm." She cups the back of my head to hold me in place.

I seal my mouth over the little bullet and suck, pressing my erection against her thigh. I begin to caress and explore her body. "You're so sexy, A." I kiss down her abdomen to her inner thighs. "So delicious. I want to taste your sweet pussy."

"This is my favorite way of waking up." She moans when I nip her inner thigh.

I lift her legs at the knees and settle them over my shoulders and study her pussy, which is puffy and engorged from all the sex we've been having lately. I can't get enough of her. My dick is perpetually hard. "Well, how convenient because it's my favorite way to wake you up."

Rather than tease her, I start out by sucking on her clit until it's hard and pulsing. Astrid nearly bows off the bed but I push my hands under her ass to hold her in place as my mouth covers her pussy. God, I love going down on her.

Now it's time to draw it out for a bit. I fuck her with my tongue. Suck, kiss, and nibble her lips. Press the heel of my hand over her pubic bone to stimulate her clit, but avoid licking it directly.

Astrid clings to the sheets, gasping for breath. "Ohmygod. I'm so fucking sensitive. That feels incredible."

"God, I love you, Astrid Gustaffson." I grin up at her from between her thighs.

She points at her pussy. "If you love me so much, stop edging me and make me come."

Oh, game on. I flick my tongue against her clit, lick down her wet slit and Astrid gasps when I plunge my tongue inside her.

"Good?" I hum against her.

She's barely coherent. "Yes...*God*, yes."

I resume, loving the breathy moans slipping from her lips. Reveling in the way she presses her hands on my head to keep me in place. No matter how many times I go down on Astrid, it's a mind-blowing experience. My cock throbs against the mattress as I resume licking her clit, which pulses in my mouth.

When her thighs clench and release in a steady cadence, I know she's on the edge so I capture her clit between my lips and suck hard like it's a piece of delicious candy and she explodes. Her cream coats my mouth, lips and chin as she writhes through her orgasm.

I don't stop, though, because I want to draw out every last drop of pleasure from her body before we start all over again. When I lift my head, Astrid's eyes are glazed. Her breasts are heaving from the aftershocks of release, pink nipples distended into hard points.

"You're way too good," she eeks out.

Satisfied with my efforts, I kneel between her legs and swipe my cock up and down her slit. I'm about to plunge inside her when Astrid grabs my wrist.

"It's my turn. Let me suck on you." She licks her lips.

"Not this morning, I want to come inside you. If you put your sexy mouth on my cock, I won't last." I sit back on my calves.

Astrid leans up on her elbow. "You will."

She sits up and playfully pushes me on my back and makes a point of dragging her gaze up and down my body before setting her sight on my jutting cock weeping with precum.

"Hmmm. Where should I start?" She blinks at me faux-innocently and lowers her mouth to my nipple as she grips my hard length.

Good God. She strokes me from root to tip. Sucks on my nipple. Strokes. Sucks my other nipple. Repeats. My hips begin to piston off the bed when she kisses her way lower. And lower. When she reaches my cock, she kisses and licks my belly. My thighs. My cock strains toward her mouth but she deliberately avoids it, instead bathing me everywhere but where I need it.

Finally she drags her tongue up and down my shaft. Lifts my balls and sucks them into her mouth.

"Jesus, A." I jackknife up and nearly lose it altogether.

"Don't come," she pleads, pressing me back down. "Not yet."

Astrid repositions herself between my legs and laves my ball sac thoroughly as she jacks me slowly. I put my hand over hers to help her pick up the pace to where I want it and make a demand. "Touch yourself. Make yourself come with me."

Goddamn. Astrid obeys me without hesitation. I watch her plunge her fingers in and out of her channel while stroking my cock with my hand over hers and worshipping my sac with her mouth. It's incredible, but too slow. I'm delirious. I need to fucking come.

"Suck me. No, suck me while you ride my face," I demand. "I want to come in your mouth and you to come again on mine. Then you'll get me hard again and I'll fuck you any way you want me to."

Astrid scrambles over me. "We've done everything I can think of but never this. Let's try it."

I wrap one arm around her hips pull her down onto my lips and feast again. She grips my shaft with both hands and strokes while she sucks on the tip. Our bodies vibrate as we drive each other out of our minds. My senses are short-circuiting. I can't hold on to a single thought beyond the mounting pleasure and how good it feels to push in and out of her mouth while my face is buried in her pussy.

My balls tighten as Astrid's hot, wet mouth works me over. She gives such good head, sucking me as if her mission in life is to get me off. She swirls her tongue over my crown, takes me deep and hums.

"Fuck. Yes," I hiss against her lower lips. "So good, A."

Astrid kicks it up a notch, making sexy little sounds in the back of her throat. The hot suction of her mouth feels like heaven and when she cups my balls and squeezes gently, I nearly shoot my load but I manage to control myself because I'd rather go over together.

"Holy fuck." Astrid clenches her thighs around my ears when I swirl my tongue like a madman on her clit and press the tip of my finger into her puckered little ass. She takes me to the back of her mouth and swallows against my tip and it sends me to the moon.

We work each other like this for a couple minutes until I spurt down her throat and she bucks against my face. We're so in tune with each other, it's incredible.

Savagely, I turn and crawl up her body, capturing her mouth and grinding my half-hard cock against her center. Astrid grips the back of my head and she pulls me down for a kiss, sweeping her tongue over my bottom lip before biting it.

"Fuck me hard," she demands.

My mouth crashes back against hers and we're maniacs, devouring each other. We suck on each other's tongues, tasting each other as I ride her slickness until I'm hard again. I drive into her in one hard thrust.

Astrid cries out, "Again! Show me what you've got, B."

"Oh yeah." I chuckle, loving her ferocity. "I'll show you."

I grab her hands and shove them over her head, locking her wrists together. I pull back and thrust back into her. Hard. Fast. Piston my hips and grind to make sure my cock hits her just so. Her tits jiggle with every pass and I bend down and suck on her nipples, fucking her so hard the headboard slams into the wall.

"Come for me, A. Come all over my dick," I demand.

Astrid gasps from each sharp thrust. Every command. Her inner walls squeeze my cock. Her pussy is so wet I feel her juices coating my balls. "Fuck, I feel your pussy throbbing, you're close, aren't you?"

"Yes," she chokes out, arching her back, taking me in deeper. "*Yesssssss.*"

I see the exact moment ecstasy flashes across her face and her orgasm rips through her body. She shudders and keens as her pussy pulses around my cock. I feel my own orgasm sizzle down my spine all the way to my balls.

"Fuck, yessssss," I yell as my climax spins like a tornado through my body.

I continue pounding into her in desperate, erratic thrusts. Astrid writhes beneath me and goes over again. Our groans mingle in an epic release. Her inner muscles keep squeezing my cock, milking everything I have.

Eventually our bodies begin to wind down and I hold myself up on an elbow, still buried inside her. Stroking her hair and whispering how much I love her.

She runs her hands up and down my back, nuzzles my neck and I can't believe how perfect my life is.

Astrid's going to be my wife and I'll get to fuck her like this for the rest of my life.

We're buying a house together. We're building a business. We'll have a family someday soon.

Who says you can't have it all?

Thirty-Five

ASTRID

One Month Later

IT'S SO NICE BEING part of Brennan's family.

I truly feel like I belong. I love every single one of his brothers. His mom and dad are great. It's the type of home I wish I grew up in.

As we've done for most of this year, Brennan and I are at the McGloughlins for Sunday dinner. Tonight Maureen decided on a coastal theme. In the middle of the table, a massive cedar-plank salmon showpiece is topped with a vibrant salsa of diced mango, red onion, cilantro. She also prepared a creamy Dungeness crab risotto, flecked with leeks and fresh herbs, a platter of grilled asparagus and a skillet of herbed cheddar biscuits.

I peeked in the kitchen before we sat down because I've had a crazy sweet tooth for the past couple of weeks. I'm definitely saving room for a huge serving of the fresh peach cobbler cooling on the counter.

Well, maybe. Tonight feels different. My anxiety is through the roof. My stomach's been in knots all day. It's nothing serious, I tell myself. I'm sure it's because the reunion is looming so close and the Reuniverse partnership with Jason Deveraux is going ahead. Or, maybe, it's because we're about to close on this gorgeous house in Madison Park. Could be some bad chicken wings from The Zoo last night.

Whatever the reason, I'm pushing the food around on my plate instead of eating it. I glance over at Brennan, who's deep in conversation with Cillian about the house. He's so excited about it and, truthfully, I am too. Our home. I'm already imagining us hosting Sunday dinners like this, with our own friends and family someday.

I'll need to learn how to cook., but still…

"So, have you settled on a date yet?" Maureen snaps me out of my thoughts, her eyes dart between Brennan and me, the excitement in her voice palpable. "I know you've been busy with other things, but I'm dying to help with the wedding plans."

"Oh, we're still figuring it out." I grimace out a smile through a wave of nausea. "There's a lot going on with Reuniverse, and we want to make sure everything is perfect for the reunion. After we get through it, I promise I'll focus on all of the things."

Maureen beams. "Oh, perfect. Let me know what you need. I'm sure your mum and sisters are helping but planning a wedding takes a village. I'm happy to help with anything."

"We'll lean on you a ton." Brennan squeezes my knee under the table. "We've got a lot to look forward to but we're trying to just enjoy each moment after last year's stress."

Cillian, who's been mostly quiet tonight, suddenly chimes in. "You should totally have the wedding at the new house. Can you imagine? The two of you saying 'I do' with those lake views as the backdrop."

I have such empathy for Brennan's brother. There's still a hint of wistfulness in his eyes. I know he's been putting on a brave face about the woman who broke his heart being back in town, but the way his expression shifts when he mentions love makes me want to reach out and hug him.

"You know, I think that's a great idea." Brennan catches my gaze. "We close in a week. Depending on when we set the date, I'm sure we could have everything ready in time."

"It's close by, right? The house, I mean." Seamus shovels a bite of salmon into his mouth. He's been quiet until now. The gentle giant seems to have a lot on his mind.

"Oh, it's stunning." I shift into realtor mode. "It's a beautiful Roland Terry design, with tall ceilings and broad rooms. There's a two-story granite fireplace, and the whole place showcases breathtaking views of Lake Washington. I'm Pinterest boarding like mad figuring out how we're going to decorate it."

Cillian nods with his eyes shut, as if he's picturing it. "Big house, big views, big everything. I could totally see myself living somewhere similar one day. I'm ready, if the right girl comes along."

"Don't give up hope." Brennan pats him on the back. "You never know what the future holds."

He shakes his head. "Ship has sailed, man."

I glance at Brennan who's focused on his brother, clearly concerned. They met up the other night and

Cillian seems to be navigating the not-drinking thing pretty well, all considering. "Well, most people love to have stability in their life. A house provides a great anchor."

We resume eating until Maureen speaks up again. "You know, Astrid, I've been meaning to ask. Will we be able to meet your parents and siblings soon? It would be lovely to get to know them before the big day."

Ooof. Another wave of nausea rolls through my belly and I feel my heart drop into my stomach. "*Oh*, I'm not sure..." I eke out.

But, she's already pressing on. "Maybe they could join us here next week for Sunday dinner?" Maureen continues, smiling warmly. "Tell me what their favorite food is and I'm happy to cook it. We'll make them part of the family."

"I don't think they'll come, I'm sorry." My cheeks flush. I can feel Brennan's eyes on me and I wish I could just vanish into the chair.

"Why not?" Rory's eyes bore into me, gentle but curious. "We don't bite."

I swallow, feeling queasiness rise up again and feel the need to flee.

"The thing is, we're not close. I introduced them to Brennan and it was the last straw. I don't want them in my life anymore," I blurt out, surprising even myself with the admission. "They've hurt me deeply for many years, especially my mom. She has her reasons, but I'm tired of being a punching bag for something that's not my fault. Brennan and I have been through so much, I don't want them to tarnish my new life. Or my relationship with all of you."

Every pair of eyes is trained on me at this point and I hate feeling so exposed. The table goes silent and for a moment, all I can feel is silent judgment.

"Oh, A. I wasn't sure if you knew. Don't worry, you're one of us now. She can't hurt you anymore." Brennan's eyes search mine, then he glances around at his family. "She's not Astrid's biological mother."

I freeze, stunned. The words hang in the air, and suddenly my entire world feels like it's tilting.

"*What?*" I whisper, my voice barely audible. "What are you talking about?"

Brennan's expression shifts from confusion to horror. I know the exact moment he realizes he's made a horrific mistake. "I thought...uh, I thought you.... I thought that's why you haven't..."

I stop hearing anything he's saying because the room is spinning. I know I'm going to be sick.

"What did you do?" My voice shakes with utter devastation. "Even though I asked you to leave it alone, you didn't listen. Have you been investigating my family behind my back?"

"Astrid, I—" he starts, but I can't let him finish.

I'm going to throw up. *Right now.* I shove my chair back and bolt for the bathroom, barely making it before the nausea overwhelms me. I collapse over the toilet, my stomach heaving, and I can hear someone's footsteps approaching, but I kick the door shut and manage to lock it. I don't want to see him. I don't want to see anyone. Not in this state.

However long it is later, when I stand up, I'm shaking uncontrollably. I splash water on my face and stare at my reflection in the mirror, trying to understand why Brennan would press forward when I begged him not to. It's such a violation. Unforgivable, maybe.

How long has he known? Why didn't he tell me? How could he do this?

There's no way out, I realize. I'm locked in the McGloughlin's bathroom and the only way to leave is by walking past all of them. How *mortifying*.

I tentatively peer out the door and Brennan is there. Waiting. Leaning against the wall, his face pale and stricken.

"Sorry doesn't cut it." He reaches for me but I avoid his touch. "I wasn't trying to hurt you. I wanted to give you answers to make things better. When I found out, I figured you already knew and it's why you felt so strongly. So, I dropped it."

"Make things *better*?" I repeat, incredulous. "Brennan, you withheld information from me again. *Deliberately*. I told you to drop it and you didn't give two shits. How am I supposed to process this? I'm so fucking mad. And hurt. And devastated."

He looks like he's been punched in the gut. "It wasn't malicious. I really thought I could help. I wanted to surprise you."

"Let me make one thing clear. You *don't* get to make my decisions for me," I snap, my voice rising to a yell. At this point I don't care if his entire family hears me because I cannot *comprehend* where his mind was at. Hyperfocus or not. This is *wrong*. "I'm a grown woman who *trusted* you, Brennan. For what? You have no respect for me. None. What else have you been keeping from me?"

His look of distress doesn't faze me.

"I haven't—A, please. I'm wasn't trying to hurt you," he pleads. "I thought if you had the information you wouldn't be so hard on yourself about your relationship with your family. I hate seeing you hurt. It kills me..."

"I told you I don't need you to fix me." I shake my head, tears stinging my eyes. "I needed you to *listen* to me. You didn't." My voice cracks but I'm beyond being worried about appearances at this point. My emotions are raw. Real. Legitimate. "I can't marry someone who'll disregard my capability to choose how I conduct my own life."

I pull off my engagement ring and hand it to him. He makes no move to take it from me so we stand in the hallway staring at each other. I can see how badly he wants to fix what he broke.

It's too late.

I love Brennan with all my heart, but I'd lose respect for myself if I were to brush this off. "I need to be away from you." I grab his hand and press the ring into his palm. "To rethink what I want. Right now it feels like our entire relationship is ruined."

He collapses into himself at my words. The pain in his eyes shatters me, but I can't let myself soften. Not this time.

"Astrid, please." Tears stream down his cheeks. "I love you."

"I need space." I walk past him, back toward the dinner table. "And I need you to respect my wishes this time."

As I approach the family, who are obviously uncomfortable witnesses to our abrupt breakup, I keep it simple because there's no way they haven't heard every word we've said.

"I need to go," I manage, knowing my words land heavy in the room.

Maureen's eyes flick to Brennan, who stands behind me shellshocked. She looks back at me. I can tell she wants to say something, *anything*, to help. But she doesn't.

Cillian glances between Brennan and me, clearly worried about his brother. Seamus shifts in his seat awkwardly, his mouth half-open like he's about to speak, but he closes it again, probably realizing there's nothing he can say that won't make the situation worse. Even Rory, who usually can't keep his thoughts to himself, stares straight ahead. His expression is a mix of shock and sympathy.

Maureen is the one who eventually speaks. "Oh, sweetheart, are you alright? Can I do anything?"

"No." I shake my head. "Thank you for a lovely meal. I'm sorry it came to this but I need to go home."

I make it to the door and step outside, shutting it behind me. Thank God I'm the one who drove tonight.

As I get into the driver's seat, I hear Brennan calling my name, but I don't turn back. I need to get out of here, away from all of them, before I fall apart.

I don't know what to do.

I don't know what to think.

Everything I thought I understood about Brennan, about us, has just been turned upside down.

We're not coming back from this.

Thirty-Six

BRENNAN

Present Day

PREGNANT.

I can barely process what Astrid has just told me. Or the kiss she instigated.

My heart is pounding so hard it feels like it's echoing off the brick walls of the cafeteria where our classmates are engaging with Reuniverse.

All I can hear is the word "pregnant" hanging in the air between us like a bombshell.

Astrid stares at me, her eyes wide and guarded, like she's bracing for my reaction, but I'm frozen, my mind running a thousand miles an hour and not moving at all. It's like I've stepped out of my body, watching us from above.

Two people whose relationship blew up as we were planning our happily ever after, standing here. Alone on the lawn. My world has shifted under my feet.

The past few weeks have felt like I've been living in some kind of nightmare. At first, I couldn't help myself. I stalked Astrid at the houseboat, waited there for hours. Paced around the deck. Stared out at the water. Prayed she'd come home and we could talk.

She never showed.

I tried calling, texting, emailing—anything to get through to her, but every time, it was like hitting a brick wall. She wouldn't answer. Wouldn't give me the chance to apologize or explain. I drove around the city like a lunatic. Tried to figure out where she was having a showing. Hoping I'd find her car parked outside The Zoo.

It was a long shot, of course. Seattle's a big city, and I was just one guy yearning for a miracle.

I know I screwed up. I've been desperate to make it up to her, but she shut me out. Definitively. I've been losing my mind over it.

Being without her is the most painful experience in my life.

At some point, I ended up at Cillian's place. I poured out my heart. Detailed the mess I'd made. I didn't realize how badly I needed a sounding board and Kill is my best friend in the world.

He told me, "You did screw up, Bren. But don't think for a second this is the end. You're not a quitter. Turn your ability to focus on winning her back and you can't go wrong, even if you have to do it one step at a time."

When I lamented she wouldn't give me a chance, wouldn't listen, he set me straight.

"Then you *make* her listen," he advised like it was the simplest thing in the world. "I'm not saying force your way back in, but don't you dare throw in the towel. She's scared and she's hurt, but she's not *gone*. Show her *you're* not going anywhere."

I've always respected Cillian's advice, even when I didn't want to hear it. He's been through his own share of ups and downs, and he knows what it's like to lose everything and try to build himself back up too. So when he told me not to give up, it stuck with me. He reminded me of something I'd lost sight of.

Love isn't just about the good times. It's about fighting through the hard ones, too.

The next day, I went back to Astrid's houseboat and left a note under the mat, telling her I'd be at the reunion and I'd wait for her there if she wanted to talk. It wasn't much, but it was all I could think to do. I just needed her to know I was still here, still fighting for us, even if it felt like I was swinging at shadows.

I also paid into the earnest money on our house to obtain an extension on the house closing, citing a personal emergency. The sellers were annoyed, but I put money where my mouth was. There was no way I could buy a place without her. No way I was losing it when we work things out.

When, not if.

I'm manifesting our reconciliation.

It's hard to stay positive, though. Everything feels so fragile. Like one wrong move will make it all fall apart for good.

My mind kept rewinding to the morning before the dinner, where we made love and talked about turning the house into our home. I was so sure nothing could ever tear us apart.

Now, I know different. Thanks to me, once again our life together is hanging by a thread and I'll do anything to stop the unraveling.

"Brennan?" Astrid waves her hand in front of my face. "Did you comprehend what I said?"

Her beautiful face snaps back into focus and I stare at her, slack jawed. Finally, I clear my throat, and try to form a coherent sentence. My words come out rough. "It's for sure? You're pregnant?"

Astrid nods, biting her lip as she searches my face for something, *anything*.

"Yeah, B." She rubs her flat belly. "I took a test. Well, about ten tests. Every single one of them confirms it."

There's a tiny, irrational part of me that's almost relieved. We're tied together forever now and at least she's here talking to me, instead of shutting me out like she has for the past few weeks. I shove the thought aside because, damn it, this is huge. I'm always gonna fight for her. Now I have every reason to double down—our child.

"I'm overwhelmed, but so happy. I can't even..." I manage to catch my breath. "When did you find out?"

"Yesterday." She glances down at her shoes. "I haven't been feeling well for a while. I thought it was just stress. Heartbreak. I've been a mess since...and it didn't occur to me because, well, as you know I use an IUD for birth control." She sucks in a whistle, like she still can't believe it herself. "Then I bought a shit ton of tests and, *well*... Here we are."

"Have you been to a doctor? Is everything okay?" I can see how scary this is for her now. The last thing I want is to make it worse.

"No, I have an appointment in a couple days." She runs a hand through her hair. "I've been doing some internet medical sleuthing and the odds of me getting pregnant are so miniscule. You seem to have super sperm. Right now, the scariest part is the IUD. They're going to remove it, otherwise there'll be risks to our baby." She hesitates, like she's not sure if she should say the next part, but she steels her resolve. "Brennan, I want this. Badly. I hope you do too."

"Of course I do." These words come out easy. The rest do not. "I'm sorry. So, so sorry, A. For everything. For not listening, for going behind your back—"

"I know," she interrupts. "You have to understand, this can't happen again. *Ever* again. I told you not to dig around and you did it anyway. Without even thinking about the consequences. You found out things about me I didn't know. Why did you do it?"

"I wanted you to have your family." I shake my head sadly, recognizing how stupid I've been. "You've been so incredibly supportive of me through all of my bullshit, I wanted to be the one to give you something you could hold on to. I didn't *ever* want to hurt you."

Astrid is still conflicted. "I know you didn't mean to hurt me, but it *did* hurt, B. It's *devastating*. Do you know what's *more* devastating? The fact you didn't respect my boundaries. You took my choice away." Her eyes search mine. "Then, if that wasn't enough, the icing on the cake was dropping this bombshell in front of your entire family, like it was no big thing. I'm completely mortified. How can I face them ever again?"

I cringe, remembering how it all unraveled at dinner. The shock on Astrid's face. The stunned silence at the table.

"I screwed up. What I did was inappropriate." I caress her cheek. "I don't expect you to just forgive me because you're pregnant. I'm willing to do whatever it takes. I love you, A. I'll never stop loving you. Or our child."

She looks away and I can see the tears welling up in her eyes. "It's not so simple. There's so much we haven't dealt with, so much we still need to figure out. And now...this." She gestures to her stomach and her voice catches. "I'm scared, B. I'm scared of what it means. Of what it will change."

"We'll figure it out together." I mean the words with everything I have. "I'm not going anywhere. I'm all in. I'm not running away from this. From you."

She blinks. A single tear slips down her cheek. I want to reach out and wipe it away, but I hold back, not wanting to push her.

"You're not getting off easy." She manages a hint of a smile. "I'm still mad at you and we have a lot to work through. But I love you. I love our baby. I want the life we were planning and appreciate you're willing to be there for us."

A wave of relief washes over me, even though I know this is the beginning of a much longer conversation. "I'll do whatever it takes. We can go to counseling. We can start over. We can close on our house. Whatever you need. Please don't shut me out again."

"Okay." She nods. That one little world feels like a lifeline. "We're going to have to take this one step at a time. You've dropped a bomb on me and I'm still not sure how to handle it."

My chest tightens with a mixture of hope and fear. She's giving me all I could expect. A chance. "We'll take it slow and figure this out."

We stand there for a moment looking at each other and she steps forward into my arms. God, I've missed her. Missed this. Even in the middle of all this chaos, Astrid's the one person I want by my side and I'll do anything to keep her here.

"I want to be at every doctor's appointment." I kiss her forehead. "For everything."

She looks up at me, surprised. "Yes. Of course I want you to be with me for everything. Going forward, though, we have to be honest with each other, B. No. More. *Secrets*."

"No more secrets," I agree

I feel her hand slide into mine. "I missed you so much," she whispers.

"Me too." I lean down and kiss her and place my hand on her belly. "We're going to be okay. One day you'll hopefully forgive me for being such a dumbass."

Astrid leans her head against my shoulder and my entire body relaxes. I only feel complete when she's by my side.

"Jury's still out." She covers my hand with hers.

As we stand there, with the music from the reunion playing in the background, I make a silent promise to myself.

I'm going to be the partner she deserves, no matter what it takes.

I'll be here for her. For our child. Unconditionally,

For the rest of our lives.

Thirty-Seven

ASTRID

Two Months Later

I NEVER THOUGHT I'D be back here.

Let alone be sitting here with no fucks to give and nothing to prove.

Brennan and I are in my parents' living room. I'm about to face down the past I've spent most of my life trying to avoid. Everything seemed impossible before—family, stability, love. Now, it's my real life. Except for one thing. This looming shadow of my past I need to confront and put behind me.

So, here we are, at the house I grew up in, surrounded by ghosts I thought I'd escaped.

Since the reunion, a lot has happened. My whole world has shifted. I'm five months pregnant now, with a nice little baby bump.

Once I got my IUD removed and the doctors confirmed our pregnancy was viable and normal, it felt like the universe was giving us the green light to move forward. To continue what we were building before things nearly imploded. Brennan and I closed on our house in Madison Park, with the incredible lake views. We've been diving into Reuniverse headfirst. His role at CognifyAI is almost nonexistent now, thanks to the agreement he brokered after his brutal legal battle. He's free, and we're knee-deep in making our own project come to life.

Best of all, we get to spend every waking moment together. For some couples, our dynamic wouldn't work. For us, it's heaven.

It helps we've been in counseling, both individually and together, trying to untangle the mess of our pasts so we can build a future. It's not easy, but it's worth it. And today feels like a test of all the progress I've made.

I sit here, holding Brennan's hand, about to ask my parents the questions I've been afraid to ask for as long as I can remember.

"Mom, Dad." I feel the knots tighten in my stomach. "Thank you for having me over after all this time. I'm hoping to talk to you about my birth. I learned Mom is not my biological mother."

My dad shifts uncomfortably in his chair and glances at my mom. She sits stiffly across from me with her normal, icy composure. Today it feels like a wall. A barrier I need to get through. Brennan's thumb traces gentle circles over the back of my hand, reminding me he's here. I'm not alone in this.

"We didn't see the need to explain." Mom's voice is cold and sharp. "You were Jens's daughter, so I raised you. That should have been enough."

I take a breath. This is it. "Why didn't you at least tell me? These are things I should have heard from you."

"It doesn't matter." Brigitte waves her hand as if there's a bad smell in the air.

I lean against Brennan. "I guess it explains why I never felt like I was part of this family. No matter how hard I tried."

My dad looks stricken. His usually placid face tightens into something resembling guilt. "We were doing the best we could. Maybe we failed, but we fed you and put a roof over your head. Got you through school."

Mom's eyes flicker to my dad and we witness a silent communication passing between them.

She sighs so deeply it sounds like it carries the weight of years. "You were born to a woman who wasn't ready to be a mother. She left you with your father at a week old and I was there. I took care of you because he couldn't do it alone. When your birth mother came back, wanting to take you, we said hell no."

"Really?" I feel like someone's knocked the wind out of me. I didn't expect this. Didn't expect to feel sorry for my coldhearted mother, but there it is—a flicker of sympathy, something soft I'm not used to feeling for her. "So, you kept me. But you never wanted me, did you?"

Her eyes widen and, for the first time, I see a crack in her icy facade. "We may not see life in the same way. I always wanted you. I was scared you'd be taken away. I probably distanced myself to avoid further sorrow. I thought if I didn't get too close, it wouldn't hurt as much if you were taken from me."

I swallow hard, trying to process this. I always thought she was cold, but hearing this, I realize her emotions are deep-rooted. Fear. Grief. Things I never considered.

"So, then what? Were you going to keep me at arm's length, forever? I grew up feeling like I didn't belong, like I was a visitor in my own home. Maybe, in many ways, I was." I cross my arms over my chest.

My dad leans forward. "I don't understand why you'd say something so dramatic. So what if we don't talk about all of our feelings. You were fine. Got good grades. Your generation needs to toughen up. I can't, for the life of me, keep up with you girls. Always some excuse for poor behavior."

A silence, heavy and thick, hangs between us. All this time I thought it was my mom who was cold. Only to find out, no. It's my dad. I feel Brennan's hand tighten around mine, grounding me. I don't dare look at him or I'm liable to burst into tears.

"Your birth mother," my mom continues, "didn't disappear completely. We kept in touch over the years. Once the court ruled in our favor, she backed off. I kept her information...just in case. I never wanted to hide it from you, but I didn't know how to tell you."

She gets up, reaches into a drawer and pulls out an envelope, worn and yellowed with age. She hands it to me. "This is the last contact info we had for her. I don't know if it's still valid, but it's yours if you want it."

I glance down at the envelope. It feels like Pandora's box because opening it could change everything, or nothing. I look at Brennan, who meets my gaze with a steady, reassuring calm. He already gave me this information weeks ago, but he's letting me decide what to do. Giving me control over an uncertain future.

"Thank you." I take the paper. "I don't know if I want to reach out to her. Not yet. Maybe not ever. But I appreciate you giving this to me."

There's another silence until my dad clears his throat. "Astrid, I know we've made mistakes. But we do love you, in our own way. We always have."

"I believe you." I surprise myself with how much I mean it. "It doesn't change anything. As you can see, I'm pregnant. Brennan and I are planning our wedding. I'd like to find a way to include you both but I'm still figuring out how."

"We want to be in your life. Be grandparents to your baby." My mom glances at my dad, who nods.

We leave their house in a kind of truce. It's not closure, not by a long shot, but it's a start. Maybe this is what healing looks like—messy, imperfect, with a lot of unanswered questions. As we walk to the car, Brennan wraps his arm around my shoulders, pulling me close.

"You okay?" He kisses my temple.

"Yeah." I lean into him. "I mean, it went about as well as could be expected. It's not...fixed, but I don't feel as angry. Progress, I guess."

"It's a lot. You did great in there." He takes my hand and leads me to the car.

God, I'm grateful for his constant support. I'm also glad to have the discussion over with. My mind is already moving ahead, though, thinking of the future. He helps me into the passenger seat and takes his place at the wheel.

"I'd like to focus on us now. Our family." I place my hand over my small bump, still not entirely used to the idea there's a baby growing inside me or we're going to be parents and make a million mistakes with our own kids. "We've got so much to look forward to. Let's not waste time on the past."

He puts his hand on top of mine and, together, we caress our little one. "I love you. I love us."

As we drive back to our new house, I daydream about our baby. Imagine the future we're going to have. Vacations we'll take. Memories we'll make. There's still fear, still uncertainty, but there's also hope. Peace. Acceptance. Things I never thought I'd find.

"I'm proud of you." Brennan breaks the comfortable silence as we pull into the driveway. "For everything. For facing them, for being so strong."

I smile, leaning over to kiss him. "I'm proud of us. We've been through a lot, and we've still got a long way to go. But we're doing it together, which is most important."

As we step into our sanctuary, I feel a sense of tranquility I haven't felt in a long time.

The past will always be there. It's a part of me. But, it doesn't have to define who I am. I'm starting to understand it's okay to let things go, to focus on what matters.

I have my own family now and don't need to hold on to the pain of the past. I'm letting it go, bit by bit. Focusing on the miracle ahead.

Brennan and I spend the rest of the evening curled up on the couch, talking about baby names, about the nursery we're going to set up, about everything and nothing. It feels normal. Perfect.

When he falls asleep, hand resting protectively over my belly, I find myself thinking about how far we've come. An unexpected connection. True friendship. A thriving business. Passion beyond my wildest imagination.

Now, a baby and a wedding.

We dared to take a chance on each other. Or, maybe destiny led us here.

Either way, we're exactly where we belong.

Epilogue - Four Months Later

HOLY SHIT.

The day has arrived. I'm about to be a father.

Our hospital suite buzzes with a quiet, tense energy as I sit beside Astrid, clutching her hand. It's been over sixteen hours since her contractions started, and we've been through the whole roller coaster together—breathing exercises, position changes, the occasional joke to ease her nerves, and a million ice chips.

I thought I was prepared for this. I had everything planned down to the smallest detail, but watching her endure this kind of pain, I feel totally powerless. My heart aches for her, and I wish I could take some of it away, but all I can do is be here, hold her hand, and remind her to breathe.

"Alright, my love." I brush back a few damp strands of hair from her forehead. "Just like we practiced. Deep breaths in and out. You're doing great."

Astrid's eyes have been flickering in and out of focus through her contractions, but the look she gives me now is somewhere between exasperation and affection. "Brennan, I swear to God, if you tell me to breathe again..." Her voice trails off, breaking as another contraction grips her and she winces with pain.

I flinch at the contraction but bite back a smile. I've been expecting this, knowing full well she'd be sick of my well-meaning instructions by now. Still, I squeeze her hand tighter, hoping she feels my support, even if my words are starting to grate on her nerves.

"Okay, okay, I'll stop with the breathing reminders," I whisper. "Just...keep doing what you're doing. You're amazing."

"Much better," she grits out, her face contorting again as a contraction rips through her. Then her grip on my hand tightens and I can practically feel her strength bleed into me as she rides out the wave. She's always fierce, but rarely this vulnerable. It's awe-inspiring and terrifying. My chest swells with a love I didn't think could get any stronger.

I steal a quick glance at the clock. Nearly seventeen hours now. I've lost track of how many contractions she's had but it doesn't matter. Time feels like it's standing still. Every second draws out as we wait for the moment we've been imagining for months.

The nurse checks her again and nods, her smile reassuring. "We're getting close now, Astrid. You're almost there."

"Thank fucking God." Astrid breathes out a low, frustrated moan. "I can't... I don't think I can keep doing this." Her voice is raw with exhaustion.

I rub her temples, lean down and press my forehead to hers. "You can. I know you can. You're the strongest person I've ever met, and you've got this. We're so close. Just a little longer, and he'll be here."

Her eyes well up and she grits her teeth. Fear. Pain. Determination. All shine through her beautiful face.

"I love you, B," she moans. "But I'm also going to kill you if you say 'breathe' one more time."

Oh, I can't help it. She's bugged by everything. I burst into laughter and it feels like a release. Her words break through the tension.

"Noted." I kiss her nose. "I'll shut the fuck up now if it makes you feel better."

The doctor steps forward, glancing at Astrid. "Alright, Astrid, this is it. I need you to push. Hard."

I hold her hand, bracing myself for her grip, and she does not disappoint. Her nails dig into my skin, but I don't let go. I can see the effort it's taking, every muscle in her body straining, and I wish I could do it for her. I say to myself so she can't hear me, "You're amazing, my love. You're incredible. Just a few more minutes."

She pushes again, gritting her teeth, and I see her face transform. All determined effort. Sheer will to bring our son into the world. I don't think I've ever been prouder, or more terrified.

A sudden cry fills the room. Raw and sharp and impossibly beautiful. I blink, my eyes stinging with tears, and the doctor holds him up, tiny and wriggling and so unbelievably perfect.

"Congratulations," she beams. "He's perfect in every way."

Astrid collapses back against the bed, her chest heaving, but she's smiling through her tears, eyes fixed on him.

"Bairre," she whispers, barely audible. "Our little Bairre."

The nurse places him gently on her chest. I stand there, staring down at them, completely undone. He's so small, so fragile. I'm afraid to touch him. Afraid I'll break this perfect, tiny person we made.

Astrid looks up at me, her eyes shining, and she says, "Brennan, meet your son."

I reach down, my hand trembling as I brush his cheek with the back of my finger. His skin is so soft and he makes a tiny noise, almost a sigh. I lose it. Tears spill over, and I don't care. I don't care about anything except this moment, and them. My family.

"He *is* perfect," I choke out, and Astrid nods, tears streaming down her cheeks too. "I love you both so much."

"I love you both so much too." She leans up toward me and I kiss her, our lips meeting over the top of our baby son's head.

We stay huddled together for what feels like forever, the three of us cocooned in a priceless moment. I hate to break the spell because I know I'll carry this with me for the rest of my life. No matter what happens, no matter how chaotic things get, this is what matters.

They are my everything.

There's a gentle knock on the door, and a nurse peeks her head in. "Your family's going crazy out there. All of them. They're anxious to meet him. Let's get Mama and baby cleaned up and ready, if she's up for it."

I laugh, wiping my eyes. "Yeah, sounds like the McGloughlins." I look back at Astrid, and she nods, tired but radiant.

"Let's do it," she says. "Let's introduce him to his family."

"Okay, Bairre." I kiss the top of his tiny head. "You've got a lot of people waiting to meet you. And they're going to love you as much as we do."

Want more Brennan & Astrid? Scan the QR Code below for a Bonus Scene.

When ambition and passion collide, will love find the way? Seamus & Marcella's story is up next in Wistful Whispers. Preorder now scan the QR code.

Connor's story launched the McGloughlin brothers' tale in Fearless. "I've never met anyone like you, Connor McGloughlin. I'm in way over my head."

Discover more read it here.

Behind the Scenes

Dear Reader,

Writing Daring Destiny was a privilege that felt, in many ways, as unexpected as the story itself. As with many of my books, my best laid plans took a turn as I got to know Astrid and Brennan on a personal level.

Through a series of twists and turns, the words poured out of me. I loved exploring love as a force that dares us to face our past, embrace our flaws, and build a life we may never have thought possible.

Astrid and Brennan's love isn't about perfection—it's about bravery. Astrid, with her fierce independence and quiet insecurities, and Brennan, with his brilliant yet deeply private nature, show us how love can challenge us to see ourselves more clearly.

Their connection is powerful. Playful. Filled with respect.

Love evolves as they both find courage to take risks and trust each other while unravelling layers of hurt and past trauma.

Daring Destiny is ultimately a story about two people defying the odds and choosing a life neither saw coming. I hope it brings you laughter, a few tears and the sense that sometimes the love we need is waiting in the least likely places—daring us to step forward and claim it.

Thank you for stepping into this world with Astrid and Brennan and for embracing The Charming Irish Series. May their story leave you with a sense of adventure, courage, and a belief in the beautiful, daring possibilities that await us all.

With gratitude,

Kaylene Winter

Maureen McGloughlin's

Roast Garlic Lamb & Pan Gravy

INGREDIENTS

- 4 1/2 lbs leg of lamb
- 2 garlic cloves, cut into thin slivers
- A few sprigs of fresh rosemary
- Good olive oil
- Salt and freshly ground pepper

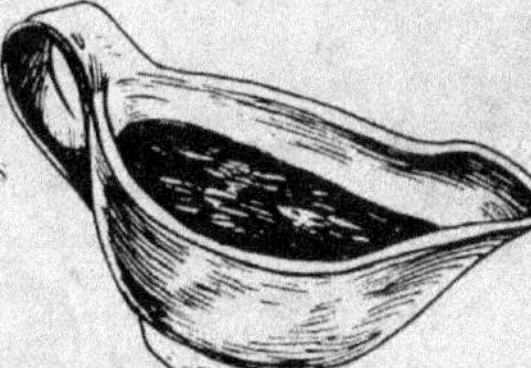

Ingredients for Gravy

- Pan juices from the roast lamb
- 1-2 tablespoons plain flour
- 1 cup lamb stock or beef stock (more if needed)
- Salt and freshly ground pepper, to taste

DIRECTIONS

Ah, love, there's nothing like a proper roast lamb for Sunday dinner. This recipe has been passed down through the family, and it's as simple as it is delicious. It's hearty, full of flavor, and just the thing to gather everyone around the table.

Lamb Directions:

Preheat your oven to 350°F (175°C).
Take your lamb and, with a wee sharp knife, cut small slits all over, top and bottom.
Into each slit, tuck a sliver of garlic and a small sprig of rosemary. This will infuse the meat with beautiful flavor as it roasts.

Brush the entire leg with a bit of oil, then sprinkle generously with salt and a crack of black pepper. Place the lamb on a wire rack inside a roasting tin. Pour about 3/4 cup of water into the tin—this will keep everything lovely and moist.

Roast the lamb for about 2 hours, giving it a good basting with the pan juices every so often. The aroma will have everyone wandering into the kitchen for a look. Remove the lamb from the oven, cover it loosely with foil, and let it rest for about 15 minutes. This is key to keeping the meat tender and juicy when you carve it.

Pan Gravy Directions: This recipe is simple, made right in the roasting tin, and absolutely bursting with flavor. You'll never go back to packet gravy after this, I promise you.

Once you've taken the lamb out of the roasting tin to rest, place the tin over medium heat on the stove. Skim off most of the fat from the pan juices, but leave just enough for flavor—maybe 1-2 tablespoons.

Sprinkle in the flour, stirring it in with a wooden spoon or whisk to make a paste. Cook this for a minute or two to get rid of the raw flour taste.

Gradually add the stock, a little at a time, stirring constantly to keep things smooth. Scrape up all the lovely browned bits stuck to the bottom of the tin—those are your secret weapon for flavor!

Let the gravy bubble gently for a few minutes until it thickens to your liking. If it gets too thick, add a splash more stock or water. Taste it, then season with salt and pepper as needed.

Pour it into a warm gravy boat, and there you have it—a proper pan gravy to go with your roast lamb. It's rich, savory, and guaranteed to have everyone reaching for seconds.

Acknowledgments

COVER/GRAPHIC DESIGNER/FINDER OF HOTTIES: Regina Wamba

Editor: Grace Bradley Editing, LLC

Proofreading: Letitia Delan

Formatting: Willow Yanarella

Sensitivity Reader: Tawny Gratto

PR: Wildfire Marketing

Literary Agent: Stephanie Phillips, SBR Media

Website Maven: Sherri Kiarsis, Ruby Moon Designs

My Right Hand: Willow Yanarella

YAY to KAYLENE'S KREW!!!

Dedication

To my husband Gareth. There's nothing like being part of a big, feisty, passionate, hardworking Irish clan, I hope the McGloughlin's capture the love and loyalty I've experienced in my found family.

About the Author

KAYLENE WINTER IS A best-selling author of steamy, contemporary romance.

Each character-driven novel is filled with snappy dialogue, pop-culture references and enough steam to make you fan yourself. Kaylene weaves authenticity, emotion and angst into a turbulent rollercoaster ride of love, passion and soul-searing romance always ending with a delicious HEA.

Kaylene lives in Seattle with her amazing Irish husband and her Pomsky, Phalen. She loves creating art of all kinds.

Other Titles

www.ingramcontent.com/pod-product-compliance
Lightning Source LLC
Chambersburg PA
CBHW070403310726
48977CB00003B/545